# PLUNGED

## SHILO CREED

*To all who are searching,*
*who know there is more.*

A huge thank you to Navy SEAL Nathan Wilkins for your incredible insights on this book. Thank you for your courage and service to our country.

To Peter Last, a skilled writer, and an amazing developmental editor, thank you. Your eye for plot and character are second to none. Thank you as well for your military service and selflessness.

Are you a writer? Maybe you will get a chance to have Peter Last beat up your book, it might sting at first, but your novel will shine so bright afterwards!
peterlast.com

# 1
# JACOB

OUT OF EVERY ONE HUNDRED FIGHTING MEN, TEN SHOULDN'T BE THERE, EIGHTY ARE JUST TARGETS, NINE ARE REAL FIGHTERS AND WE ARE LUCKY TO HAVE THEM. AH, BUT THE ONE, ONE, IS A WARRIOR.
~HERACLITUS ON ARMIES; FIFTH CENTURY B.C.~

Battle has always been my story. From the first time, as a five-year-old, when I threw my body in front of my brother's, guarding him from our father's heavy hand, until now, with an M4A1 rifle gripped across my chest. Maybe it always will be.

"I got a bad feeling about this." Rivera frowns at the massive generators bolted to the ship's deck. We've served together since Basic Underwater Demolition training.

Tucking the rifle closer, I stand steady against the familiar sway of the ship as I frown at the machine. A technician in a white lab coat jabs a voltmeter through a cable as thick as my thigh. The numbers it shows are not comforting. *What's their plan for all that electricity?*

The ship dips again in the light swell of the open ocean, throwing the technician off-balance. Rivera snatches him by the back of his coat right before his forehead smashes into a metal corner. He frowns as the tech cringes at him.

The two couldn't be more opposite. Steve Rivera, one of the most capable men on earth as a SEAL Team three operative, and the lab tech, whose mental faculties outweigh his physical prowess. At least I hope they do; I have a sinking feeling that our lives are in his pale hands. Out across the brilliant-blue water, a fleet of anchored ships surrounds the LCS *Engage*.

"You figure they're counting on trouble?" Rivera looks at me, his tone sardonic.

"We wouldn't be here if they weren't. Question is, what kind?" I say, following the ominous wire's path to where it dives over the starboard side of the ship.

Rivera nudges me with his elbow, jutting his chin across the deck. Two precise rows of personnel form near the railing, standing at attention. Military medics, every single one.

I look from them to the generators, ready to feed high voltage around the ship. Swallowing hard, I suppress the unease rising in my mind; it's a tactic that's as familiar as the rifle in my hands. Rivera and I laughed when they'd pulled us from the op in Qala-i-Jangi, figured we were in for a vacation of sorts. But with the New World Order rising to power worldwide, free choice is a thing of the past.

I'd prefer the front lines to the heavy sense that the *Engage* is heading for a catastrophe. Rivera's hungry eyes remain locked on a pretty blonde nurse at the end of the line.

"Two Navy SEALs, two Delta Force guys, twenty-four medics, and a bunch of scientists. Sounds like a bad joke." His voice is low, with a dangerous edge to it.

"Or a disaster waiting to happen…" I say, sweat soaking under the full battle gear our orders had demanded. The *Engage* is in U.S. waters, with minimal personnel, no visible weapons, or enemies, with an entire fleet of friendlies anchored around it. As a SEAL, having a clear objective is absolutely necessary; we play to win every time, keep getting up until we reach the goal. The mission's nebulous nature is not an asset. There is no enemy to take down, no hostage to extract.

We continue patrolling the open rear deck of the *Engage*, trying to put the pieces together. At 387 feet long with a beam of 57 feet, the *Engage* is a mid-sized littoral combat ship, one of the most versatile in the Navy.

Forty percent of the ship's area is reconfigurable, and right now, it's set up for what I can only classify as an experiment—one that's got me more on edge than mortal combat. The rules are clear then. Live or die. We cut under the shadow of the control tower, enter the empty helicopter hangar, and pass out of sight of the abundant medics.

"Four soldiers on board, armed to the teeth. For what? We're anchored in 259 feet of open water. Never a good idea, especially when the weather changes. Why hide just offshore like this?" He shakes his head. "There's no fight here. Nothing about this *mission* is adding up."

"We're due back to normal duty in three days, so whatever's going down, it'll be soon."

Rivera swears under his breath.

We stand at attention as a lieutenant commander escorts the rows of medics through the ship, his voice booming in the metal interior, "There are four decks below, two of them are open format."

The blonde nurse studies me as they pass, her brown eyes solemn. She seems as apprehensive as we are, her oval face filled with concern.

"Guess I'm not having any luck with that one." Rivera frowns when her eyes don't stray from me until the group clips down the stairway to the next deck.

I grunt in response to Rivera. The *Engage,* a type of ship usually well outfitted to protect U.S. coasts, is utterly devoid of weapons. Of course, now every border is blurred, and the turbulent change of power to the New World Order affects us the most. We're the boots on the ground, enforcing the bloodiest world peace in history. "Thirty minutes till the debrief. Think they'll shoot straight about this?"

Rivera gives a harsh laugh. "Not a chance, Jacob Carter, not a chance."

I nod as we continue through the hangar. I frown at a black puddle seeping from a control panel.

"What...?" Rivera dips his fingertip into the puddle and sniffs. "Oil."

I crouch next to him, scowling. At the far end of the expanding puddle, I find a distinct set of paw prints. Rivera and I share a sharp glance. A surge of adrenaline rises and I force it away with slow, steady breaths. Annihilating fear had been one of my main reasons for joining the SEALs, and I won't let it touch me now.

I stand, inspecting the prints as they fade where the massive animal had strolled down the hall, tracks gradually disappearing.

"Look at this." Rivera holds his hand over a print; his fingers, spread wide, still can't quite cover it.

"Remember South Africa? What? Two years ago? There's no denying these are lion," I say, forcing words through the thickness in my throat.

If there's tracking to be done on an op, it falls to me. It's in my blood. I'd grown up hunting deer through the Virginia woods.

There's a sheen of sweat on Rivera's brow. I blink hard, the air pressing in. Unable to resist the weight of it, I drop to one knee. A long slice runs through the wide main pad of the lion's print. *A boot print underneath? No, it's repeated in every single one. Must be a scar.*

I shake my head against the gripping sensation, as if I'm chained to the spot, locked in a battle of wills with the floor. Snarling, I free myself from the unseen force and see Rivera in the same struggle.

"Why would they have large animals aboard?"

Rivera doesn't answer, his eyes still riveted. I follow the tracks a few feet, finding them clearer here where the oil is almost worn off.

"Overgrown lab rat?" Rivera stands, but his attempt at a joke falls flat as we scan the metal hallway. He shoulders his rifle, finger hovering over the safety.

Footsteps echo around the corner, and we spin to find a midshipman flipping a 50-pound bag of cat litter onto the oil spill. Pieces skitter far down the hall.

"Hey!" Rivera's shout makes the midshipman jump.

The cat litter collects around Rivera's boots, obliterating the tracks. Any hope I'd had of further study is gone now. Demanding answers from the brass is tempting, but that's risky on a good day.

"I'll get it cleaned up, sorry." A gesture accompanies his words.

Rivera snarls at him, stomping off the clay as we continue down the hall.

"We've entered the circus." He clenches his jaw as we round the far turn, ready for anything.

Dropping down the ladder to the next deck, I stop short. A mass of silver tubes and wires takes up most of the large room, surrounded by eight technicians in white lab coats. I scowl at the round symbol with DARPA in the center. Three of them are arguing.

"The particle decelerator must be tuned to the right frequency in order to…" Sensing Rivera and me, they fall silent, turning to glare at us.

We stare back, the air crackling.

"Decelerator?" Rivera growls under his breath.

I grunt, senses peaking the way they do before engaging live fire. The technicians turn back to the control panel with wires arching in every direction. We walk past the mass of pipes, dropping down to the next deck to find it empty, unlike my racing thoughts.

"Didn't give much credence to the clause at the bottom of our orders about complete secrecy till now. DARPA? Being a science experiment ain't gonna fly." Rivera's right eye is tight, which usually means someone is in for a bad time. But this enemy is as elusive as our mission.

"Why would they have a particle decelerator?" I squint, pulling knowledge from my hobby study of quantum physics.

Decelerators contain molecules of antimatter, which are separated by lasers or proton beams. For each molecule of matter, an identical molecule of antimatter exists, only with an opposite electrical charge and spin.

"They had a generator alongside the decelerator, so the gens topside aren't feeding this." Mind churning, I watch the medics file back up the stairs.

The commander directs them into a transport vessel as the *Engage*'s massive rear door opens, greeting the gentle swell of the sea. Hydraulics hum and push the loaded boat into the embrace of the ocean. The door reverses, giving me enough time to watch the small craft reach the nearest ship and disappear inside.

"They're keeping the medics close enough, but not on the ship. Carter, I think we should have stayed on foreign soil."

I nod in agreement.

"Debrief in five," I say, setting out for the top deck, rejecting concerns, clearing my mind. The crisp ocean air is welcome as we take our place with the skeletal crew of the LCS *Engage*.

"Is that Admiral Ash?" Rivera's voice is hushed.

I groan inside. "Sure is."

Ash has a reputation for pushing the envelope with his super-soldier projects. He's the guy everyone talks about under their breath. At least that explains the DARPA technicians. His presence is the final blow. I didn't sign up for this; but the New World Order doesn't take complaints. I study the rows of medals on his chest, glaring at a pin I don't recognize with an ellipse and a triangle behind it.

"I reckon they're going to fry some fish, or we're going to get a chance to become something special," I say, glancing at Rivera, whose right eye is squinting tighter.

"I'm already special." His voice is a low snarl as they start the debrief. The apprehension in the air is palpable.

"Rear Admiral Adam Brooks," a warrant officer barks out the name while standing at attention. Brooks steps forward, brown eyes scanning.

"Project 157 is now underway, the primary goal of which is the continued testing of a ship-cloaking device known as *Covert Force*."

Rivera sighs, a disgusted sound.

*I'm not taking that bait any more than he is.*

"At 1200 hours, the crew of 22 will proceed with the project. You may experience intense sensations of sound and light. All personnel will file a full report covering the scope of the project. The confidentiality agreement will be strictly enforced."

"They're blowing smoke," I mutter. Rivera nods, but the fact remains…we're both locked in to the Navy. Despite my skepticism, I can't back out of my commitment; it's who I am.

We watch another boat carry the two admirals and the extra officers to the safety of the surrounding ships.

"Ten minutes," I say, watching the lab techs skitter to their posts. The two Force Recon Marines join us, uneasy, and we spread out across the deck near the helicopter landing pad. Watching.

*For what?* Why do they need elite fighters aboard for a cloaking experiment? I grit my teeth, forcing my mind to remain clear and in control. Making decisive decisions under pressure is a huge part of what I do. I let years of training and live ops give me confidence to face the unknown.

The hum of the massive generator's startup module vibrates through my boots. A sharp click echoes across the deck, then the machine roars to life. We tighten up under the clear blue sky, searching for whatever enemy the brass is expecting.

Another vibration joins the first until the hull of the ship pulses with it. The numbers on my watch roll to 1200. With slow, deep breaths, I enter the familiar state where fear is contained, thoughts are clear, and action is fluid.

A high-pitched whine jumps to life along with the generators. I glance over my shoulder; the Marines hunch, searching. The sound rises, reverberating until it pierces my focus. I resist the throbbing frequency as pain grips my head. Still, it grows, accompanied by an intense volume rattling in my chest, as I fight the urge to roar in pain while the punishing sound doubles its crushing grip.

Blood trickles from Rivera's ear. His face is a mask of agony, eyes darting. Images flash like rifle fire, broken by the pulsing energy, the glaring sky, the dull-gray ship, the vibrating air. We writhe as the noise streaks through us, beyond bearing. Rivera crouches low, his expression savage.

The red streak oozes down his neck; in hunter mode, an unnerving light flashes in his eye. His rifle is tucked tight to his shoulder, muzzle sweeping back and forth erratically. I hit the deck as three rifles go off at once, their loud report lost in the chaos.

Everything in me wars to do the same, to stop the sound before it tears me to pieces. I bite my tongue hard and force my rifle ahead on the deck, fighting for control.

My muscles tremble, absorbing the energy that's flowing through the deck and streaking through the air. It invades every cell and engulfs me in a deadly grip. The ship's temperature spikes, its blistering heat inescapable. The heavy air is a punishment in my lungs.

Rivera falls to the deck, twitching beside me, swinging at unseen assailants. His mouth is open, face a mask of terror, but I can't hear him scream. There's only the agonizing sound, the hammering energy ripping through every cell.

I blink hard as an eerie green haze rises from the deck, engulfing me. The glow turns my thoughts into syrup, transfixing me. I buck erratically in the surging pulse. The green haze burns into my eyes as I thunder against the agony of it. I clench my fists in front of me, limbs rigid. Terror grips hard as I watch the quavering image of my hands melt into the deck.

"No!"

But the shout can't stop my body from sinking into the molten metal; it won't slow my disintegration. I gasp hard for a breath of searing air as my chin sinks through the burning deck. I grimace, the ship no longer supporting me; my right arm drops into the shivering air beneath. I scream as I plummet through the space of the deck below, glimpsing the technicians, glassy-eyed and stiff on the floor next to the particle accelerator, descending.

The next floor is the consistency of peanut butter. The green haze sucks me forward till I'm falling faster than a high-altitude parachute jump, still gaining speed. It strips away more of my being until I hit the ocean below. The shock of the cold water courses over me, the surging energy escalating at its touch—like gasoline waiting for a match.

The sudden deafening silence leaves me stunned. But I'm still falling, sinking, *no, rising*. Orientation lost, I struggle, holding my breath, but the speed of my travel sucks me forward. I flail in the chaos.

Then the pain disappears, peeled away, and an awareness of freedom comes that I'd never imagined. *The absence of my body.*

Loosed from all its input, I'm a clean slate. No past, only intense movement and energy. Time has released me and I fall for an eternity, though the acute grip of the green energy doesn't fade, nor does the forceful, blasting wind of my motion.

Something catches my face. I search for its name through the fog. *Tree branch.* Another, thicker limb clips my ribs; now there's a crazed tumult of branches and leaves ripping everywhere, slapping in quick succession, hissing past.

I land hard on a solid limb, void of air. Gasping at the sudden stop, mouth working like a fish as I dangle, arms and legs hanging from the unforgiving wood at my waist. I suck in a breath; the air tingles in my lungs as I struggle for balance, twisting on the wide bough until I'm draped over it lengthwise.

A flush of bitter cold washes through me; I shiver, mind empty, clinging to the wood. The rough bark scrapes my stomach as I clutch it. The forest floor is far, far below.

I take in a steadying breath and a barrage of scents fills my mouth: the warm forest loam, the spicy hint of the tree bark, the tinge of something sweet, like flowers.

Searching my mind, the wild speed of my arrival and the thrashing branches are clear, but only blank space exists before that. Turning my head, I'm entranced by the leaves wavering in a light breeze.

Their color is so intense, the shades of green captivating. I stare at the nearest leaf and, as I do, a humming sound comes to me and the soft scent of growing things curls into my nose. It has a fresh green taste.

Colors with sounds? Scents? I blink hard; the volley of sensations is overwhelming. A tiny bird lights on the end of my branch, its chest a deep-purple hue that shimmers in the dappled light. Spindly, coal-black legs glitter like diamonds; when it opens its beak, the sweet sound pierces me. Then, in a flutter of wings, it dives off the branch. Every sensation is magnified, like an exposed nerve.

A weighted hush falls over the forest as my gaze falls to my hands and forearms, white-knuckled on the branch. I resist the urge to gasp; my bones stand out, pale skin stretched over atrophied limbs. Disgust rises. *That's not right.*

My legs tremble, confirming that the condition affects me from head to toe. My stomach lurches as I search past the sensation of my wild fall, but the green haze conceals everything else.

A twig snaps, the sharp sound making my hair stand on end. A stench of rotten flesh makes me recoil. Sweat breaks out as I search the forest for the source of the sense of dread seeping into me. *There.* The leaf litter reveals the outline of a massive paw in the dim brush. I raise my eyes until they fix on a massive snout and one dark eye revealed among the cover. A rusty, unhealed crust lines the edges of the wound on the wide bridge of the lion's nose. I cling tighter to the branch, longing to disappear.

The beast steps forward, leaving a streak of bright blood on the brilliant-green leaves. Fear crawls through my skin. Wounds crisscross its hide, stinking patches of fur rubbed off. It's a male, but it lacks any thick glory of a mane; instead, scraggly locks cover its neck and chest. It's thin, pinched even, but that does nothing to diminish the sense of the innate power it exudes…or the terror enveloping me as I watch.

A second lion steps up next to the first. This one's right ear dangles, sliced almost through, and he's far larger, dwarfing the first.

His appearance makes me flinch, bringing an alarming revelation. The branch I'm clinging to is dead. Its empty dry fingers stand out from the health of the forest. The dried bark has slipped at my motion. Heartbeats pass like days as the sheath grates against the damp wood beneath it. Wincing, I lean the opposite direction, willing the motion to stop.

A third lion enters the clearing, swiping at the first with its massive paw. They growl and spin, the air vibrating. The sound is an agony in my ears, a sickening taste. They settle straight below, broad snouts in the air.

They've caught a scent. *Me.*

"No," I whisper as the bark under me lets loose, and I twist in slow motion.

Flailing, I grip only empty bark; then I land hard on the back of the largest lion. He takes the punishing impact with a savage hiss, claws scraping the ground, dirt clods flying high.

I hit the ground, lungs empty, scrambling to a crouch. We lock eyes for a breath. Fear clamps down, paralyzing me.

The largest one with the tattered ear shifts back, coiling, eyes pinning me. I lunge to the side, but the full extent of my weakness is crushing. My legs wobble, trembling as I run downhill, the incline forcing me forward more than anything else.

I dodge through the trees, the crashing sounds of pursuit too close. A branch lashes my face, drawing a hot line across my skin. Up ahead, the light intensifies—*a clearing.* I grimace; they'll have me there, in the open.

Sharp claws catch my pant leg, pitching me forward. *Can't slow down.* I break into the openness. There is no field; there's nothing but a chasm. I scream as my feet lunge in the air, plummeting toward whitewater far below.

I drop for long seconds before smashing into its depths, its icy embrace too tight as I crumple hard against the rocky bottom. Pain shoots up as the water's swirling energy rips at me, the current impelling me forward.

I break the surface, gasping for air, catching sight of a lion dangling from the cliff high above, his claws sunk deep in a tree root as he scrambles up. The river sucks me under, its thunderous voice ringing in my skull as I slam into a protruding rock. The froth reddens as the current tumbles me, its touch against my skin like an electrical current.

I make desperate grabs for air as I sweep around a sharp curve; the cliffs give way to rocky shores. I struggle toward the bank, washing up. The rocks rake my stomach. I flop on my back, the current still tugging at my scrawny legs as I drag in insufficient air.

On hands and knees, I crawl up the beach, empty without the surging of the energy of the water. A streak of blood stains the rocks behind.

Without the delicate cover of the trees, the light is piercing, making my eyes water. Forcing empty muscles to function, I roll over; the clinking, raking sound of the rocks makes me wince.

Memories explode in my mind, so fresh they mix with reality. A thin veil of green haze hedges around my vision.

*I am six again, in the frigid dark on a riverbank, blood coursing down my cheek. Our crumpled car lies on its roof, only the wheels showing above the icy water.*

*"Save him, Daddy!" My throat is raw in the frigid air from screaming at the limp form of my father.*

*I shake him, red fists small against his shirt collar. He groans, and a blast of familiar alcohol-laden breath hits me. Cars stop on the bridge high above, the guardrail dangling, a testament to our path. They're too far away to save my little brother, Ruben, still trapped in the car.*

*I run, rocks clinking, back to the car, and plunge myself into the deadly cold water, searching for a way past the twisted metal.*

*"Ruben!" My scream echoes over and over, tearing me to pieces.*

I open my eyes, struggling out of the intense grip of the memory.

*Lion.*

Breath hisses through my throat, the air fetid with the creature's rank scent. Massive yellow-stained fangs open, inches from my neck; his head is as wide as my shoulders. I crab-crawl backward over the rocks, but it's a futile effort.

One massive paw pins my chest to the ground, crushing me against the rocks. I'm too weak to resist. The thick black lips open; *this is it. I'll see Ruben soon.*

A wild bellow pierces the silence and the lion's massive head snaps toward advancing footsteps. His growl rattles my chest, saliva splattering my face.

A flash of light reflects off metal that draws a bright-red slash down the lion's flank. He shrinks back as a wide-shouldered man rains blows on him. I scramble away from the wicked claws as my rescuer shouts again. His muscled arm lofts a deadly sword; the lion spins, paws spitting rocks as he makes for the tree line.

Chest heaving, the man turns toward me. A thick dark beard hides most of his face, but his green eyes brim with life.

I groan, empty, exhausted, lion bait next to his virile strength. He wipes his sword and looks me over.

"Aye. You've got the light about you, Boy."

Blinking, I stare at his skin, which glistens with a faint glow. He stretches out a wide hand and I take it. At the contact, everything comes back with a jolt. I'm Jacob Carter, a Navy SEAL. *Strong.* Able.

*What happened to me?* I grit my teeth, hating the fear my condition produces. I waver on bony legs. The man slaps my back, and I almost crumple. Hands on knees, I struggle with the green haze, the sound, the crazed speed of my journey here, stealing everything from me.

"When did you last eat, Boy? You look like a wet rag." He scowls down at me.

One side of my mouth pulls up in pain. "I'm not sure."

"You're in no condition to be traipsing about the woods. Lions are never far off. And there's worse than them lurking. Follow me, Boy. I'll bring you to the table." With that, he strides off, his long legs eating up the distance.

I push through the loose footing, struggling to keep him in sight. He walks through an old-growth forest, wide shoulders swinging, one with the wild nature of it.

My legs burn, calf pulsing where the rock had smashed it open. My breath is too short. I hiss through my teeth, desperate to keep up. As we travel, the sounds that have scents, colors with tastes dilutes the sharp awareness of my past. Experiencing the moment is overwhelming and easier than grieving for my former self.

Minutes pass and as I fall into a painful rhythm, my awareness expands. The trees are massive—older than any I've ever seen. Pausing mid-step, I press my hand against one, hear a deep, steady hum. *Growth.* I jerk my hand away. The word had been loud in the forest's hush, yet no one had spoken.

This forest has little undergrowth and I can see for a surprising distance. The man is coursing over ancient hills and gullies at a punishing pace.

My legs cramp as we descend toward a small creek. The sound of its rippling water raises goose bumps on my skin; *I can smell it.* Vigor returns as we near the water. The air above the thin rill seems electrically charged.

He spreads his hands, held under the fast-flowing water. His head cocks, as if listening. Then he looks up, sniffs the air, and grunts. His green eyes are bright. "Drink, Boy! It'll do you good."

Kneeling, I cup my hands to draw water. As my skin immerses, shock waves ripple through my body. Terror had cloaked it earlier but it's familiar from the river. Sounds like muffled voices seem to travel through my bones, energy surging. Hesitating, I raise the water to my lips and find it sweet and refreshing. A shiver of power runs down my spine, and relief floods me at the sensation.

"I'm Demyen. Glad I came upon you when I did." He nods across the stream. "A pride of lions is two clicks south, heading this way. We better get moving." He leaps the stream and strides away up the far hill.

I'm surprised to find the water's surge of energy still coursing through my veins. Still, the disturbing weakness of my frame eats at me.

When I top the rise, Demyen is leaning against the tree. *No, wait.* I search the area, spotting a hut behind him. The well-concealed forest dwelling is almost indistinguishable from its surroundings, made from branches, mud, and logs. Weeds, brambles, and sticks break its outline, jutting out as they naturally would.

Demyen pulls open the door as I draw near, his sharp eyes scanning the woods beyond. A soft light and a mouthwatering aroma flood the air. Ducking through the low entryway, I find a tidy interior far larger than I expected.

A massive, roughhewn table splits the length of the single large room. Neatly arranged bowls and platters covered with lids sit steaming there. Two people turn at our arrival; I'd guess there are often larger gatherings than the hut hosts tonight. They both smile on seeing Demyen's stout frame.

"Demyen, welcome! I was hoping to share the board with you today," a slender man with sandy blond hair and slate-blue eyes says.

Demyen nods, reaching to grasp his outstretched hand. "The pleasure's mine, Ian. I see we've arrived just in time."

A petite woman sets down a platter; her dark hair and eyes remind me of my mother. The thought gives me pause as I try to grasp her image in my mind, but it's as if the memory is sky-bound: beautiful, but unreachable. Her image mixes with the reality of the woman before me.

"And who is this you've brought around today?" A bright smile accompanies her quiet voice.

Demyen turns, gazing down at me.

"I'm…Jacob." The name on my tongue seems foreign, like a puzzle piece with the colors misaligned. "What is this place?" I swallow hard; the implications are heavy. "Where are we? Is this a dream, or an alternate reality?" Suppressing a shiver of dread, I force the question: "Is this permanent?"

My words seem to hang in the air as Demyen, Ian, and the woman exchange an intense glance.

Demyen turns back to me, clasping a meaty hand on my shoulder with a forced smile. "Well, Boy, this is no *alternate* reality. This *is* reality, stripped of…the finite. But we'll have clearer heads once we've partaken."

I follow Ian and Demyen to the table. The woman guides me to sit on the long bench, placing a thick wooden bowl before me.

"I'm Myah. Be at ease here and eat your fill." She settles on a stool, and the scent that's rising from the bowls consumes my thoughts.

Ian lifts his hands to the heavens. "Almighty, we thank You for Your Word that sustains us. Guide our steps. So be it."

My mouth waters as they lift the lids and steam drifts upward. As it clears, I scowl: the plates are not full of meat and bread, but *scrolls*. They fill every platter, different sizes and shades of tan and brown, their damp edges curled. The words, written in tight script, are unintelligible to me as I glower at them.

None of my dining partners seem to see anything amiss as they reach out, ripping hunks from each platter. My mouth is watering, my frame desperate for fuel. I watch Demyen rip his pieces even smaller. Then with practiced ease, he rolls them inside a larger section, opens his mouth, and takes a bite. Ian as well is chewing with gusto as he mops his bowl with a scrap of scroll.

Myah nods at me. "Don't be shy; there's plenty more."

Driven by the urge in my stomach, I reach out to the nearest platter and rip off a corner. The soft scroll tears, then I take a deep breath and put it into my mouth.

An intense bitter flavor bites my tongue, tingling and burning. It seems to catch fire in my throat. Uncontrollable coughing racks me, and I feel the exact location of the scroll as it slides into my stomach.

Demyen leans over, slapping my back, "Here now, Boy! That's a hard one to swallow all by itself. Let's add a bit of the others."

Through watering eyes, I watch Demyen's expert assembly of another roll, then he stuffs it into my hands.

"No fear, Boy. This will soothe the burn."

This time it pays off. Layer upon layer of flavors roll, from deeply satisfying, almost meaty, to smooth and buttery, then a burst of sweet, with only a tinge of the burn. A solid sensation spreads through my stomach, replacing the emptiness.

Ian glances over at me. "You wondered if *this* is an alternate reality. It's an interesting question."

Myah smiles at him. "One of your favorite subjects, Ian."

"True. It's the foundation of everything. If you don't take the first step, you can never ascend the stairs." He shrugs, "The real question is, what is *reality?* Here, we experience the cause, *there* the effect. Life originates in the spirit. This 'reality' is the source. The physical order overshadows the spirit for most. Some never even know the spirit exists. But it dictates all things." He leans forward, intent. "The Lawgiver…His words change everything. They are the code upon which everything runs. One can go a lifetime without knowing the code, the law, the way. The right knowledge determines your success or failure." He goes back to eating, now on his third helping.

Demyen wipes his beard. "Boy, if you want to survive the morrow, you'd better eat."

I sigh, battered by the import of Ian's words. All I want is to go back. I force another piece of paper into my stomach, determined not to retch. I must survive until I find a way.

Morning breaks over the forest hut, and wisps of smoke rise from the firepit, the scent bringing a distant memory of the "physical order," as Ian called it. Of running, fighting, *winning*. The opposite of me now.

I draw the memories closer, studying the time frame leading up to my arrival here. An icy sensation spreads across my chest, and my peripheral vision blurs with green. Something's off; the strange symbol on Ash's uniform comes into sharp focus, forcing the adrenaline higher. There's significance to it I can't quite grasp. But it's like water in my hands; that world won't stay in focus long enough.

Frustrated, I shift toward the fire. *The experiment must have created a tear between realities. Is the rift still open? Did the memories slip through the fog that divides the two worlds?*

Fists clenching, there's only one thing that's certain: *this is real.* Every sense is heightened here, intense to the point of pain. The most poignant experiences of the physical are dim compared to this place, this breath, this second.

I reposition, side tender where I'd rolled into the hilt of a sword at my belt. In the quiet dark, I'd drawn it, remembering Demyen's impressive weapon. But I'd burned with shame to find just two short inches of blade showing above the intricate, jeweled hilt. With a deep embarrassment, I'd sheathed it, lest anyone see. Somehow, it's too personal—not just a weapon, but a reflection of me.

Pulled from my thoughts by movement, I follow Demyen through the rickety door. Outside, the sounds of birds' wings and voices are everywhere. The mossy wet scent of the forest floor fills my lungs; I can taste the clean, dark aroma, hear it.

Demyen turns his head as I stop beside him. "Ready for the day, Boy?"

I meet Demyen's eyes and answer with painful honesty, "Not at all."

A slow smile spreads across his face. "Then let's seek He who is."

He heads down the hill, back toward the stream we'd drunk from last night. This time I'm certain Demyen is listening as he spreads his broad hands under the water.

I whisper, "Do you hear something?"

I'm desperate to grasp the rules of this place, to gather the intel he does.

"Rest your hands in the water, Boy, and open your ears."

Needing his perception, I plunge my hands under. First comes the sense of energy surging, flowing, tingling up my skin. A whispered hint of an airy voice follows. The swirling current mingles with the sounds.

"With time, you will understand. The Almighty…He is always speaking. If you can hear and understand, all things become possible."

Nodding, I decipher words as I wait, intent on the communion with the water. It's in this quiet, with shivers of exotic life racing up my arms, that I'm caught by the sight of a familiar pugmark on the far shore. It's large and crisscrossed with scars. The twisting tension in my chest returns; clear in the firm mud, the print's scars form the symbol I'd seen on Admiral Ash's chest.

My mind contorts over the immense distance, the other reality vacillating, peaking again, gripping. *A dark puddle, expanding, the same huge paw prints lead off down the cold metal hall. A man crouches next to me.* I search for his name, but it eludes me, the knowledge fading like fog before the heat of day.

"Boy!" Demyen has been calling.

"What?" I blink hard, the difference between worlds so clear, that world so flat and gray, lacking the 5-D scope of this one so vibrant, so full of piercing life.

"Aye, he's a brute, that one. You've seen his print before, no?"

I nod, glad to have a reason to look elsewhere. "Yeah, I have. Was he hunting us?"

One of Demyen's thick eyebrows goes up. "They are always hunting, Boy, especially for the likes of you, fresh into the spirit. Best move along now."

Demyen points to the far shore to one side of the print. "Can you see your way? That faint incandescent line? It's golden. Almost like a crack in the ground?"

"I *think* so."

There's a glowing thread in the soil across the stream. Impossibly thin, it traces away out of sight.

"Let me tell you truth." Demyen raises three fingers in the air. "One. That line is your path. The perfect will of the Almighty." He drops one finger as he continues. "Two, it only takes one step to get off your path." Another finger goes down. "And three, the path *never* terminates."

I grunt. "So, I'm to follow it always?"

Demyen's head dips. "Aye. It looks as if our paths run together a bit longer. It's strange that I've been able to see your path this whole time. Usually, you only get a glimpse of someone else's path. Can you see mine? Running there, to the right of yours?"

I don't see another thread per se—only a distortion in the ground, as if light isn't settling, or maybe it's vibrating.

"Almost."

As we set off through the woods, with every step, it's easier to see my golden thread running ahead of me.

As the woods thin out, a gathering of people becomes visible. Most of them are thin with sallow complexions, looking as if they'd blow over in a gentle breeze. I wish I differed from them, more like Demyen with his solid muscular bulk.

Most hurry forward, lost in their own reality. Many wear dark clothing, gazes shifty; they make the weakness of the first group seem like strength. Their eyes are hollow and a strange darkness is in their skin. Only a few, like Demyen, are strong, fit, and able-bodied, skin glowing with a healthy luminosity.

One girl catches my eye in particular; her bones protrude and her brown hair hangs limp. Pain is etched in the creases near her mouth, the tension around her eyes; whenever someone walks by, she smiles, but it can't cover the truth of her emaciated condition, or the darkness that emanates from her skin.

Two more figures emerge from the distant woods. A head and shoulders taller than any man in sight, they exude light. Heavy swords hang from their sides and they wear pure white.

Demyen whispers. "Never seen a Watcher before, eh? Well, you'd better hope you see plenty. They serve the Almighty and help His people. So, I must be off. Looks like our paths diverge from here. Be careful, Boy. Keep your sword at the ready; hold to the path."

I cringe at his words about my sword, thankful he doesn't know. With that inadequate advice, Demyen sets off, and I feel conspicuous. I try to ignore the sweat that pops out on my palms as I step forward onto the path. As confident as I had grown walking with Demyen, now I stagger along as if on a tightrope.

My strides lengthen when my path turns left, veering through the crowd. Many of them stand or walk with their right hand stretched before them, staring down at nothing, empty, unaware of their surroundings. Their thumbs twitch back and forth over space. The oddness of their behavior and the emptiness in their eyes make a shiver run down my spine.

A man stands on a stump up ahead, his voice rising over a small crowd. He lacks the mass of Demyen, but his physique reveals him as a fighter. I'm drawn to him, longing for the quiet confidence I'm missing in this reality. As I draw closer, I catch his words, mid-sentence.

"…the law of seeds. When the Almighty created you, He made you triune, like Himself. You are a spirit, you have a soul, and you live in a body. He gave you the seed of His Word, when this seed bears fruit, you will defeat all enemies and live in victory."

A man next to me sniggers; he is so thin it's painful to look at him. "Law of seeds…like words will shut the mouths of lions." He turns away through the crowd; the darkness that clings to him gives him a harsh edge.

"But your spirit is dead, cut off from life by the darkness. The Almighty has life for you! Come to the light and live. Everything you need is in the light: strength, health, abundance. Turn from the darkness now; be made new and live!" The crowd shifts, their murmurs growing louder at the man's words.

But the girl I'd seen earlier has tears in her eyes as she listens, an expression of rapture on her face. In her condition, it seems hopeless. Could she have life like Demyen's? Can I? Her gaunt face makes me cringe. The man steps down from the stump, and I lose him in the crowd's swirl, wishing I could ask if he meant that literally.

I frown at my path, its wavering light creeping away through a thick forest ahead. Perfect cover for lions. I scan the crowd; most people don't focus on the ground ahead of them, clueless about the way. I stare down at my traitorous one, fading into the underbrush. Demyen's words find me again. *It is your path, the way you are to follow.*

The first step into the dark woods takes me a while. Senses on fire, I stalk through the thick scrub until it gives way to the relative openness of the forest. Heart slamming, I move from tree to tree.

A memory slips through; the barren, war-torn streets of Ramadi. I am stalking through hostile territory—able, ready, deadly, the self I have lost in this place. It seems real for a moment. Tantalizing, the memory of confidence. My legs tremble as I lean against a tree; growling, I slam my fist against its bark. I hate my condition, and this crazy place where the rules aren't defined.

With a steadying breath, I move forward, wincing at the snap of twigs under the thin sole of my shoe. I'd have been invisible in my other life, would have loved this challenge instead of cringing in fear. Sweat pours as I press ahead.

A large bramble drapes its long tendrils over my path. The flat area on the left is easier to traverse. Scanning hard, I decide to rejoin my path a few feet ahead, avoiding the bramble.

I ease out, searching for lion sign. Everything's quiet. Sliding my foot forward, I ease into the open. Two more steps and the ground beneath me shifts. I spread my arms, but the sound of the dirt shifting grows. A heartbeat passes as I fall, screaming. Logs, dirt, and leaves pile over me as I hit the bottom of a deep pit. Groaning, I struggle, leg pinched tight under the heaviest beam. I peer up through the choking dust; I must be fifteen feet down, and the sides of the shaft are sheer.

"Aha!" It takes all I have to shove hard enough to pull free. My leg throbs, swelling already setting in as I pile the wood to one side. Maybe I can build a ramp out.

I imagine lions finding me here; one simple pounce; the end of Jacob Carter. Working faster, sweat turns into a muddy slurry as I try to climb the pile. Everything shifts, too loose to hold my weight. A sharp protrusion jabs my foot. My mind screams to get out; this is the worst possible scenario.

Noise above makes me crouch, jaw clenched, but I see a man's silhouette. "Hey! Help me, will you?"

He disappears, returning with a long pole, a noose at one end. I reach up and the man expertly snags my wrist, and the noose tightens until the skin threatens to tear. *It's better than dying in here.*

Belly flopping over the top, I cough in the dust, rising to thank the man, but he yanks my arm back down to the path, his heavy foot on my neck.

With my cheek on the ground, I shout, "Let me up!"

The noose twists hard over my back till my scrawny shoulder screams in pain, tearing.

"Shut up and listen. You fight, I'll kill you outright. You obey, and you get to live."

The man's words ignite rage. Overriding the pain, I twist toward his weight-bearing leg. As he crumples on top of me, I grasp the pole, swinging it hard until I hear its satisfying crack against the man's skull. I roll free, chest heaving. The man scrambles away, eyes dark, holding his head. I back off farther, scanning the woods. Sure enough, two others appear, wary.

"Stay back. I don't want a fight."

The sheen of their skin holds the wavering dimness that tells me I'm in dangerous company. I back away into the undergrowth, pitch the pole deep into the brambles, and rejoin my path, keeping a careful ear out for pursuit. By the time I'm sure I'm alone, the elation of having fought him off gives way to wracking pain in my overused muscles.

I press on, exhaustion building; a smear of rotten scent mars the pine forest I've passed into. Senses on fire, I search ahead. Something's out of place: *human skin.* My breath comes heavy; a limp hand lies stark against the leaf litter.

Nothing moves, not for many breaths, so I approach, vigilant. It's the girl. She'll be lion bait out here, collapsed in the woods. I crouch next to her, feeling way too exposed. Rolling her over, my gut churns. She's already dead, neck mangled.

The pitiful, wistful expression in her eye as she listened to the man settles like a brick in my stomach. Hoping for strength isn't enough. Longing for it doesn't do the job either, or I'd not be wavering here, endurance gone. I have to figure it out. Survival here demands it. What's the difference between Demyen, the teacher, and me? We have *the light,* but it isn't affecting us the same way. I seem closer to this girl than to them.

I draw back as the girl's corpse seems to waver, translucent bands moving in waves. Then her skin blackens and a choking sulfur scent rises as the translucent streaks flash red. I jolt backward as she disappears, a smear of blood all that remains on the forest floor. The hair on my arms stands on end.

I blink, lock eyes with the dark, dead gaze of a lion, its mouth wreathed in dripping red. It hadn't gotten to eat before she disappeared. Its massive jaws open. I crouch, desperate to run but unable to…until it lunges forward. All that keeps me from being overtaken right then is the wonderful grittiness of my leather shoes and the wild, ineffective scrambling of the lion's paws on the damp leaves.

My atrophied legs propel me through the trees, my lungs struggle to haul in air, and I long for my former strength. The pursuing sound of claws raking the turf behind me raises goose bumps on my skin.

*My path! When did I leave it?* There, its golden glimmer is straight ahead. A high sheer face of rock rises in the distance, and my path heads straight toward it. I tuck my head and run, lungs wracked with pain.

I reach the base of the cliff at top speed. With a desperate twist to the right, I use my ricochet to propel me along my path. The sharp bite of claws rips through my calf. Driving deep to regain my speed, I hear the massive beast slam into the cliff face, piling up against the rock, not making the turn, snarling in pain.

My legs are giving out; I can't keep up the pace much longer. Searching the path, my heart almost stops. There, not far ahead, its wavering golden light ends. *Does the lion eat me? Do I die right there?*

Demyen's words return, "The path *never* terminates."

The ground vibrates under the lion's next leap toward me. As I run, high above I see a vine dangling, a golden thread weaving up its length.

With a shout, I leap for it. The lion swipes one massive paw, and my pant leg whips flat, *way too close*. My hands close on the thin vine, as my stomach muscles scream, forcing my legs up. With a savage growl, I make slow progress up the vine, grip slipping. Eventually, I can use my knees to clench the bottom of the vine. I dangle, trembling like a leaf, sweat pouring.

The lion circles below, burning eyes riveted on me. He leaps, front paws reaching high. Terror forces me higher. Branches reach out, entangled with the vine. I fold myself over one, groaning. The lion claws the trunk.

Darkness is coming, and its arrival pushes me to escape, making a wild leap for the next tree. Then I waver, arms flailing for balance as I tightrope across the center branches. Wrapping my arms around the trunk, I give my empty muscles a second to recoup. The warm scent of the bark brings a wave of clarity. If I can work back toward the cliff face and exit the treetops onto its height, I'll evade the enemy.

I force myself to push off again, hands gripping branches as I rush along. The lion keeps pace below, its stench rising, mouth open. Up ahead, the rock face comes into view; even its dull gray hums with a peaceful sound in the fading light. Hope surfaces. *I'm close.* Coiling back, I launch over open air before thought can keep me from action.

I shout, slowing at the high point of my leap. *I'm not going to make it.* Stretching, willing myself forward, I grasp at the branches; their thin tips give way under my weight, fists full of leaves. The sharp snap of them shearing off the tree fills me with dread. I plummet, my shout morphing into a scream of terror as the lion surges; there is no way to escape.

A rippling energy surges in the vibrant air, pulsing through me. My fingers, still gripping leaves, tingle with it. I blink hard, trying to clear the green haze clouding my vision. My legs buckle as I slam hard into a small stream; energy explodes from the chilled water like a lightning bolt. *Thud.* Through the green fog, I see the lion land a few feet away, one more leap and I'm done.

Halfway through his next leap, his eyes go wide, and he lands half-turned, his heavy head searching. *He can't see me through the haze.*

I'm still falling from the tree. *No,* rising. I grip my head as the energy spikes, unbearable. The sense of motion is disorienting; there's nothing but green haze burning my eyes in the crazed rush. Pain. *Body.* So foreign. I open my eyes, vision narrowed, trapped in my flesh that's shrieking in agony and bucking on a metal table.

Foam bubbles from my mouth, but through these sensations, it's the flatness that crushes me. This world is gray, only three-dimensional. Sounds without colors.

The green haze dissipates, and I'm seized in a body that's determined to jerk off the table. *The lion.* Determined to fight, I strike hard. Hands try to hold me down as I roll off the cold table. A face appears above me, warm brown eyes holding mine…must protect her.

# 2
# SAGE



The second my foot hits the deck of the LCS *Engage,* a deep unease grips me. I shake it off, lining up next to another female nurse. The lieutenant commander shouts in my ear as I stand at the front of the line.

"Your duties will include full med checks of all personnel assigned to the *Engage* at 1215 hours. You may find them anywhere on board, and a full search of the ship will be conducted."

My mind races; *find them? Won't they all be at their research stations?*

"We have assigned each of you a specific patient; as per orders, you should be completely familiar with their medical records."

I gaze across the deck. My patient and his buddy are watching me right now.

Jacob Carter, six feet tall, brown hair, blue eyes that are even brighter than his photo. Elite operative doesn't seem to encompass who he is. His files, even without the redacted information, were well over five inches thick. I've studied every word for the past two weeks. Top scores on physical fitness, unbelievable lung capacity. Mental aptitude test scores that make me feel well below average, even with my medical degree. Multilingual. He's been shot twice while on duty but recovered from both. All said, he's the cream of the crop in every area. The line beside me moves, touring the ship. The officer continues spouting information, but I've already studied the ship's schematics, so none of it is new to me.

I pass Carter and the other SEAL, Steve Rivera, as we walk through the hangar. I can't tear my eyes away from Jacob. From his helmet with the night vision goggles perched and ready to his heavy, bulletproof vest loaded with ordnance, he brings back my tour of duty in Afghanistan in vivid detail.

The memories pummel me: standing in the stinging sand and choking heat as my first medevac helicopter returned from the field. I'd only flown into the country six hours before. When that helicopter shifted to land, blood spilled from the still-closed rear door, falling in a wavering crimson sheet through the air, splattering over my fatigues. My stomach clenches; the responsibility has never lifted. Whatever wounds were in that bird were mine to fix. Most of them were unfixable.

I guess it's the reason I'd been close to receiving my general medical license, but opted for more training in radiation therapy before finishing. Deep down, I wonder if I could handle the stress.

My eyes lock with Carter's, and I shiver, hoping his med check will be quick and simple.

I force myself to focus on the stairs before me, thinking hard about the crisp sound my boots make as I step down, the coldness of the metal railing under my hand. *Real. Now.* This is reality. It's a trick I've learned to use whenever the past takes me. Concentrate on the present; experience it, re-centering.

We pass a crazy-looking machine on this deck without a word. The officers' silence only adds to the ominous foreboding. Soon enough I'm gripping a transport vessel's sides as it rides the swells back to the heavy cruiser called *Olympia* with its bristling silhouette of cannons.

Aboard, we're released for a twenty-minute break. I head straight for A27, my ship's hospital room. I'd spent two days setting it up just the way I like it and wondering why I'd been issued an entire room to complete a 30-minute health check. I step in and, even though I've seen it plenty of times, the first thing I notice is the metal plate bolted to the wall with thick leather straps and heavy buckles at the height of a man's neck, waist, wrists, and ankles.

I stare at it for a moment. Straps on a med table are expected. I had used them plenty of times when a patient was in… I shake my head. But the vertical set on the wall is straight out of a horror film. This room also features a metal exam table with a pivot joint under it to keep it steady in high seas, a tiny corner bathroom, a small prep sink, and a desk.

One wall is packed floor to ceiling with lab equipment. I run my fingers over familiar but rare radiation-testing equipment. A small cart with an EEG machine sits in the corner. *That's new.* Someone must have rolled it in while I was touring the *Engage.*

Sighing, I open all the drawers under the exam table, triple checking my tools. After completing med school with honors in radiation and chemistry, I'd planned on at least a short leave. A moment to rebalance after the New World Order and U.S. alliance. They both claim peace but everyone knows it's a takeover.

I laugh—it's more like we are all dancing to their tune. There is no more leave now; the government doesn't promote freedom anymore. Not with a group they call the Collective ruling the world. Ten men and women, from each continent, who supposedly have world peace as their main goal.

I clench my fists; the rules are undefined. What would happen if I said no to serving in the new hybrid military? Nothing good, that's for sure. I glance at the shackles; it seems medical consent is a thing of the past too. Whatever the government orders, you do. I shake my head, turning from the dark reality.

Radiation and its effects in the body always fascinated me, but after the fourth pandemic, part of me wants to hide from the regulations and rampant fear. This duty seemed safer, sheltered. I pull my eyes away from the wall shackles that scream I was wrong.

I chew my lip. Hiding from the tail end of the latest pandemic at sea has its appeal. With global unrest at its peak, and the shift to digital currency propelling us into a new age, this assignment seemed heaven sent. Oversee one man during a three-day project called "157." Eyeing the specialized lab equipment, I wonder what they expect me to find at 1215.

I pick up the list of medical equipment I'm required to carry back to the *Engage* in 40 minutes. I double-check my pack, including a portable defibrillator, oxygen mask and mini tank, EpiPens, nitrous oxide pills, suturing kit, two large doses of morphine and Xanax. The last one is a powerful sedative.

But it's the handheld gamma-ray detector that gives me real pause. I run over the symptoms for radiation poisoning: nausea, headache, dizziness, low blood pressure. When I'd gotten these orders two weeks ago, I'd seen the radiation equipment listed, so I'd started rubbing iodine over my stomach every day to block anything I'll be exposed to. The thought makes me smile.

It's something my dad had always done to my brother Peter and me growing up. Whenever he thought the country was in danger, he would start rubbing us with iodine. In all my training, I've found nothing to refute his country wisdom.

I sigh. Jacob Carter has one of the strongest bodies on the planet, and I'm having trouble matching the required medical equipment with the man whose image is so fresh in my mind. What could happen on board a weaponless ship to make him need my attention? And why did seeing him today affect me so much? Maybe it was the quiet confidence in his gaze, or that simply walking past him made me feel safe for the first time in ages.

I grip the handle of my med pack, frowning. None of this is adding up. Maybe this will be the easiest assignment ever. Check his pulse and blood pressure, smile, fill out the paperwork. I nod, willing it to happen.

I report to the same deck we'd entered the transport vessel on. Lining up next to the boat, a sailor hands out heavy ear protection. I settle the muffs over my ears, enjoying the solitary sense of total silence. I don't want to connect with anyone here, just finish the job and move on, heal from my time downrange.

Lieutenant Smith stands in front of us, flashes five fingers. We wait, time seeming to stand still. I check my watch; the digital readout flips to 1200. A high-pitched buzz pierces the muffs' shield, rising until I can't resist lifting both hands to press them against my head as we stand on the loading dock.

Now the sound grips my chest, pressing inward until I curl forward, desperate to protect myself. An odd green fuzz creeps into my vision. I blink hard, any logical thought driven down by the pressure; but still, the haze intensifies. It's coming through the heavy closed door. I drop to my knees, the air too weighty as I fight the terror scrambling through my mind. I clutch the muffs, clenching my eyes, blood almost at a boil.

Diagnosis surfaces through the chaos: air embolism of the lungs. Sustained long enough, it will travel to the heart, resulting in death. The pressure increases again and I crumple forward. Imploded lungs from the increased pressure is also possible. I open my eyes, but everything vibrates so hard it turns my stomach.

Seconds before I fall face first, the sound fades. Its grip eases and I kneel, panting. Five other medics pitch forward on hands and knees, vomit streaming. Another lies prone on the cold metal deck. I crawl over to her. Her pulse is weak and irregular. I dig her own oxygen mask out of her pack and fit it to her face with trembling hands. The fitful pulse under my finger stops. I read the name stitched onto her lapel.

"Simmons! Listen to me, Simmons. It's over; come back now." My voice is shaky as I dig through her pack and pull out the nitrous oxide she'd been required to pack and force one tiny pill under her tongue. I count to ten, prepping to defibrillate, but her pulse jumps to life under my finger.

"Medics, in the boat!" Lieutenant Smith bellows at us. I ignore him, already treating a patient. His fingers clamp down like iron around my upper arm.

"Emerson! Front and center."

"But…" I resist, gesturing at Simmons.

He points to another staggering nurse. "Jones, take over on Simmons."

"I gave her nitrous oxide," I say as Smith forces me into the transport vessel, my med pack too heavy when he pitches it at me. Coughing grips me and I taste blood. The nurses double over in the boat, hacking.

I focus on Jacob Carter. If the intense sound and green haze originated from the *Engage,* then his symptoms will be far worse. I run through emergency procedures as the boat greets a far rougher sea than it was forty minutes ago. He'll need resuscitation first off. I force myself to stop coughing and breathe, tasting blood. What condition will his lungs be in?

Pulling out the radiation detector, I find the red needle at the top swinging from zero to maxed out. The digital readout follows suit. I grit my teeth as I watch it, struggling against the intense fear that cloaks me as we near the *Engage,* sitting so serenely under the darkening sky.

"No! Take me back," a female nurse shouts. Smith's grip on her uniform is all that keeps her from diving into the sea to escape the unreasonable fear that rolls from the *Engage.*

"Pull it together!" Lieutenant Smith fires the words at us, but the sheen of sweat on his brow gives him away. "Once on board, your number-one priority is locating your patient; life support is second. Radio for backup should you need it."

Now their reference to finding people is clear. Whatever chaos they had experienced on the *Engage* was likely deadly and would have prevented any usual thought processes, which means they knew what was coming; they knew they would need more nurses than patients.

The boat gains speed toward the *Engage's* ramp as I grip its side. My chest heaves and I tense, far too close to losing it.

When my boots hit the deck, a pulsing energy shoots up my legs, as if the ship is electrified. A wave of heat engulfs me, forcing its way into my agitated lungs. I cough hard once and then cut it off, ignoring the sensation, focusing on my patient.

The others stand as if rooted to the floor; the sense of terror is even heavier inside the ship. Jacob Carter's pleasant face overtakes my thoughts, and I push forward. The seconds are ticking; I have to find him.

I take the stairs two at a time, burning up excess energy. The strange mass of tubes and wires has imploded; nothing is left on this deck except a charred heap. I scan the room; it's devoid of personnel. Then I rush up the next flight of stairs. I enter the hangar; it's even hotter in here, and the energy flowing through the thick soles of my boots makes me jumpy, as if I drank ten energy shots.

Gaining the open rear deck where I'd been told Jacob was stationed, I release a sharp breath. *It's empty.* I rush to the railing; smaller boats are zipping back and forth in a search pattern. I sprint across the space, heart pounding. *He's not here.*

I can't imagine anyone living through what happened. About to rush down to the lower decks, a shout catches my attention. I lean over the rail. Footsteps echo behind me, but I can't pull my eyes away from the surfacing diver who's pulling a limp figure from the depths.

Ropes snake over the side of the ship next to me. A squad of soldiers is ready to haul the listless soldier up from below. Somehow, I'm certain he's mine.

Seconds later, the heavy stretcher, shedding water, gains the deck of the *Engage*. The men strain to haul it over the rail. I've spread my equipment out. *Ready*—except for the tremor in my hands. The men lower the stretcher and stand, crowding it with gawking looks at the body.

"Move!" I command, forcing them aside. "Jacob Carter, listen to me, you're going to be fine. Come on back now, Jacob."

I grasp his wide jaw, tilting his head up to open his airway. Glassy blue eyes greet me. My urgency doubles. I force his head back, close off his nose, and push five breaths into his lungs.

"Here! You." I point to a sailor. "Keep his head tilted back like this." He moves too slow. "Now!" I roar as we trade places.

I check his pulse. *Nothing.* Shifting, I put my palms over his heart, hands clasped together. I jam down hard, but his thick muscle and equipment resist me. Harder now, I compress his chest. Still no pulse. Frantic, I unzip his heavy Kevlar vest. Straps and buckles slow my progress.

"Get me the gray box!"

A soldier leaps to do my bidding. The heat rolling off the deck is burning my knees. Grasping Jacob's black T-shirt in both fists, I rip it down the center. The defibrillator appears beside me.

I crank the voltage dial to 150, force the paddles hard against the skin on his chest. The loud beep of the charging paddles sounds, and the sailors instinctively step back. I nod at the man holding Jacob's head. He lets go; I double-check the skin contact readout. It's in the green.

"Clear!"

I press the flashing shock buttons. Jacob twitches at the jolt, the heels of his heavy black boots slamming the stretcher. The skin on his wrists is cold and still. I hiss under my breath, transferring back to his mouth for five more breaths and chest compressions. *Nothing.* He was underwater too long, even without the injuries that got him there.

"Jacob!" I shout into his face. "Wake up!"

Nurses skid on their knees around me; help has arrived. I crank the defibrillator as high as it will go.

"Clear!"

Hands go up around the body, and I press both buttons. A nurse takes his wrist as I administer more chest compressions.

"I've got a pulse! It's weak, but we've got it."

"Thank You, God," I mutter, reaching for the oxygen mask. I force it tight against his square jaw. "You got this, Jacob Carter! That's right, fight for it!"

I run through potential issues we're facing: severe lung embolism, hypoxia. I check my watch, fifteen minutes at least since the experiment had reached peak intensity. *Possible brain damage.* I've got to raise his temperature and elevate his oxygen levels, stat.

I lift my head as a punishing sound descends on the deck. The sailors twist, searching. It's like the roar of a furnace, mixed with a guttural snarl. A wavering image appears at the far end of the deck, solidifying into a man. His arms flail as huge, unsteady strides carry him into reality. He's translucent for a moment, then visible again.

He's screaming, sending waves of terror ahead of him across the deck. His expression is pure horror. Time seems to slow, as if it doesn't have a tight grip on the man I'd last seen standing next to Jacob.

I watch, open-mouthed. As he runs, smoke billows off him, his standard-issue boots melting into the deck, leaving steaming rubber footprints. He convulses, snapping into full speed, pitching face first across the deck, limp. His red, blistered skin still smokes; no one moves, caught in the grotesque sight.

"Randall! Mobilize!" Lieutenant Smith shouts.

Grimacing, the girl holding Jacob's airway open gets to her feet, her cargo pants smoking at the knees.

"Now!"

Trembling, she pushes forward. The stench of burned flesh and sulfur fills the air, flowing from Rivera's ruined body, turning my stomach. I'm so glad Jacob has his mask on, unaffected by the smell. Randall and four others roll Steve Rivera over, gasping for air in the noxious cloud his body is emitting. One of them twists away, stomach heaving. I turn back to Jacob, thankful for his smooth, pale skin and too-cool temperature.

I force myself to focus. *How deep had he sunk under the water?* Checking the seal of the mask, I finish pulling off his heavy vest. *Even free divers can face the bends from surfacing too fast.*

"Immediate transport of two med patients to the *Olympia*." Smith's voice hammers into his radio.

I readjust the straps holding Jacob to the stretcher.

"Ready!" I say, as four male nurses grip the poles of the stretcher.

I walk by his side, fingers reading a now-steady pulse. I am so glad to see his chest rising on its own. Glancing back, I'm thankful Randall doesn't have Rivera on a stretcher yet. I want to keep Jacob as far from him as possible. The tight, steep staircase presents a problem. I trot ahead, turning backward, ready to catch if someone trips.

I breathe a sigh of relief as they settle him into the small transport boat. I pull out my IV kit; in one well-practiced jab, I hit the large but deflated vein in his arm. I hold the bag high until another nurse takes it. The boat lurches forward toward the rolling waves. It's going to be quite a ride. Tucking my legs in tight against the stretcher and the side of the boat, I anchor myself next to Jacob against the wild writhing of the sea.

By the time I get him settled on the metal table in A27, I've regained some composure. Plus, I'm happier with only one other nurse in the room. Too many hands equal miscommunication, and it's imperative that I monitor all his symptoms.

Wires and tubes lie in all directions from Jacob; I double-check all the equipment, nodding to myself, staring at the radiation tester. There's got to be a reason they required me to carry it. I wave it over him, the numbers jumping erratically before landing deep in the red zone.

The small machine shows the highest content over his stomach. Woodenly, I turn to the tall stack of waiting paperwork and enter the number on page five. The awful whine of a heart monitor gone flat sends a shot of adrenaline through me. I whip the heated blanket back and prep the defibrillator. The room fills with people.

"Clear!"

Hands go up and I press the shock buttons. I wince as he flinches but the steady blip on the screen makes it worth it.

"You've got to stop pulling that, Jacob," I whisper, as I inspect the monitor's connections to his skin.

"Core temp's up to 95°," a nurse says.

"We're in the clear, people. You can head out." My tone leaves no room for argument.

Needing more information, I wheel the EEG machine close and slide the white cap over his head. I adjust it until there's a good connection. When a patient is in a coma, especially if it's not medically induced, brain waves are almost nonexistent. He'd been underwater so long…my stomach rolls as the readout scrolls across the screen.

Tears jump to my eyes at the nearly straight lines. There should be a mixture of waves: delta, theta, alpha, beta, and gamma. I bite my lip; this might be a death sentence. Trembling sets in, my stomach quivering. He'd been so alive, the aura around him so steady just an hour ago. I bite the inside of my cheek, locking down hot anger at what's happened.

*Wait.* I frown at the screen; his gamma waves spike, a sharp peak on the readout. Gamma is the least known wave; technically, the frequency of these waves is too high for the brain's neurons to create. They are associated with perception, consciousness, and the quick processing of new information.

My finger follows the section tracking theta waves. "What?"

They jump to life, indicating a dreamy state, a mental place where learning and intuition are in control. I spend the next hour holding Jacob's wide hand while watching his brain defy all known processes. Gamma, theta, and a powerful burst of beta waves roll like a stormy sea across his brain. I'm delighted to see any activity; maybe one day he will use basic communication, but the surging rise and fall is unheard of.

"Well, Jacob, you don't follow the rules, do you?"

The door swishes open, and a new officer enters, carrying a laptop.

"I'm Brooks. I'll be overseeing your care of Carter."

I nod, assessing his clean features and toned physique. He's got some serious clout behind his name. *Why would a rear admiral be directly over a nurse? And why would he leave off his status on the introduction? He's got an angle I'm not aware of yet; that's for certain.* Project 157 was labeled as an equipment test on my orders, but the hospital setup and medical equipment suggest it was about the patient, not the ship.

"The brass ordered you to have communication with Randall, so you can compare patient stats. Document everything. *Twice.*" He sets the computer on the desk, clicking through till I have a bird's-eye view of an identical room with Rivera at the center.

*Note to self: you're on video, Sage.*

"Here's the list of tests we need on him by 1900 hrs."

I take the stack of papers. "Yes, sir."

He looks at me a moment. "Nice job bringing him around, Emerson."

"Thank you," I say. The compliment would have meant a lot if I weren't looking for anomalies. He'd separated himself from "the brass" when, it's obvious, he is one. *Why pretend to be on my side?*

He turns, the door clicks shut, and I sift through the tests, scowling. Half of them measure potassium-40 and other forms of radiation. A heavy pit settles in my stomach as I glance at the machine a Marine had rolled in behind Brooks.

It's a rare piece of equipment; I've only used one like it a single time in medical school. It's the very latest in radiation testing. One. Two. Three. The pieces are coming together. They had chosen me for this duty because of my obscure qualifications in chemistry and radiation. They knew what type of nurse they would need and which equipment.

I cross my arms, turning from the screen. Jacob is so pale on the table: someone *did* this to him. I flip through the rest of the papers; these tests also focus on brain activity. The EEG continues; we need to understand what's happening. A sharp beep makes my heart rate spike, but it's coming over the laptop as Rivera's room floods with more staff. Randall presses the paddles on Rivera's swollen red chest; the paddles break open the blackening blisters that cover his skin.

"Clear!"

"Nothing!" another nurse shouts.

I press the green transmit button on the screen.

"Crank it up to 200 joules. Go!" My voice penetrates the frantic action in Rivera's room. Randall turns the knob.

"Clear!"

Rivera convulses. Someone taps the monitor screen; they've got a faint beat. The nurses swirl, focusing on steadying the singed man on the table. One of them turns away, hands on her knees.

I turn back to Jacob, watching his chest rise and fall. I'm almost happy with his blood oxygen levels. Methodically, I continue to fill out his paperwork, moving on to the tests. Every result furthers my suspicions that the Navy knew what would happen. I lay a hand on Jacob's shoulder.

"What have they done to you?"

In the lonely silence of the room, I wonder at the attachment I have toward him. Is it the fact that I'd seen him alive and well, walked past him with only a few feet separating us? Caught his eye, and looked at him. *Connected.* Felt the quiet vibe of strength he gave off. So different from other patients I'd only known as broken; that was easier to accept somehow. Now there's only pulsing urgency that I must save this man.

I blink the heaviness out of my eyes. Forty-eight hours of constant supervision have left me drained. Twice, I'd gone down the hall to grab a quick nap on a cot; but each time Jacob had coded, sending me rushing back. I won't leave him in anyone else's hands. Not after pulling through all this. I rub more burn ointment on my knees, still blistered from kneeling on the *Engage*'s super-heated deck.

Any spare moments I'd spent at his side, researching. His EEG results continue on their crazed journey, still leaving alpha waves flatlined. They control waking functions, so it's no surprise. Still, even a brief flash would be great.

For about seven hours, his brain waves had flatlined. I'd worried the entire time, hovering over him, talking as if he could hear me. Then, his gamma came to life, starting whatever strange path his mind is on. At least he has activity. I don't know what to expect if he wakes up.

I release a slow breath of relief; he's breathing on his own, which is huge, considering the intense damage his lungs had received. I scan my phone; turns out the nurses assigned to Rivera graduated with similar skills to mine, adding to my conviction that Project 157 had a distinct purpose that I haven't grasped yet. They handpicked us for this duty. Reading through Admiral Ash's previously rumored "success" with his super-soldier program and deep connections to the N.W.O. leaves me queasy. I turn back to the safety of my familiar charts.

All my findings from the endless tests I've performed on Jacob lead straight to positrons…and potassium-40. I scroll through the jargon of a medical journal article on antimatter. Potassium decays into a positron, which, as far as science knows, is antimatter.

For every molecule in our universe, an exact match of an antimatter molecule exists, which has a negative charge instead of a positive one and spins in the opposite direction but is otherwise identical. Studies have revealed that every molecule of antimatter contains enormous energy, and the antimatter scientists have been able to capture and contain over years of study equals less than a thimbleful.

The problem with harnessing this enormous energy? As soon as antimatter connects with its physical counterpart, it decays into pure energy called *annihilation*. I scroll down the page as the image on the screen makes the hair on my arms stand on end. It's a mass of tubes and wires with the words "particle decelerator" printed underneath. It's the only machine that can contain antimatter or positrons. It's exactly what I saw on the *Engage* before the experiment.

I watch Jacob, toying with the idea that a massive annihilation of different classes of radiation energy is what he survived. Yet, he has no symptoms of classic radiation poisoning like Rivera. Theories bounce like ping-pong balls in my mind. Brooks steps into the doorway.

"How's he doing?" he asks, brown eyes sincere.

Brooks is likable, and I'm glad to have him between me and Admiral Ash, even though I'm still calculating his every word. He reminds me of my older brother, Peter. Thinking of him makes me smile; I let it cover my unease in his presence.

"Well, he's stable. Not sure how. The thing I don't like is how he's coded so abruptly. He's gone from stable to dead in seconds." I cross my arms as Brooks enters the room.

"Did you complete the spinal tap?"

I swallow hard at his question. "I'm glad he was already out for that, made it easier."

"There was a radiation level of 300 REM in the bone sample you took?"

I clear my throat, turning to straighten the wires on the heart monitor to cover my expression. I haven't submitted the results from that test yet. In fact, the papers are sitting right next to me. I cover my agitation, forcing an answer.

"Yes, that's correct. But that reading's inaccurate, more of a guess. I ran it three times, and that's the average of the results, they were so vastly different." I shake my head. "We are dealing with something new here."

I run over the past twenty minutes in my memory. The first reading had been so high, I had muttered it aloud. *A27 is well fitted with audio-recording equipment.*

"You'd expect him to be deep in severe radiation poisoning with those levels." His statement is more of a question. They'd offered me a full radiation suit, but I'm wearing only the vest and my iodine.

"Well, time is a factor, but he's doing great, considering." I hand Brooks the report, holding his eye, letting him know I'd called him on knowing the numbers. *Here's the info you already know.* He turns on his heel and exits.

I guess that explains the reason I've enjoyed so much freedom in caring for him; they're right here, watching over my shoulder, listening to every sigh, monitoring everything. I wonder if they are scanning the searches I've done on my personal phone. I shiver;

privacy is obsolete in today's world. Everything is traceable. The thought makes me clench my jaw.

I settle into the only chair in the room, close to Jacob. It also explains why they'd pulled my assistant. The wavering radiation results are a major issue. I run the meter over Jacob again. The needle jumps between zero and max a few times before landing in the high red zone, as usual.

I checked online a few times, and it's not supposed to behave like that. It should give a clear reading straightaway. I rub my forehead, trying to get all the pieces to fit together.

Jacob was one of the healthiest men in the SEALs, the strongest. But he keeps trying to die, and it's wearing on me. The test results don't sit right. Brooks is correct; Jacob *should* be dying from radiation poisoning, like Rivera. And I've had higher exposure than is safe even with the vest, if indeed it's a harmful strain. But I'm not sick; in fact, although I'm tired, I've gone almost three days without sleep, and I'm still functioning well. It's as if there's extra energy in the very air around Jacob's inert form.

They had to pull and replace Randall within hours because of her severe nausea and low blood pressure, despite wearing a full radiation suit. Of course, the stench Steve Rivera is giving off could have caused that.

My head snaps up. *Had Jacob moved?* I stand, running my eyes over his powerful physique, covered in a thin sheet and heating blanket. Maybe I am too tired to function. His thumb twitches. I go still, entranced.

"Jacob?" I lean closer, willing him to move again. His face contorts; I suck in a breath and lean closer. "Come on, Jacob! That's right. Wake up." My voice is loud in the room's stillness, desperate to connect with him.

His arms clench, muscles standing out. He bucks, his body flopping hard. I wish I could reach his head to keep it from slamming the table as I lay over his chest, fighting to keep him from pitching off the table. It gets worse. He's popping my feet off the floor as he thrashes. Foam builds at the corners of his mouth. The room fills with people. Brooks slaps a syringe into my hand.

"Valium."

"NO!" I shout, knocking it away. The syringe spins to the floor.

"No?" His voice is tight, eyes piercing as he tries to lock down Jacob's other arm.

Foam is bubbling down Jacob's chin. It sure looks like a seizure; but deep down, I *know* he's coming back.

"No. He's coming to. If you give him that, he may never surface again." I watch the heart monitor as the numbers spike.

"Emerson! You're going to lose him!" Brooks shouts in my face as we wrestle with Jacob.

Jacob's wide mouth is now forming words. I can't tell what they are, but it's a function I never hoped for in him.

"Look!" I yell as his hammering muscles slow to a rock-hard tension; his blue eyes snap open, making me gasp.

As I hold down his chest, he curls forward like I'm not even there, grappling with him. He swings his legs off the table, gains his feet, and sweeps the wires off in one smooth motion. The heated blanket I'd covered him with falls away as his chest pumps huge breaths. He grabs my shoulders, fingers like steel, eyes darting around the room.

"Where is he?" he pants, forcing me behind him as he swipes a scalpel off of the exam table. Now he's armed, the muscles in his back bunching. He turns, one arm keeping me centered behind him, the small knife out ahead. *Protecting me.*

Personnel press against the walls, hands held high. He heaves a deep sigh, then turns back to me, confusion on his face. Evaluations fly through my mind; the brain damage I'd feared is nonexistent. I wince at his grasp on my upper arms. Jacob blinks hard, searching, jaw clenching.

"Why is everything so…gray?" he asks. Then he groans, veins in his wide neck standing out.

"Where are my clothes?" Then his eyes roll back in his head, and he crumples to the floor. We rush forward, and Brooks confiscates the scalpel as we struggle to get his heavy, limp form back on the table. His pulse is steady; blood pressure is great.

Brooks steps forward. "Is he dead?"

I shake my head. "No." I laugh. "He's asleep. Actual sleep, instead of the state he's been in. He spoke! Against all odds, we've got full brain function." The stress of the last two days fades into relief at his surfacing.

"So, he's stable?"

"Yes, sir. Solid as a rock." Hands fly over him, reconnecting monitors. "Look at that; these are some perfect numbers, just what I'd expect from a twenty-six-year-old in top shape. I say, let him sleep; he's been through a lot."

Brooks's shoulders drop the tension they've carried. "All personnel clear out."

The nurses file out at his words.

"Brooks, I want a cot. I'm not leaving him."

He nods his assent. "You should really wear a suit."

"I have the vest. What's done is done. The worst exposure was on the ship, anyway, and it's not like you offered a suit then. That's my decision."

I expect him to insist; it would be procedure. But as with everything else that sits cockeyed about this, he lets it pass. Honestly, keeping Jacob Carter alive has become my entire universe. The heavy suit will slow me down in an emergency. Deep down, with all the numbers swinging wild, I can't quite believe normal radiation poisoning is a part of this strange case.

"Fine. You'll have a cot."

I marvel at the leverage they've given me. Nothing about the situation is normal military function. The cot arrives and, in seconds, I'm asleep next to the medical miracle named Jacob Carter.

The disturbing beep of a flatline wakes me. I'm out of the cot with paddles in my hands before I'm fully awake. I stare at Jacob's face, full of healthy color. His monitor blips in a steady rhythm, and I release a breath. It's Rivera again. I turn, watching the third new nurse struggle to move in his heavy radiation suit.

"Come on, Rivera," I mutter; but the truth is, it might be a mercy if he never wakes up. His insides are as burned as his skin, and his hair has fallen out. He regains a weak heartbeat. I press the transmit button.

"Burkehold, run your radiation tester over him, will you?" He nods and I squint, longing to see the needle.

"589," he reports.

I wince at the number; life is unsustainable with those levels.

"Did the needle ping back and forth before it gave you a reading?"

"No. It spiked straight to 589 and stayed there, just like always. This guy's in the last stages. Thing I can't figure is why he smells so bad, like sulfur." Burkehold's voice is hard to decipher through the suit.

"Thanks," I say. I'd already requested two fresh radiation testers, but all of them had done the same swinging needle act when giving a reading on Jacob. All the information from the bigger machines along the wall matches its wild rhythm.

I turn to find Jacob staring at me. I cover my shock with words as I search for balance.

"Welcome back, Jacob Carter. I'm Sage Emerson, your nurse." Smiling wide, I force my usual bedside manner as my hands move to his wrist, finding a strong pulse. *I've never been more unqualified to take care of a case.* "You gave us quite a scare."

His blue eyes search my face, intelligence shining, clarity instead of the confusion I'd feared. "Why is everything so flat?"

"Flat?" I cock my head, remembering how he'd called the room gray.

He grunts, looking around. "Where am I?"

I nod at his logical question. "You're on board the *Olympia*."

"Commissioned in 1995, 550 feet long, displaces 9,600 tons of water." He rattles off the stats, defying all my worst fears.

My brows rise; he's lost none of his smarts. I smile. "That's right. So, tell me how you're doing."

His bright eyes come back to mine. "Breathing is not a comfortable experience." His voice is deep, a little raspy from the lack of use, but pleasant.

"Breathing, for you, is a miracle." My honest delight at his consciousness is uncontainable.

He murmurs, "How did I get here?"

I can see him trying to patch together the memories.

"Well, it's been three days since the experiment," I say, and his brows go up. "Went by quick, huh?"

I keep my voice light as he grunts an agreement. His gaze lands on the wall shackles; he stares at them before sitting up. I restrain myself from steadying him; his motions are smooth and strong. *He doesn't need your help, Sage.*

"Those are less than comforting," he says, referring to the restraints.

I look at the floor; what can I say?

"Where's Rivera?"

My eyes dart to the laptop, giving my thoughts away.

Jacob leans forward, squinting at the screen. "What happened to him?"

I lick my lips. "He's in the final stages of radiation poisoning."

Jacob's eyes shift to mine. "Final?"

"Yes, I'm sorry." I clench back tears, watching the sorrow on his face as he looks at Rivera.

"Divers pulled you from the ocean, but Rivera appeared on the deck of the *Engage,* billowing smoke."

His eyes narrow, thoughts rolling.

"Do you remember what happened?" I probe.

"Yeah," he whispers, but it's clear he won't share. "What do you mean, 'he appeared'?"

"Just what I said. I was defibrillating you when he materialized out of thin air."

"What about everyone else on board?"

I'm quiet for a moment, wishing I could change the past. "There are no other survivors."

Jacob nods. He looks down at his arms and chest, flexes his muscles, and nods again, as if he's relieved. "I need some clothes."

"Uh." Honestly, I didn't figure he'd be off the table for months. "I... I'll order some." I raise my voice, although I know I don't need to. "Brooks, requesting a uniform."

Seconds later, the door opens, and a Marine shoves a neatly folded stack of clothing through the opening. I take them and he shuts the door hard. I narrow my eyes, looking over my shoulder at Jacob.

He juts his chin at the door, and I know what he wants. Pulling my lips to one side, I grasp the handle; it's locked. I turn back to Jacob, adding everything up to a bunch of negatives.

I put the clothes in his wide hands and turn to my desk, filling out a stack of paperwork and giving him as much privacy as possible. I don't know what I write. My thoughts race; he's suffering from none of the side effects I'd expected. I need to run another EEG. I'd love to see the readout right now. His alpha waves are back in full force, that much is clear.

"Got any food in here?"

I turn at his deep voice; he's intimidating standing there, seeming to fill the entire room. One of the top operatives in the military.

"Brooks," I say as I dig into my bag, pulling out a candy bar.

Our fingers brush as he takes it, making my eyes snap up to his. My skin tingles where I'd touched him; the energy seeping down my arm is fresh and clean, not from my imagination. He rips open the bar and devours it.

"Thanks."

"Brooks will have a meal soon if he's on his A-game." I can't resist the dig at our surveillance team. "I need to take your vitals."

He nods at me with a quiet thoughtfulness in his eyes.

"Let's get your weight first."

He steps on the scale, the readout steady at 200. I write the number, then flip to his stats from before the experiment. He taps the digital readout, frowning.

"You're heavier," I say.

"I've weighed 195 for years," he says.

"I was expecting a weight drop after three days of unconsciousness."

"Must've been the candy bar," he says, still staring at the number.

I cover a smile; I hadn't expected the sense of humor. The door opens and a Marine delivers a tray of meatloaf, mashed potatoes, and green beans.

I set it on my desk, offering him the chair. He sits, black T-shirt stretched tight over muscle. He devours the food in the time it takes to get his blood pressure.

"I need more," he says, but I know it's not to me.

His perception and intelligence give me pause; *this is not a man to underestimate.* Another plate arrives and I bury myself in paperwork, trying to explain to myself how he's sitting there eating like a machine when medically he should be clinging to life like Rivera.

I look up to find him staring over his empty tray at Rivera on the screen. He's swollen, skin tight and seeping. Of all the horrendous wounds I've seen, I pity Rivera most of all. Living must be torture.

"I have to go for a run," Jacob says, flexing his arms.

"Uh. I'm not sure you should take that sort of action right now."

He gives a polite nod at my words and repeats his own. "I have to go for a run. Around the deck is fine, but I can't sit here anymore."

I shrug; it's Brooks who will decide. Jacob slips off his chair, dropping into a series of fast-paced push-ups. I count fifty before he questions in mid-motion, "You said you had to defib me?"

"Four times." I smirk down at him, so alive; it seems like a year ago. "I'd really appreciate it if you didn't do that again."

He laughs at my comment, still breathing easy, switching to sit-ups. "Well, I sure appreciate your help. I was in the water, right?"

"Yes, glassy eyed and all when they got you to the deck. You were under for at least ten minutes."

"Hanging out with sharks." He laughs, and I wonder if it's an old joke.

"Where was Rivera?" he repeats, trying to get something more from me.

"He appeared, screaming. Was like time couldn't grasp him; he was running full out, but in slow motion. Then he crashed to the deck and required the same lifesaving efforts as you."

He looks back and forth as I speak. I sure would love to know what's going on behind those eyes. The door swings open and Brooks sets a pair of boots on the floor.

"You're in luck, Carter. We've got an entire deck fitted for physical training. Let's move."

I resist the urge to interject my cautions, but I can't deny that Carter doesn't seem to need any coddling.

"Emerson, bring a blood pressure cuff and some blood-collection equipment," Brooks adds.

I nod, relieved to stay with Jacob.

I pause in the hallway; six armed Marines line the tight space. They fall into step around Jacob. *Are they expecting a fight?* I watch Jacob's smooth movement; as he walks, his square jaw shows to the left over his shoulder, scanning his escorts.

Two decks below, we enter a wide room that spans the massive ship. A running track lies around the edge, and an obstacle course takes up its center. I scowl, taking in the course's difficulty.

*Admiral Ash*. His reputation gives me a queasy reaction as I stare at the training area. *Super-soldiers*. Watching Jacob pull tension from his limbs, I swallow down emotions. They'd been more than happy to bring him here, and Brooks holds a clipboard with lap and course times to record on the first page. A large DARPA logo sits at the top of the page, along with another I don't recognize.

Jacob takes off as if a pack of wolves is at his heels. Had he signed up for this? I would have to guess no. I'd read the unease in his eyes before the experiment, full of the same questions as me.

Halfway around the track, he's settled into a punishing pace that he holds for the next fifteen laps. I fret, wishing I could stop the madness; he should be resting. The damage to his lungs could cause him to drop at any second. Brooks is timing him, cataloging numbers, an air of amazement veiled on his face.

Brooks hails Jacob as he barrels toward us like a freight train, sweat rolling. Jacob stops in front of him, chest rising easily as if he'd been doing a light jog. It's the expression of satisfaction, maybe even delight, that I didn't expect in his eye. I lean over, a half a mile in a minute eighty flat! That's a few seconds better than his fastest time on his records. *After three days of intensive care, how can he be doing this?*

"Emerson, take his vitals."

He stands like a statue as I move around him.

"He's good," I state the obvious.

"That all you got, Carter?" Brooks taunts.

"Psht." Jacob makes a disgusted sound as he takes off again. He puts his head down, arms pumping as he speeds around the track; I can sense his elation in the power of his motion from here.

I've been around these elite soldiers enough to know how fiercely competitive they are by nature, and I wish Brooks had kept his mouth shut. My main concern is his lungs, the only thing he complained about. My own still seem tender and they hadn't received the full punishment of Project 157 or been drowned.

"Sir. You should stop him, sir."

"He's pushing himself. Look at him. Almost as fast as Tex."

A sharp glance reveals Brooks frowning down at his chart, regretting the slip. Jacob whips by, increasing his tempo again, hauling in air, maxed out. He grabs a rope hanging from the ceiling at the far turn. One-handed, he lets the motion swing him over the first hurdle, sprinting up to the twelve-foot wall. He leaps, stretching high, fingertips catching a small lip three-quarters of the way up. He completes the rest of the course in like manner. Brooks gives an enthusiastic click on his timer as Jacob leaps from the last wall.

Panting hard and soaked with sweat, he walks toward us, hands on his hips. I repeat his vitals, comforted by the perfect numbers.

"Satisfied?" I ask, close by his side.

"Much better." A smile plays on half Jacob's mouth.

Brooks nods, hand outstretched the way we'd come. Filing up the stairs, the niggling sense of missing something solidifies into a number. Potassium-40 decays with a half-life of $1.19 \times 10^{10}$, which means the radiation meter should pick up a solid reading since potassium-40 has such a predictable nature.

I grip the railing hard; the lab results have shown concentrations of potassium-40 in unheard-of proportions, then the next round is lower than normal. All humans have some levels of K-40, which we accumulate from food and the environment. But K-40 is toxic, admitting a positron, sort of like a gamma ray every time a molecule decays.

Jacob's lab results show that his levels are well past severe radiation poisoning. But he's not sick. Neither am I, even after such close contact. Meanwhile, Rivera's on his third nurse, the first two still suffering acute exposure even with the full suits.

What if Jacob doesn't have too much K-40? What if he's got a different type of potassium? I run through the chemical charts in my mind. Known elements are K-39 through K-57. Our bodies require sufficient K-39, a.k.a. *potassium,* to sustain life. Brooks ushers Jacob and me into A27 but my thoughts are flying. I need to study his charts and double-check his numbers. Jacob stands with his hands on his hips.

"You still good?" I ask, pulling out of my thoughts.

He draws a breath to respond, but an anguished scream erupts from the laptop. Gasping, I turn, unable to rip my eyes away from the unfolding scene. Rivera is sitting up on the table, face contorted in horror, screaming, blood trickling from the corners of his mouth, his ruined lungs unable to sustain the effort. His nurse's movements are awkward in the suit as he tries to force Rivera back onto the table.

"No! Don't let me go back!" His raw scream raises goose bumps on my arms. Smoke flows off him. Jacob stands close to me, transfixed by the ghoulish scene. Trembling starts in my stomach and spreads to my limbs. Rivera's next scream echoes live, straight through the walls, raising my hair.

"No! The worms! Don't let them eat me! No, no!" He squirms as if something approaches from the right but nothing's there. It's the expression in his eyes that's so terrifying, *pure fear.*

"The claws! They have me! Please, help me! Don't let me go!" He clings to the nurse, who's desperate to escape the dying man's grasp.

*"Nooooo!"* Rivera's long shriek sears itself into my mind and he goes limp, head thudding against the table, eyes empty. The nurse runs off-screen as Rivera's body blackens before our eyes.

I reach out and slam the laptop shut, unable to see anymore. My chin trembles as the knowledge descends that I've just witnessed a man's entrance into hell. The terror and the inevitability of it—the *eternity.* A sob chokes me. I shut my eyes, but the images are worse in my mind; the worms are eating him.

Jacob's strong arms surround me, the human connection life-giving. I let my face rest on his thick chest.

"Shh," he whispers, but he's trembling too.

Pulling myself together, I look up at him.

"Is…is that where you went?" I whisper, needing to know.

He shakes his head, sorrow and relief running over in his blue eyes.

"No. No, it isn't," he says, blinking back tears. I back out of his embrace, aware of the unseen eyes. We stand in silence as time creeps past, trying to find equilibrium. Jacob groans. I turn, shocked to find him curled forward, muscles tight. His face contorts as he forces himself straight.

"Jacob?" But he can't hear me, his eyes are far away. His arms jerk. He frowns, trying to control it. The contortion takes his torso.

"Jacob!"

He leans forward, gripping the stainless exam table, growling. The air vibrates as he struggles; the bolts holding the table down squeal as he wrenches it from the floor. My tools shiver loose from their drawers with sharp metallic pings.

The veins on his neck stand out as a green haze blurs my vision. He sinks, legs buckling. No, wait. I blink rapidly; his boots are missing! He's sinking through the floor. He looks over at me, teeth clenched, grimacing as his hands meld into the metal table. I rush forward, snatching at him, too late. He drops through the solid metal floor, and my hands spread over its hard, hot surface.

"Brooks!" I shout. "Get the divers! Find him!"

The radiation meter bounces crazily through its range where it's landed face up on the floor. I leap up and hit the door to find it locked. A savage scream rips my throat. "Open the door!"

I snatch my med pack and run out the second it opens. *Not again.* I stand where the ramp meets the foaming waves, legs wet as the transport vessel pulls in. Glassy blue eyes greet me.

# 3
# JACOB



Night will fall soon. Darkness comes. I must not spend it here where the lions prowl. As I creep through the forest, its vibrant colors and smells are like an assault—too bright, too fresh, too alive. I nod; I'll adjust until it's intoxicating again.

A twig snaps beneath my foot, making me cringe, *stupid*. My skin crawls and I freeze, waiting for the rush of an unseen enemy. Nervous sweat trickles down into my eyes; the tearing weakness is back, bones protruding.

Gritting my teeth, I push myself forward by willpower alone. I'm glad to see the vibrant wings of birds flutter; it means no predators are waiting ahead.

Being back in my body was incredible once I adjusted to the restriction of it. The energy, strength, and ability had been a relief.

Squinting, I consider the preacher's words as I clench my fists, hating my powerlessness.

In my body, I'd been able to push the envelope, with more energy and speed than ever before. Now I'm *in* the spirit, and the awful truth is, my core, my spirit, is malnourished. I scan the forest ahead. I think that can change. Clenching my jaw, I vow *it will change.*

The trees thin and the gentle dish of a meadow shows in the distance. Peering past the tree line, I grimace; crossing open ground is dangerous. A neon-green lizard rounds the tree. Seeing my face so close, it stops, looks at me with one eye. Its tiny chest puffs up.

"Chirp!" Its skin flashes brilliant red as it emits the sound, then fades to green. A smile curls half my mouth; the *life* here will rub off on me.

There is movement beyond. In the center of the meadow, a man rises. He'd been napping in the deep grass. He stretches, pulling out tension. Another movement catches my eye; three tawny heads freeze as they catch sight of the man. They drop to the ground, disappearing from my view.

Sweat pours as I stand rooted to the spot. I should climb; they're circling closer, but the unfolding scene renders me immobile.

Two lions split off. I wish I could call out, but my voice betrays me. My breath comes in shallow gasps as they cut toward me. But the closest one halts fifty yards distant. At some invisible signal, the three rough-coated beasts erupt from the cover of the trees, converging.

The man in the center of the field turns, his face paling. He fumbles for the jeweled hilt of his sword. I cringe at seeing its pitiful length. *Just like mine.* His quaking arms loft the short sword before him and he falters, unsure against the three.

The man makes a good sweep of his pitiful blade, catching the first across the jaw, turning its oncoming rush. From the left, another swipes his long, wicked claws and draws four deep red lines across the man's thigh. He drops the sword, clutching his leg.

The lions circle, growling and hissing, ears flat against their heads. The bright grass is smeared red. The man stands horrified at their gaping mouths, so close. My heart pounds as they relish the moments before the kill.

A wild rebel yell pierces the air, making me flinch. A slim figure emerges from the far trees. Uttering another war cry, the woman… *Myah?* She barrels toward the center of the meadow. Her gentle smile and soft words don't compute with the firebrand closing in like a freight train.

Gaining more speed, she meets the largest lion with deadly intent, fearless. She fights karate-style, forcing the lion to back up. Dwarfed by the massive beast, she advances, rage on her face. The lion's growl shakes the trees; yet her arms flash in and out, forming an impenetrable barrier. They unite, rushing forward as one; she turns them aside, unyielding.

I see no weapon in her hands, yet the lions are wounded and bloody as they circle her. She whirls, on the offense, landing a solid blow on the spine of the foremost lion. It falls, writhing and growling as the other two leap onto Myah.

I groan, hating to watch yet unable to tear myself away. All I can see now is a blur of dull, matted fur and Myah's long black hair. The ground shakes at the concussion of the battle. Myah regains her feet, shouting, irate, raining punishing blows. She shows no signs of quitting or hesitating.

I jerk as memories descend like a cloak, thick and heavy, as if they've slipped through the veil. I'm deep in enemy territory, in hand-to-hand combat, landing punishing blows till the enemy falls, ignoring intense pain. Under heavy fire, pushing forward, gaining ground.

I groan: *your real self is hiding in the woods while a woman does the rescuing.* I grip the tree next to me, humiliated, yet too anemic to take a step.

Myah leans forward, roaring her defiance. The lions retreat, leaving red tracks in the green grass. She stands, chest heaving air, with fur mashed into her dark tunic, but she seems unharmed. She bows her head a moment, then reaches out to lift the man from the ground as he clutches his bleeding leg.

Soon, his arm is around her shoulder, and they hobble into the shelter of the wood. I stare at the wreck of trampled grass streaked with blood. She did it. Slight, quiet Myah saved that man's life. *How?*

Galvanized, I turn, looking for my path, disturbed to see it glistening a good twenty yards away. *How have I gotten so off track?* The depth of my attachment to my glittering trail is startling. Creeping along, there is only staying alive and not being eaten by lions.

My legs tremble with relief as I push open the moss-covered door of the hut. Warmth and golden candlelight soothe my tattered nerves as I slip inside. Myah's arms are loaded with cloths as she kneels by the man she rescued.

His leg, extended on the bench, is a mass of swelling. Blood is still seeping from the four ragged gashes. The man clenches his teeth, skin a pale pallor. Ian rounds the corner, a steaming bowl of water cradled in his hands. Ian and Myah go to work cleaning and wrapping the man's leg while I crumple on the floor nearby. A deep sense of shame crushes hard; I'd left her to make war on her own.

All my shortcomings, frailty, and frustration at being ambushed by this reality bubble up, simmering with an uncontrollable nature. *Why am I being punished like this? I hate being hunted. I hate the fear and my inability to handle it. I want my world, where I'm able.*

The door creaks open and Demyen squeezes through the opening. His presence fills the small room with a crackling energy; his emerald-green eyes take in the scene and he grunts, "When? Where?"

Myah looks up, her mouth set in a straight line. "A few hours ago in the south meadow."

She goes back to work and Demyen grunts again. He vanishes into the darkness without a sound.

My voice comes out too loud. "Where's he going?"

Myah's compassionate gaze finds me. She sees more than I want her to. "He will return. He does not fear the night."

"This place is crazy. What's the point? Only to end up like him?" My questions brim over shotgun-style, too harsh in the quietness of this safe place.

Myah's gaze is solid, then she turns back to her work. "Let me tell you a story… Long ago, when I was young, Demyen was stung by a scorpion on his left shoulder and became very ill. His strength waned, and he drew closer and closer to death's door.

"Many came to pray over him; even so, he did not recover. Only later did we learn Demyen had awakened at the scorpion's sting and crushed it. Sometimes, the tip of the stinger will break off and remain embedded. The venom had rendered Demyen unresponsive, so none of us knew what was wrong.

"For three days, he neither ate nor drank. We gathered, already mourning. I stood by his bed as his breath came in gasps and quivers; my hands trembled with fear, *so blind to the laws*. His dull green eyes slid open, struggling to speak. I leaned in, trying to understand what he wanted. 'Meat...' he rasped.

"I ripped some scroll into tiny pieces and laid them in his parched mouth. He retched and I thought the silver cord would be broken right then. But a wild light shone in his eyes. He opened his cracked lips for more. Cringing, I put a smaller piece in his mouth, and he fought the convulsions." She shakes her head.

"He opened his mouth again; the more he forced down, the brighter the odd light in his eyes grew. 'Water.' I thought to give him all he wanted in his last moments." Myah's eyes are far away, deep emotions swirling on her face.

"He gulped the water, holding it down by sheer force of will. That's when Aseph, the lion with the tattered ear, stalked in. Every one of us backed away at his presence. Now, I wonder what we were thinking. Leaving the weakest one to him? But fear locked me down." She makes a deprecating sound of disgust that I can relate to.

"I knew so little then. We pressed ourselves against the walls, hoping he would be content with just one victim." Tears prick her eyes, shame making her drop her gaze. "Demyen's eyes widened as Aseph loomed over him, dripping hot saliva on his chest, enjoying the moment. When his huge jaws opened, I shut my eyes, unable to bear the sight.

"'Get!' Demyen wheezed. Despite the weakness, his voice had authority. His fingers shook as he reached for more scroll right below the massive jaws. Aseph growled; the walls shuddered; my bowels turned to water. Demyen somehow got the scroll to his mouth, took a bite, fought it down.

"'Get out.' His voice was stronger. He plowed down another giant mouthful. His throat constricted, trying to reject the words. I'm still not sure which battle was more intense: Aseph's, standing over Demyen, trying to disobey, or Demyen's, forcing that scroll down. But Aseph sank to the ground, growling and slinking out of the house. Later, Demyen's shoulder erupted, spewing out that splinter of scorpion's tail. He hasn't stopped eating since then."

With uncanny timing, the door swings open, and Demyen's presence makes the hut seem full. Another man enters. He's shorter, but with a definite aura of strength I long for. His tunic ripples over muscle as he strides forward. I flinch, realizing it's the man I'd listened to in the crowd.

Myah smiles at him with relief. "Welcome, Peter. I am glad Demyen found you."

But Peter only sees the injured man. "What is your name?"

The man's pale lips move with barely a sound. "Solomon."

His straight-brown hair looks too dark against his deathly pale skin; he's lost a lot of blood. Peter reaches into a small pouch in his tunic. His thick fingers cradle a small glass bottle. Peter leans over Solomon. "Do you want healing?"

It seems like such an odd question. *Who wouldn't if he were dying?* Yet Solomon struggles, frowning, pride and need at war. In a reedy voice, he says, "Yes, I need the Almighty."

Peter nods and opens the small bottle. He pours the amber oil into his cupped palm. Its scent wafts over me, clearing my mind. He bows his head as words flow, changing the atmosphere.

"Almighty, I bring before You Your servant Solomon. I thank You that You brought his healing and carried his pain so long ago, for by Your stripes, we are healed. You are power, and nothing is too difficult for You." Peter lays his palm against Solomon's forehead. "Be healed."

Two small words, so forceful, so impossible. Yet the command ripples the air. I can feel it in my bones. Every nerve is on fire; there's a fold in the fabric of the world; a smear of green haze is visible, like heat waves over the desert.

Peter leans forward, pouring the oil onto Solomon's forehead. It runs, glistening, over his temples, between his nose and eyes. Everywhere it touches, color and life appear in Solomon's skin. The healthy blush spreads down his neck under his tunic.

Sound draws my gaze to his wound. It sizzles; the seeping blood and ragged tissue are boiling. Solomon groans, gripping his leg. The sound grows louder, and I watch new, supple skin stretch over his wound.

Solomon relaxes. A scent like honeysuckle and jasmine fills the room as he swings his leg off the bench and stands. His dark-brown eyes glisten with tears as he lifts his scrawny arms to heaven.

"Praise You, Almighty!" he shouts at the top of his lungs, making goose bumps race up my skin.

Everyone else seems to enjoy the light, the worship. But the emptiness inside is acute. If I don't figure out how this world works, I'll end up like the girl in the woods. Everything here seems backward, defying logic.

We gather around the board. Demyen, as usual, is packing away massive amounts of scroll. Myah is brilliant, filled with joy over last night. Peter's ice-blue eyes crinkle at the corners as he laughs at Ian's comment.

But Solomon is the one who draws my eyes. His hair still glistens with the anointing oil. He's tall, and far too slim, but *alive*. Brimming with life. Devouring an incredible amount of scroll, keeping right up with Demyen. He nods to himself as he eats.

"You know, I hadn't eaten for two days before the attack. Was so busy, so tired too. That's when they struck." He shakes his head in disbelief. "You'd think I'd know better."

"They're always seeking an opportunity, watching for weakness. Especially Aseph," Ian says, nodding.

"Aseph?" I ask, the name pricking like a sword's tip.

Peter responds, "Old Aseph. He's the biggest lion, the only one with scarred paws. Torn left ear. He's the strongest, the most devious. Never misses a chance to attack children of the Light, as Solomon discovered."

Peter laughs again. "We've all been there, Solomon. I'm glad I was still here. I was supposed to travel yesterday, but I had so much trouble getting things settled I didn't leave. Guess I know why, now."

I sit there, at war with myself. In my world, life and strength would pulse through my veins. I had a plan, a future. My other existence surfaces, making me yearn for it. Yet, somehow, I'm certain, this version of myself has always haunted me. *The truth.*

I grit my teeth as a new thought explodes in my brain. If I could thrive here, what would the other world be like? What if I were strong in both places? I blink hard; it's an enticing thought. Being fully alive. I can't hold the vision long before the other world fogs out and I'm left with the grim reality of this one.

I look down in disgust at my atrophied arms. Sweat breaks thinking of going outside. *I don't want this.* Myah telling Demyen's story comes to mind.

I glance over at his muscled bulk. Chewing massive mouthfuls of food, he's the most alive person I have ever met. Demyen is… everything I have lost coming to this world where colors are too bright, my senses are on overload, and death is around every corner.

I contemplate the piece of scroll in my hand; it smells so good—like Gigi's roast beef. But paper is not satisfying. I punch down the hunger in my belly with my sour attitude. The awareness of being watched dawns on me.

I glance up to find Peter's bright gaze on me. Color creeps up my neck, knowing he's read the thoughts on my face. His words are like arrows, piercing and well-aimed.

"The battle comes for you, Jacob. Your testing draws near. Your time to be proved. The Almighty has called your name to see what you will choose. Your eye must be single. Faith and fear cannot occupy the same space." He leans forward.

"Remember the law of seeds. The heart is the most fertile soil; each word and thought is a seed. There are only two kinds: death or life. Be sure of this: every seed allowed to remain within will grow. Be careful what you are sowing, Jacob. It's what you'll soon be reaping. When battle comes, what you've planted will determine whether you live or die."

I blink. *Battle?* I'm the man—the fearless, the Navy SEAL—who brings it. What a farce: here I'm the weakest. I have no response, so I give none, unable to care if I'm being rude. Nervous sweat once again appears on my face, longing for my world. But there is no going back; I've seen too much to return unchanged. I am forever marked by this place.

I might jump to earth again, but I can never go back. I can't *un-know* what I experienced here. Who I am is altered, different. The only solution is to grow, to become strong, and to claim victory in it. It seems miles away.

Demyen slaps the table, making me jump. "Aye! It's a good day for battle. It's high time we went about the Almighty's work."

Everyone stands and begins clearing the rough wooden board.

"Boy, I could use a hand today. What say you, we see if our paths align?"

I nod at Demyen's comment, desperate to get away from myself, forcing my watery legs to support my body.

"Yeah." My voice cracks; I clear my throat. "Yeah, sounds good."

I'd agree with anything that gives me a moment to hide from Peter's words.

Birds. It's baby birds that separate me from Demyen. We've been traveling quiet and fast through the woods. Apparently, this is heavy lion territory. I'm panting pathetically to keep up with Demyen's punishing pace when I almost step on an overturned nest. Two ridiculously large-beaked chicks are trembling on the ground.

Without thinking, I gather them against my chest for warmth. *Great. Now what?* The chicks emit a cheeping protest, far too loud. Scanning the trees, I find a crotch in a branch where I can stash the nest.

Grunting as the rough bark scrapes my arms, I scramble, using only one arm. A brilliant flash of color; *Mama is here.* Her plumage is the deepest red I have ever seen; each feather tipped with glittering gold. She hops on her impossibly skinny legs and looks at me with one critical eye.

"Easy…I'm on your side," I whisper as I push the nest down into the crook of the tree. The chicks open their purplish beaks wide in hunger. She hops closer, glaring at me.

As my feet hit the ground, reality returns. Scanning the forest, I rush forward, but Demyen is nowhere in sight. Ahead, the trees thin. *Not again.*

Demyen stands in the middle of the field, watching a lion stalk up to him.

"No." Not when I'm the only help for miles.

Demyen's posture is relaxed, chewing a mouthful of scroll. He swallows, watching the massive beast approach. His hand drops to his side, *his sword!* But no, he fishes out a tiny stick, puts it into his mouth, and starts picking between his teeth.

The lion's in full hunting mode—low to the ground, piercing eyes riveted on Demyen's neck. I catch the stench of him; it makes my skin crawl. My breath comes hard as the lion slinks nearer. Even crouched, the beast stands almost as tall as Demyen and many times heavier. His wicked eyes gaze right into Demyen's.

*Not like this.*

Its left ear is torn. *Aseph!* The beast slows to a stop, his bloodstained fangs inches from Demyen's face. The lion's lip curls as his growl makes the leaves in front of me tremble. Demyen withdraws the pick and flicks it to the side. *How can he stand there, unflinching?*

Aseph's ribs expand, causing blood to seep from an unhealed wound on his side. His roar explodes; and even though I saw it coming, the sound knocks me back like a hammer blow.

A disgusted expression contorts Demyen's face at the lion's vile blast. His voice is steel. "In the name of Yeshua, I rebuke you." He leans forward into the lion's space. "Go!"

Aseph's eyes widen. I scowl. *Is that fear in the beast's eyes?* Still, Aseph shifts closer, mouth gaping, a hair's breadth from his throat. But Demyen holds the line, eyes blazing. The lion shrinks back, and Demyen steps forward.

Claws extended, the lion tries to hold his ground, but Demyen leaps forward, hand upraised. Long claw marks mar the ground as the lion writhes, vacillating between attack and retreat. A few feet away from Demyen, he's rolling and swatting as if Demyen were beating him. The ground trembles under his punishment. Finally turning tail, he disappears into the undergrowth. Demyen's voice makes me jump. "Boy! Come along; we're late."

I'm running before I'm aware of it. The warmth of the open meadow embraces me as I arrive, panting, though I've only run a short distance. Demyen grunts at me, not quite in disgust. I must be pitiful in his eyes.

We set out again as I mull over my experiences here. If Demyen began so lacking and grew into such strength, there's hope.

My weakness still bothers me on a deep level, like knowing a tick is burrowed in but being unable to remove it. This has always been a part of me—unseen in my world, cloaked by mental and physical strength, but lurking within. *At my core, this is what I am.* I would have venomously denied it, but it is *true.*

*This is the real me I'm seeing now,* what my eternal identity looks like. As Demyen said, it is stripped of the finite, deprived of the physical—all my covering, ability, my goals. This is my spirit exposed, and I hate its malnourishment.

Demyen leaps up the base of a steep, wooded incline from rock to rock. His long sword slaps his thigh. My legs burn as I scramble up the same place a second later, fighting for balance. *Maybe I don't have to remain this way.* Gritting my teeth. I vow I *will not* remain this way. I will overcome. I must, to survive.

Pushing Peter's words out of my mind, it's down to only one burning question, and I must break the silence with it.

"Why didn't the lion launch a full-out attack, Demyen? Why did it get in your face like that?"

Emerald eyes smoldering, Demyen looks at me. "We've tangled many times, Boy. He's afraid of my sword, what it's made of." Demyen's words raise more questions.

*What is it made of?* I've seen his, and it's sharp and full-length compared to my sword's embarrassing size. *Why didn't I get a real one?*

With sudden sharpness, the oily prints, far away in my gray world, grip me. *Tracks with scars crisscrossing them hunting me there.*

My head snaps up, torn between realities. "He's the only one with scarred pads? The big lion with the torn ear?"

Demyen responds, "Aye, Boy. He's a fighter, won't yield an inch."

I grunt in response. *The biggest…the strongest…the worst has been hunting me in both worlds.* I clench my teeth at Demyen's next words.

"Aseph will come for you when you least expect it—when you are weakest, empty. He has killed more children of the Light than any other." Demyen's eyes spark fire as he looks over his shoulder at me.

"You must defeat him, Boy. He will skirmish with you first, test your strength, try to frighten you before the actual attack. Watch, be on your guard; defeating him is the single most important battle you will face." He pulls out a wad of scroll.

"Eat, Boy!"

I frown at him as he narrows his eyes.

"Suppose a lion came at you like this." He crouches, instantly menacing, and comes at me, wide hands like paws. I jump back and deflect two of his sudden blows, but he twists, coming back lightning fast to rake his fingers across my exposed stomach. "What would happen?"

"He would have killed me." The mental picture of my guts exposed is crystal clear. "But I should have expected that move."

Demyen cuffs the back of my head in disgust. "The TRUTH is, no." He sifts through his small leather pouch, slaps a piece of scroll in my palm. I chew it, savoring the flavor.

"Nothing shall by any means harm you." His spoken words seem to echo as I chew.

"Right. But that's not literal, is it?"

"If you believe the lions can hurt you, they will, every time. But if you take the Almighty's Word and honor it above your own expectation and especially above your experiences, then you receive what *it* says. Even if a lion gets inside your guard, the damage is soon reversed. Now, you can't jump off a mountain in a foolish act and expect protection. But *within the covenant*, it's completely literal."

Demyen leaps onto a large boulder. "Here's one that will mess with your head. You." He points down at my emaciated frame. "Could have defeated him the same as I."

I grunt in disbelief. "Look at me, Demyen, there's no way that's possible."

He shrugs. "Aye."

His agreement makes me groan in frustration.

"You're right. It wouldn't have worked for you. Not with that belief, but..." He points at me, driving home his point. "It *could* have. You have the light about you. When you stepped from darkness into the covenant, you, intrinsically, can defeat every lion, scorpion, or worse. In that moment, He gave everything to you. You have the raw material, the authority. You only lack the knowledge to use it."

I fold my arms across my chest.

"The physical order, everything there, flows from this reality. Every wound sustained here reflects there, as sickness, anxiety, death. Children of the Light, without knowledge, differ little from those of darkness. How pitiful, when they have been given everything by such a great blood covenant." He grimaces. "You hear, Boy? Everything you need for life and godliness belongs to you. Yet, without knowledge and belief, you suffer just like the defeated."

Half his mouth pulls back at my denseness. "Ever wondered why my sword is so sharp, Boy?" He doesn't leave me time to answer. "Have you noticed how much I eat?"

I snort at his question.

"I can't tell you *how* it works, Boy, but there's a direct correlation between how much you eat and the length of your sword."

My face screws up at his comment.

Demyen shrugs his shoulders. "Life will teach you it is so. You must train yourself to eat. Constantly so." With that said, he stuffs in a big bite of scroll.

His deep voice breaks the silence again. "What did you see in the meadow, Boy?"

I shrug my shoulders. "I saw the lion stalk you with every intention of killing you. Yet he didn't. Then he fought your words tooth and nail. Next, he took off with his tail between his legs."

"Huh," Demyen comments. "Not what I saw. I saw a defeated beast covered with wounds of defeat, trying to get me to run. But I saw the Almighty; I saw HIM. Right here." He points to his chest. "You've got your eyes in the wrong place, Boy. You keep looking at the enemy, and you'll end up in his gullet."

We've traveled far without further incident. The forest is thick. Steep cliffs appear, and there is a lack of any sort of path other than our glimmering lines. Slapping at another biting fly on my sweaty neck, I ask, "Why are we here?"

"Had a dream last night. Small village needs water. Children are dying. Judging from the terrain, it's this way. I smell water ahead, though; let's find it."

After pushing through the thick, pricking undergrowth, we splash into a small stream. Demyen takes up his usual stance, hands underwater. Taking a deep breath, I mimic him. The coolness of the water is a pleasant shock. Strength flows up through it. The air above the rill crackles with energy.

Only after these sensations pass do I hear snatches of a silvery voice. I close my eyes and search for its source. It's more than a trickle; it also has a deep thunder of mighty falls and the tinkling notes of rain on forest leaves. There are words, but their meaning evades me.

Thirst drives me and I scoop water, sucking it down. Filled with energy, I sigh, jamming down the desire to turn back. Finally, Demyen rises; it's clear, he's received more from his communication with the water than I.

"The village is yet a few hours' journey north." The sharpness of his gaze combined with his words unnerves me. "Watch for scorpions. There are plenty hereabouts."

"Great," I sigh.

"Come on; let's eat lunch." He settles on the bank with his thick-soled boots still in the stream. He opens his satchel and draws out a fragrant wad of scroll. I fight the surge of disgust at the thought of putting it in my mouth. He splits it, holding half out to me, catching my hesitation.

"Teach yourself to eat, Boy." He flaps the wad in front of me till I reluctantly take it. Thinking of scorpions, I force it down. *Maybe if I don't chew…*

*Pitiful.* The village sits atop a crisp, parched hill. Dilapidated huts sit crookedly here and there. The creek we'd crossed was the last water for miles. The landscape has dried up in a few hours' travel.

And scorpions… Demyen pegged that one. They scramble closer, wicked-looking, tan scorpions as thick as my wrist with stingers poised over their backs, and tiny black ones faster than my eye can track.

People and children from the village swarm about Demyen. They look like me, weak against Demyen's strength. The emaciated children are like puppies about his heels.

"Come along, Boy. They've got shovels and picks."

"Perfect." My muscles are empty from the punishment of trekking here. I smash a tiny black scorpion with my shoe before following. When Demyen lays the rough, badly crafted wooden handle of the pickax in my hand, it's like a lead weight.

His eyes sparkle, filled with purpose. "These people travel all the way to the stream for water. Scorpions are too thick to move closer. Let's get to work."

I grunt in response. Shaking a scorpion off the pick, I trudge into the woods after Demyen's retreating frame. The trees here are almost dead, leaves brittle and brown at the edges.

A deep bark of laughter echoes. "This is the place from my dream! Boy, you dig a trench for the water to flow through. Follow the curve that way."

Instructions completed, he attacks the soil with such vigor that dirt sprays in all directions. I shake my head. The concussion of my pick hitting the hard dirt sends a painful shock wave up my arms. Children perch all around Demyen and me. Women gather with brooms. *Are they going to dust us?* Demyen has a hole two feet deep already. *Better get to it.* My pick bites the resistant ground.

Scorpions are converging from everywhere. *The vibration must bother them.* The women use their brooms like wild things, while the men line up with buckets to haul away Demyen's dirt pile; children shout, pointing out the larger scorpions for the women to get after. I double my efforts, wishing this miserable work was done. Clouds of black flies bite without mercy.

Time crawls, and the frantic activity of the women doubles as more scorpions flow from the surrounding areas. I pant hard from the exertion as I lean for a moment on the handle of my pickax.

"Whew." Stinging sweat pours down my brow into my eyes.

A twinge of green invades my vision, and I brace against the onslaught of the physical order. Hell week, during SEAL training, only two hours of sleep per night, constant, extreme physical effort, soaked in frigid surf, chafed with sand.

While others drop out left and right, Rivera and I dig in, refusing comfort, *beasts*. Where is that determination now? The point of my shoulder joint smarts where the bone rubs the pick. *Empty.* The painful reality settles hard, trapped in my weakness.

Demyen's voice echoes from the crater he's dug. "Eat, Boy!"

I roll my eyes but obey, forcing the wad into my dry throat. The longer we dig, the thicker come the scorpions. The ground undulates with them. Mothers send their children home to the huts.

Sweat evaporates in the dry punishment of day. The women separate into circles around Demyen and me, frantic motion beating back the deadly creatures. Demyen sends up great mounds of dirt; the hole he's dug is so deep I can just see the top of his head.

"Eat!" Demyen knows he's driving me crazy; I can hear it in his gleeful tone. Still, I mimic Demyen's style and stuff in another huge mouthful, chewing as I plunge the tool down. The flies continue their persecution.

The cry of one woman interrupts our toil as she clutches her leg in pain. Demyen's head pops up, gopher-like, at the sound. He looks to the sky, noting the oncoming darkness.

"All right, we finish in the morning." Demyen's words bring a collective exhale of relief.

We form a miserable knot and rush for the largest hut through a sea of scorpions. My eyes adjust inside to the dimness to find twenty children staring at me. They lay the woman who was stung on a crude pallet in the corner. Already she shows signs of fever, her skin flushed and her eyes glassy. The older children surround her.

All I can think about is water, parched from our toil.

"Well, brothers!" Demyen's booming voice commands attention. He jumps to the side and smashes a renegade scorpion. "When did your water dry up?"

The leader, Simon, leans forward. "Water's always been scarce in these parts."

"Don't think they settled this village with the land in this state," Demyen says, crossing his arms.

"Every year, it gets drier. Still, we will serve the Almighty through all our suffering." The entire group nods, eyes desperate in the firelight.

Demyen makes a face like they said they don't eat scroll, pulling his chin back, one brow lowered.

"He brings His children through the valley, and we must endure with patience," Simon continues.

I admire the depth of their commitment—to the death.

"And you suggest it's the Almighty's desire that you wither here?" Demyen questions.

"Aye, He works in mysterious ways, and He works all things for our good." A chorus of agreement echoes.

Demyen grunts, pulling out scroll till he finds the piece he's after. "'And we know that all things work together for good to them... ' See, here you must judge whether you meet the requirements to receive the promise. 'To them that love God, to them that are called according to His purpose.'" He holds up a thick finger. "I know you love Him, but are you living in His purpose for you?"

"I hope so." Simon's head bows; the others agree.

"Hope alone will leave you dead."

Demyen lets this grim statement hang in the air. It crushes me as well as them; hope is all I've been running on.

"Now faith is the substance of things hoped for. If you stop at hope, you lose. Faith brings your hope into reality." I lean forward as his words strike deep. "So then faith comes by hearing, and hearing by the Word. In order for you to be sure you are walking according to His purpose, you must know what it is through His Word.

"In the beginning, the Almighty gave dominion to his man, Adam. But Adam sold his rights to the lions. There was no suffering, lack, or defeat before that. So, tread carefully if you think to accuse the Almighty of bringing you darkness."

That's news to me. The girl in the woods flashes into my mind. She'd died in the darkness, and I doubt Solomon's fate would have been much different if Myah hadn't arrived. I shake my head; yet I'd seen Demyen repel the same force unscathed. I try to ignore how my tongue has glued itself to the roof of my mouth.

"Judge this, every good gift and every perfect gift comes down from the Father of Lights, with whom there is no variableness, neither shadow of turning. Take care you don't make an evil you've received out to be His blessing. If it's not good and perfect, it didn't come from Him.

"Without these truths, you'll remain a wanderer with no authority. A sheathed sword leaves you defenseless. I'll tell you truth." Every molecule in the room hones in on his next words. "Eventually, you'll receive exactly what you expect. Change your expectations to match His Word. It's the only way to a different outcome." He leans back.

His words are like a knife in my chest. I've been expecting failure and defeat at every turn.

"And the scorpions?" Demyen questions. "When did they come?"

"Scorpions have always been plentiful, but not like this. The drier it gets, the thicker they are. Where else can we go? This is our home."

A child's voice interrupts. "I need water, Momma."

"We have some, but not as much as you'd prefer." Simon shuffles over to a short barrel and lifts the wooden lid. "One ladle for each, and that's probably more than we have."

Half is all I get. My tongue is still dry when Demyen sits at the rough wooden board. "Let's eat. We can all use the strength. Have you much here?"

A slim woman with brown eyes shakes her head. "Not much left here, Mister. Mostly broken people waiting to die."

"Well. You certainly will with that attitude." Demyen glowers at her. "But I have enough for us all tonight. Come and eat." Demyen digs in his small, but seemingly bottomless satchel, drawing out handful after handful of scroll pieces. My stomach growls at the tantalizing aroma.

I lower my aching frame to the bench across the board from Demyen. These people scarcely eat or drink. Seeing their pitiful condition and knowing that, on some level, they're choosing weakness makes me keep stuffing my mouth long after I would've normally quit.

The children amuse me, flocking around Demyen. The littlest boy stares up in open-mouthed wonder at him. He gets them to eat too. Pushing little bits to the edge of the table, paying no mind when grubby little fingers reach for it.

I catch a slight movement in the shadows. *Not the firelight playing tricks on me this time.* Two evil red eyes reflect the light. Shooting up from the table, I slam my fists on its surface and somersault over Demyen, landing hard to crush the big tan scorpion with the hilt of my sword.

It's the second time I've drawn it since my arrival, and I'm shocked to see it in my hand. I hadn't intended to draw. It's a pleasant surprise to see that it seems to have grown longer. Then, beyond my sword, I see a crowd of beady, evil eyes shining.

"Hurry, bring rags!" My voice is steady, strong.

Two men hustle to stuff the hole in the wall with rags. The entire army of scorpions is searching for a way in.

"Fine move, Boy! You've got some life in you after all."

Day dawns blistering hot and dry. The sound of thousands of tiny legs scratching the outside walls makes my skin crawl.

Two children press against the legs of a woman whose soft voice breaks the tense quiet. "What will we do with the children? How will we keep them safe?"

Hers is a futile question. *Look outside, there's no way out.* Demyen stands undiminished with his arms folded across his chest. The glint in his eye says he has no intention of giving up.

Simon answers. "We'll put the children and Peace in the rafters while we work. First, we'll pray for help."

He nods, his bony arm beckoning the people together. We stand in a ragged circle, sweating out precious moisture in this oven of a hut. Quiet falls as we bow our heads, everyone hoping Demyen will start. The silence presses down.

"Almighty..." Simon clears his throat, his voice cracked and weak. "Almighty, we come before You. You are..." He pauses so long that maybe that's it. I can't stop staring at Simon. His keening cry breaks the silence, making my hair stand on end.

"AAH!" He bows his head. Face contorting in sorrow. "AH, Lord. We're most miserable if we suffer against Your will. If You would have good for us instead of this slow death, then we desire Your truth." Around the circle, people break, weeping.

The Almighty descends, as if the air gets heavier and thicker somehow. Energy races along my skin. Though I've never sensed it before, it's somehow as familiar as my own voice. The people's cries rise, anguish turning to hope. Children press against their parents' legs, eyes wide.

"Almighty, we ask that You teach us Your ways. You..." His face contorts as he struggles to speak. "You are *good.*" I resonate with his struggle to believe it. "Father, help us."

I take a deep breath; the oppressive heat has lifted. A shadow passing by the tiny window breaks our circle. Simon reaches the window first; he stares with mouth agape.

A child rescues us, crying, "What!? What is it?"

He whispers, "Eagles." There's life in his eye, as his voice grows stronger. "Eating scorpions!"

We all take a turn at the minuscule window, and I'm torn between horror at the literal carpet of venomous scorpions and awe at the enormous birds that wheel and dive, gobbling up scorpions in mid-flight. Every time an eagle touches down, a circle of hard-packed dirt appears, closing in again as the bird lifts off, its crushing talons full.

"We best fight our way to the pit while we have the eagles' cover." Everyone leaps at Demyen's command. We stash the children in the rafters.

Hefting Peace into place is harder than I could have imagined. Her skin burns with fever. Her leg looks about to burst near the sting, and her eyes are glassy and unfocused, fueling my determination.

At the door, we assemble in a tight knot. "Boy! Don't throw more effort into the trench. You'll be in the pit with me. Got to hit that water, men."

Demyen grips the crude wooden door handle.

"Almighty," he whispers under his breath. When he whips the door open, hot sunlight pours through and so do scorpions. Sticking close, we advance, stomping, the women sweeping madly with their brooms. Eagles swoop so close that the blast from their wings sends my hair flying. Their claws and sharp beaks glint like copper, a mesmerizing metallic brown with a surprising high-pitched hum.

We gain the pit, jumping in. I fight images of being covered in scorpions as I send my pickax with fury at the rocky subsoil. The ground shakes when Demyen's tool smashes down, and I hope the wooden handle will hold up to the beating.

The women shout to one another, "Here, help me!"

"They're climbing your handle!" The terror in their tone makes me double my pace.

The men grunt as they pull dirt and rocks away. Sweat pours down my back, into my eyes, stinging. A scorpion falls into our pit, lands on its back, and scrambles, drawing a shout from me. I make sure it never rights itself.

"I can't keep them back!" The woman's voice trembles from the exertion. Demyen never slows, pounding the dirt, increasing his rhythm.

"Go!" He booms at me, and I force my pick down again as I hear little claws striking the ground above, smell their sharp, repulsive scent. Time crawls by. *Will I get out alive?*

"Yes," Demyen shouts through a heavy breath with absolute certainty.

My head snaps up, certain I didn't speak aloud. My tongue is stuck to the roof of my mouth, so I can't respond.

"Close, Boy! Dig!"

I haul in blistering air, sorely lacking his rhythm and strength. My pickax falls, bites the dirt. *How much do my arms have left?* Then I smell it. *Water.* The tip of my axe is damp.

"Ha!" Demyen roars, catching the odor. "We have it now, Boy! Dig!"

Cries of relief come from above. I grit my teeth, all in, focused; there's nothing else. Now my axe comes up wet, with blue clay clinging to it. Wet muck strikes my cheek.

*"Aaah!"* I thunder like a wild man, swinging so hard my feet leave the ground. I hear a gurgling, sucking sound on Demyen's side of the tight pit. *Water!* It swirls around his shovel. With a rebel yell, I force my pickax down one more time. The floor sucks, then belches. A geyser of water blows past my head, high into the air. Every single person is shouting—shouting for all they are worth.

It swirls around my legs, sweeping up and out. My skin drinks it in and energy flows, surging up within seconds around my legs, my waist, and then my chest.

Together, Demyen and I reach up and lay our arms on the wet ground surrounding the pit. We float, anchored by our arms, water pummeling as we watch it surge down the trench I dug yesterday. Still the geyser breaks through the depth of water next to me, splattering everywhere, buffeting my legs.

Everyone's in the water—laying, rolling, and washing downstream. The scorpions recoil from it. I watch one get doused. It goes wild, stinging at nothing until it balls up, dead.

Nothing has ever felt as good. *So real.* I'd won a victory over myself, conquering something and coming out stronger, the same way I'd built my body in the foggy physical order.

"The children!" I shout. The heat near the roof must be unbearable. Demyen slaps my arm. *Ouch.*

"Aye, Boy! The light is growing stronger in you. Let's move."

He clambers up onto the wet ground, devoid of scorpions.

"How will we get there?" I ask as I haul myself from the rush of water.

"The buckets will do, Boy. We'll wet the way." He gazes down at me and opens his mouth to speak, but I beat him to it.

"Eat!" I boom. I turn toward the huts as I rip a hunk of scroll to stuff in, hiding my smirk.

Demyen's bark of laughter follows as he dunks a bucket. "A smile, Boy? That's a new look for you."

We douse the path to the hut with bucket after bucket. The ground still undulates with scorpions, but they're watchful instead of aggressive, fleeing before the water. The villagers join us and soon we splash through the doorway. Our mirth dims in the oppressive heat filling the building.

Peace hangs limp in the shawl that holds her in the rafters, fingers blue. *We're too late.* The children are listless. We must hurry. The smallest child slips free of his older sister's grasp and falls without a cry. His father dives to catch him. They land, sliding on the wet floor.

The rafters rain children. They cannot keep themselves from the one full bucket sitting at the door, and we have our hands full catching them. I climb Demyen's broad back to sit on his shoulders, struggling with the knot that holds Peace to the rafters. *Pulled too tight.* A sharp stench rises from her body in the intense heat.

"Hold on!" I shout in frustration, ripping it in two. Peace rolls free, Demyen grunts, seeking balance. Many hands receive the limp girl, lowering her. The women cover their mouths with their hands as their tears flow. *There is no life in her.* The men back away, grief stricken. Demyen shrugs me off and I land crablike at his abuse.

"Speak no words over her," he commands, scowling as he scoops her up. Her head lolls over Demyen's elbow, eyes wide, cloudy and unseeing. He takes off, bursting through the doorway like a bull, sending wood shards flying.

I follow, strength pumping in my legs. I don't want to miss whatever is going down. The dead girl flops like a rag doll as Demyen races down the path. The edges of her hair are going translucent. All the villagers herd along behind us.

The water has grown. A small river now rushes from Demyen's pit. He doesn't slow as he hits the flow until he's chest deep. Peace goes under, and he leaves her there. She's not breathing, anyway.

"Boy!" At Demyen's shout, I slog out to him through the water. He shoves the body into my arms through the current. Nothing is frantic about Demyen—no worry, no fear. His face shows intense focus. His whisper is so quiet, like a breath of wind.

"Almighty, tell me what to do."

I stare at his broad, bearded face. The dead woman's hair tickles my arm as it wraps like seaweed, more and more of it disappearing. I try not to think about holding her under. *This is not my world.*

Demyen hears whatever it was he was listening for. He disappears below the water's surface to reach a knife tucked in his boot. He stands, shedding water, a warlord from another age. Demyen grabs Peace's leg, swollen tight, almost bursting around the sting. The knife flashes, plunging into the wound. I turn my head at the stench.

"Hold her tight; she might buck." I try not to retch as I consider the absurdity of his comment. She's been underwater for over three minutes, but I remember Demyen's warning not to speak.

Slicing the wound open, he slips his knife into his belt and shakes his head as he grips her lower leg in both hands. One massive fist above the sting and one below. His fingers close like vises, and the muscles in his arms coil as he squeezes. Thick yellow puss oozes from the knife's deep stab.

He applies even more pressure, drawing his hands together, chest muscles bunching. I wonder that he doesn't snap the bone. My stomach heaves at the stench.

"Here now!" Demyen mutters under his breath. His brows knit as he works. I hear a faint hiss, as Demyen finally releases the leg. *He's gotten all the infection. For what good?*

"Raise her." Demyen's voice is hushed as I lift her pale face above the water. Liquid streams from her nose and mouth. I shrug my shoulders, defeated. Not so Demyen. He leans in, emerald eyes intent; his right arm coils, rising high.

I brace for the blow. His fist rockets for the woman's chest, but there's a blinding flash of white all around his plummeting arm, and I don't sense the impact try to rip her from my arms. The air is electrifying.

"Rise!" Demyen's roar rips through me.

She jerks, sputters, twists. I struggle not to lose her in the depths. She gasps in breath for what seems an eternity. Demyen's war whoop shatters the air. And I stare into the brightest brown eyes I have ever seen. Her red lips part, and I'm blasted point blank with a shout that matches Demyen's. She twists out of my arms, plowing water, shouting—*so alive!*

Demyen smacks the water. With his head tipped back, the veins in his throat standing out, he roars at the top of his lungs.

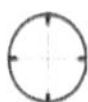

Green. It's everywhere. The landscape has come alive and I am literally watching plants grow. Children splash at the water's edge, while I sit farther down the bank, processing.

The memory of the cold gray ship slices through the edges of my mind, accompanied by the green haze. Sage is there, her deep-brown eyes full of concern. The strength of my body, who I am there; it's eons away, fading back through the haze.

I keep hold of the image for a second longer—so plain, so meaningless, so…empty. I shiver as I consider the implications. The world I longed for now seems undesirable.

I watch the water flow, a million shades of green and blue, its scent so subtle and alluring. Its voice is quiet and intricate, like icicles trembling in the wind.

I pull the memories up again; they only have one dimension while everything here has…ten. A corner of my soul knows I still belong to the "one" dimension, but it seems like a lifetime since I read that story, that it's not connected to me anymore. It's not mine; it's not me.

I run my hand over the dirt's peach fuzz of fresh growth. I can't decide which is more interesting: that I can hear and smell it growing under my hand or that my hand is no longer a pale, bony apparition. I'm tan and still too lean, but life is coursing through my veins. It makes me hungry.

Chewing some scroll is, I find, addictive. As much as it repulsed me at first, now I can't satiate my desire.

Every drop of strength in me has come from eating scroll. I will never go back.

Sitting here, doing nothing, caught by the oneness of sight, smell, and sound, inside I see...peace. Watching Solomon fight for life, I'd been so full of frustration and fear. All those feelings have vanished.

It's hard to fathom that yesterday, this spot was covered with scorpions; I haven't seen one all day. The plants grew hours after the ground took on water.

*Balance.* I hear the word so clearly as I dip my hands beneath the flow that I jerk back.

"Boy!" Demyen's booming voice draws me out of my reverie. I crane my neck, finding him striding my way. "It's time."

I nod, stretching, knowing we must be on our way. The villagers gather, sad to see us go. The children stand staring at Demyen, their little mouths still open in awe.

I stare up at the piercing white light of the stars. If I'm still, I hear their silvery-sweet voices falling from above. The cool fragrance of evening fills my lungs. *Why haven't I noticed the stars before?* I laugh. *I've been too terrified at night.*

Deeper places in me have changed than I even knew existed. My mind drifts back to our journey home. A thick brown scorpion had crept inside Demyen's pant leg on the trail and stung him five or six times before he got to it. All the blood drained from my face as out of the clear blue he had shouted, ripping off his pants, and leaping to crush the scorpion.

Yet, he'd shaken out his pants and put them back on. And we traveled hard all day with no sign of Demyen weakening.

I can't resist questioning him about it any longer. "So, are you immune to them after you got stung all those years ago?"

Demyen's brows lower. "Immune?" He shakes his head. "Immunity would imply that I have some power over them. I, in myself, have no immunity…no. It's more like light versus dark. Can you shine darkness into a brightly lit room? No? Is the room immune to the dark? Again, you see the wrong thing. It's not about the room; it's what it's *full* of. When darkness comes, I speak the healing, then I believe it."

His answer doesn't quite satisfy.

"So, do they hurt?"

"I don't know, Boy." His answer makes me angry because I'm so blind to it, yet my survival depends on understanding. My life here will be pitiful and short without it.

He must sense my need. "Boy, open up your ears if you want to learn. Most children of the Light go through their entire existence not understanding what I'm about to tell you." He pauses for effect, drilling me with his gaze.

I nod, inwardly bracing myself.

"Faith never *feels,* and faith never *looks* at circumstances. Faith *acts* on knowledge. A scorpion's sting grips the physical order with sickness. There, once the symptom, the feeling, is known, it becomes exponentially more difficult to fight it here, in the spirit. Yet, the war is won or lost in this realm." Demyen nods, savoring the words.

I squint one eye halfway shut, trying not to cast off his words as ridiculous.

"That's why I can honestly tell you I don't know if the stings hurt. Because I have *determined* to know only one thing—the Almighty's laws. His Word speaks thus, 'By His stripes we are healed."

"I only walk on words. It doesn't matter much what surrounds them. Water. Earth. Sky. Just so the Word is there. Fanaticism, however, will leap off onto any idea, or teaching, and it always fails. But faith only steps forward onto the Lawgiver's Words."

He shrugs his meaty shoulders. "People try to make it so complicated when it isn't. It's that plain; either you believe what you feel or what He said." He stuffs a wad of scroll into his mouth with a theatrical air.

When he swallows, he continues, "When I come before the Almighty for healing, I know it is according to His will. How? Because my Lord bought it by blood rights, and He is the same yesterday, today, and forever. There is no shadow of turning in Him and no variableness. He who is perfectly faithful lives in me; I am His dwelling place.

"He has never desired to dwell in a sick, broken-down temple. The ancient Words proclaim it, so I know that this *is* His will. Also, His command to me is to heal the sick. Some push this off to spiritual healing. But man's spirit cannot be healed; it must be *reborn*. My Lord healed the sick in the physical order; I am called to do His works. So, if I cannot gain such a thing for myself, how can I succeed at giving it to someone else?

"There is this… Will you know, oh, vain man, that faith without works is dead? If I came before the Almighty and proclaimed the healing He bought me with His stripes and then kept looking at the stings, lancing them, wrapping them, worrying over them, *feeling* the pain, would that be faith, Boy?

"All things"—he leans forward, intense, willing me to get it—"are in the spirit first, then the physical order follows. You must possess the promise in the spirit before you can have it on Earth. We want it the other way: when I feel, then I will believe. But we must conform to the Word. When you ask, believe that you receive, and you shall have." He waves one arm.

"Besides, it's rare to pray for healing. It has already been given; the Almighty's work for it is finished. All that remains is to call it into your being." Demyen's eyes catch the starlight, making them gleam.

"Most agree in thought. The problem comes when we feel. Pain, sickness, disease, fear, or anxiety. They believe in *those things*. Say they cannot change the way they think. Exalting the natural law over the spirit till the enemy has complete power over them. When Aseph came for me long ago, I did the same. Believed my *experience* above the Word. Some think the Almighty has failed; maybe it's not His will.

"They do not listen to 'Do not be afraid, only believe' or 'Ask and it shall be given unto thee.' They see the darkness and imagine it into their future. Faith and fear cannot occupy the same space.

Do you hear me? Faith and fear do not exist together. Faith doesn't care what is felt or seen. Faith only *knows* what the Almighty has spoken; it sees one thing—the Almighty's will." He laughs. "Faith is never surprised when its substance appears in the physical order. It already possessed it for some time in the spirit."

I grunt, wishing the words would sink into me.

"The Almighty's Words are truth," Demyen says, noting my conflicted expression. What we feel and see, those are *facts*. Many times, the facts are contrary to the *truth*. This leads to a crucial point. Will you believe the eternal, never-failing Word of the Almighty? Or will you believe what you see and feel? One is eternal; the other temporary. Finite to infinite." Demyen's eyes drill deep into mine. "Many die believing the temporary." Demyen is solid, sure. He lowers one brow. "Do you see it, Boy?"

I open my mouth before I think. "I want to get it. But how do I *do* it?"

Demyen's eyes are now distant, listening. He refocuses on me with laser sharpness. "Do you want to receive, Boy? To see?" His voice rattles in my chest.

"Yes," I say, without hesitation.

Demyen steps forward and places his wide palm on my forehead; a shiver runs down my spine.

"In the name of the Almighty, receive the knowledge of the revelation of Him! May the eyes of your understanding be enlightened."

A sweet scent fills the air, the atmosphere seems to vibrate. He pulls back, but I am now more than I was an instant ago.

*What is that stench underscoring the incredibly clean air?* I lift my nose, sniffing.

Demyen grins. "Your sense of smell's getting stronger, Boy! That will serve you well. Come, let's tell what the Almighty has wrought."

# 4
# SAGE



I stare at Jacob's body on the exam table, one hand on my hip, mouth pulled to the side. I defibrillated him once, when they pulled him from the ocean two days ago. His vitals have been solid since then, too. I need time to analyze this episode's data.

The ship rocks as I ease into my chair, flipping through reams of charts. We're dealing with something that's never been studied before. I've narrowed it down to a potassium of some sort, but it's not a form we know of. I'm clueless about how to test for or clarify it.

I turn as the door opens. Brooks stares at me. "Break topside for you, Emerson." I don't move. He knows I won't leave Jacob. "Mandatory."

"What?" I ask, face reflecting my resistance to the idea.

"You've been on duty five days. Topside. Fifteen minutes." His voice leaves no room for argument. I throw down my pen in disgust, turn back to the laptop, click the internal camera onto video, and turn it so it's got a clear view of Jacob. Then I push the chair away so no one can block the camera's view, scooping up a water bottle to cover the move. As I readjust some papers, anger boils up. I don't trust anybody, especially with Jacob.

Brooks stares at me. "Now…"

I resist the urge to look over my shoulder at Jacob as I breeze past Brooks. Gritting my teeth, I gain the top deck, starting the stopwatch on my phone. The sun on my face melts my temper a bit; the cool air coming off the water is refreshing. After days at sea, the sway of the ship seems natural. I set off at a crisp walk, the blood flow forcing thoughts to greater clarity, and facts begin to flow. Jacob shows a slight increase in K-40 levels.

It's true; I'd gotten solid readings after tweaking the tests a little. But they're not a level that would cause concern. He doesn't have high levels of any other toxic radiation either. I force my thoughts further, reaching for the connection that's been eluding me. But knowing they're doing something to Jacob after forcing me out of the room makes me clench my fists, hating my powerlessness to protect him.

I'd compared Jacob's lab results to Rivera's, and the data was shocking. Rivera's K-40 had spiked at 600 along with a few other radiation types, and all his other results had followed that diagnosis just as I would've expected—except his smoking end. I shiver, pushing away the thought. Jacob's are everywhere. One test shows K-40 higher than Rivera's, the next drawn only hours later lower than average.

If they had asked me to study Jacob's results without firsthand experience, I would have insisted the collection method or the lab process was inadequate, that the results were erroneous. But I'd collected them all myself, run them through my lab, and then sent the samples off to a larger lab elsewhere in the ship. The results on each test were identical.

I'd also run Jacob's and Rivera's labs side by side to rule out any other variables. That comparison leaves me with one answer. Jacob Carter's experiencing a huge potassium spike, the labs are picking up *something*, and if I don't get it under control, it could prove deadly.

The energy pulsing through my legs makes me wonder; the more exposure I have to Jacob, the clearer my thoughts, the better function I have physically. His impressive show on the track and obstacle course confirms the fact that whatever we're dealing with stimulates energy production and speeds healing.

The spinal tap I'd drawn closed incredibly fast, and he never once complained about it. Of course, he wouldn't. Whatever negative side effects there may be from the potassium haven't revealed themselves yet. I snort: other than occasionally falling through floors, disappearing, and coming up dead.

I glance at my phone. Four more minutes. I lean on the railing, watching the waves roll, foaming white against the LCS *Engage* still anchored in the distance. Otherwise, the ocean is empty; the vanguard of other ships long since moved on. I sigh out the fresh salt air. The coast of Wilmington, North Carolina, is a smudge on the far-off horizon. It's been easy to overlook that the world is facing its own battles over health, freedom, and government control.

Actually, it has been a relief to bury myself here, with one patient to worry about instead of watching the world implode into a communist, one-world government rule. I grimace: the chaos of the U.S., soon to be called the America's One, and Project 157 pinch me in a vise grip of stress. I inhale, clutching the high railing, wishing I hadn't glimpsed the land.

Looking around, I hear an odd sound, almost like a bee. I sigh in relief as my timer reaches fifteen minutes. I push off the railing, rushing back to Jacob.

"Ouch!" I slap my neck where a sharp burning sensation bites deep. A hard scrambling under my fingers makes me jump, and I cut off a shriek of terror. A big red wasp lands on the deck when I flick my hand. Still holding my neck, I twist my shoe over the insect with a crunch.

I swallow hard, grimacing, running past the sailors in the hall, racing for the EpiPen in my med pack. Last time I was stung, two years ago, I'd had an allergic reaction that scared me to my core. Though I'd never reacted before then, my neck is tightening, airways constricting.

Forcing my hand down, I glare at the Marine standing in front of Jacob's door. He's the same one who's been on first shift for five days, but he still makes me pull out my ID. I let the anger cover my desperation as I push past him, slamming the door behind me.

Last night I'd shut off the lights before lying down on my cot. In under two minutes, Brooks was there, switching the lights back on, scowling. "Don't do that again."

But it gave me time to sweep the room with the laptop camera. Looking through the darkness with its electronic eye had revealed two white circles staring back at me: well-hidden cameras in the walls. They're in the far corners near the door. They can see everywhere except behind the exam table, near Jacob's head.

I snatch the EpiPen from my bag with trembling fingers, trying to quiet the dragging wheeze of my breath, fighting the dizziness. They'll pull me from duty if they know I've developed a reaction, and I can't let that happen; Jacob might die. I hunker down at the head of the table, pretend I'm rummaging through drawers. I jam the pen into my upper arm.

Blessed pain at the site spreads into a cool shrinking effect, soothing my inflamed neck. I fight the blackness closing in. *Come on.* A few more seconds and it will kick in full force. I grab the table, wavering. Suck in a full breath for the first time since I took the stairs. I lean my head against the cold metal, heart slamming, fear surging. Struggling inside.

The tightness in my chest loosens, but deep in my mind, the nearness of death leaves me trembling. I hate the loss of control, the inability to stop the iron fist of the reaction. *Without that pen, what would I have done? What if it hadn't been available?* The knowledge pushes in; the reactions and side effects, until it's worse than the experience.

I blink hard, mouth dry. Better look like I had a reason to be down here. I pull out my backup blood pressure cuff, stealthily slipping the empty EpiPen into my scrubs. Still woozy, I struggle with Jacob's heavy arm as I slide the cuff around it. His numbers are perfect. I bet mine are way off.

I slide the chair back to the laptop. Pretend to enter his blood pressure on the chart while I click the play button on the laptop's video. A few minutes of stillness pass, Jacob's chest rising and falling till a dark-haired woman in a white lab coat enters, accompanied by a male nurse. My nails bite into my palms as I watch them roll Jacob over on his side, his right hand flopping hard on the table. I blink as it hits; it is like I can feel it slamming down.

They bend, inspecting Jacob's lower back. The nurse lays out a set of surgical blades. The woman selects one, works a moment, then holds out her hand for a tube of skin glue. *What have they done?* Straightening my papers, I search for a reason to roll him over and inspect the area.

My neck burns where the wasp had stung me. I push away the thought, grabbing a heating pad I'd ordered to get Jacob's skin off the table. I'd requested an actual bed for him many times, but it hasn't been forthcoming.

I smooth the pad, moving to Jacob's right side, my arms trembling as I wrestle with his limp form, the full draining effect of the reaction to the sting crashing down. I clamp my mouth shut as I glimpse a small incision right above his right hip bone; the glue is shiny. It wasn't a deep cut, looks as if she just opened his skin. Letting him roll back onto the pad, I run my finger over the spot, but I don't feel anything.

Mind racing, I go through tests and procedures she could have performed but find nothing. I'll have to monitor that spot. Rolling my neck, I wince at the sharp pain, fingers finding an angry knot. I pull my short hair over it, hoping the length will hide it.

The door opens, and the dark-haired woman enters, a sheaf of papers under one arm. The jolt of adrenaline is hard to cover. She holds out her hand; I take her grip with a firm shake that's pure bluster.

"I'm Dr. Sutton. The superintendent over your work on Jacob Carter. I've been running all the labs you send out."

I nod. *That's not all you've been doing.* I bite back the comment.

"Your instincts on this case have been exceptional, Sage."

"Thank you," I whisper. *Why is she here?* I study her face. She's pretty, older, with a square jaw, brown eyes and a wide mouth. *And why do I feel like she's an opponent?*

"I'd like to go over his test results with you."

"Yes, ma'am." I'm trying to keep the cool tone out of my voice, but I don't quite make it.

"Come, sit." She points to the lone chair. My neck feels exposed as I turn toward it. Still, I'm thankful for the chair; the past hour hasn't been easy.

"When they began operation Covert Force, you were below deck, yes?" She has a light accent that I can't quite place.

"Yes, ma'am."

"I'd like to show you the footage of the..." She hesitates. "Operation."

*Experiment, lady, just admit it.*

"Then we can compare notes." Her easy, almost motherly manner is convincing; and if I hadn't seen her sneak in and mess with my patient, I probably would've enjoyed bouncing theories around with her. I realize too late that I've said nothing.

She nods, accepting my coolness, leaning forward to insert a flash drive into the laptop. The screen splits, one half a wide view of the *Engage,* the other a close-up of the rear deck with four well-armed soldiers standing ready, rifles across their chests.

My heart clenches. Jacob faces the camera, strong and straight. I blink back tears, wishing I could stop time right then, rush out and insist that they stop this madness. The white clock at the bottom of the screen flips to 1200 hrs. The deck of the ship vibrates, and everything distorts as if the air's being ripped apart.

The memory of the intense sound, its grip crushing my chest, makes me wince as the other three soldiers twist, struggling against the blistering air. They jerk, movements uncontrolled. Faces contorted, they fire, rifles flashing bright. I grip the desk, sweat appearing on my upper lip.

Jacob hits the deck, forcing his rifle away, cringing. A mirage of heat waves ripples; the strange green haze rises from the floor. Steve Rivera dives onto the deck, striking at unseen assailants. The other two are similarly affected. Jacob, however, lies relatively still.

I watch in horror as he sinks through the floor, like he'd done two days ago, while twisting the heavy table in his hands. The *Engage* disappears. I can't stifle a gasp, hand over my mouth; the imprint of the ship remains in the water as the thick green cloud slowly clears. Then the water crashes in, filling the print left by the invisible hull.

Seconds tick past; I hold my breath. The ship reappears, whitewater boiling under it like a bath toy a toddler has thrown into the water. The ship rocks as it settles so many tons of water displacement back into the sea.

Dr. Sutton taps the screen. "Jacob disappeared at 1203, the ship returned at 1205, and then the divers pulled him from 60 feet below the hull of the *Engage* at 1213."

Boats swarm around the *Engage,* and I appear on deck, frantic, followed by a group of soldiers.

I'm frozen, watching the recording as Jacob suffers under my defibrillator paddles. I've seen it too many times lately. Rivera appears, first only a billow of smoke. I go stiff, knowing he's running straight out of hell, the terror on his face permanently seared into my mind. His screams two days later make my stomach turn. I reach up and press "stop."

"Here's what we have to figure out: why did Jacob Carter and Steve Rivera respond so differently? How could one die of radiation poisoning and the other have none? Sage, you're one of the brightest rising stars in your field. How do you explain it?"

I watch Dr. Sutton, but I see Jacob straight and tall, unstoppable, a warrior who'd withstood conditions that would have killed most during his entire career. Now he's enduring this catastrophe because of Project 157. She contributed to his suffering.

I sit back, crossing my arms. She perches one hip on the table with an air of concern. She only cares for her experiment, not the man lying comatose on the table behind me.

Getting more information from her is the key to helping him. Sighing, I rub my forehead as if giving in. "Here's how I see it. Both Carter and Rivera were so strong. Probably the toughest in the world. There were no other survivors, right?"

Sutton tilts her head. I raise a brow, insisting on the truth.

"Well, one of the Delta men, David Southland, was found in the lowest deck." She frowns, clearing her throat. "But he was fused to the ship."

"Excuse me?"

She sighs. "He was halfway through a wall, one shoulder, arm, and leg on the opposite side. He did not survive…long."

Scowling, I push past the repulsion that rises at Project 157. "And his radiation levels?"

"They matched Rivera's to a T."

I nod, thoughts racing, potassium and positrons bumping around in my mind. "So, only three survived. Jacob alone has no radiation poisoning, but his tests are all over the place." I narrow my eyes. *The image of the ship glowing green is fresh.* "Did you take readings from the ship?"

Sutton nods. "The ship spiked with radiation just before it disappeared, but it returned clean, as if it had been wiped."

Whatever stripped the ship was most likely the same experience Jacob had—the one Rivera and David Southland lacked. I remember Jacob leaping off the table, surgical knife out, protecting me. *From what? What was he running from?* I'd pushed off his reaction as a dream or a hallucination, but the fact is, the ship disappeared. It may have been transported to another location, since its hull imprint had disappeared. It's possible Jacob had too.

"What do you see from his charts?"

*Sutton is prying, but I'll play her hand to uncover the point of all this.*

"Well, the labs must be experiencing an anomaly."

"No, the labs have been ultra-controlled, plus every result has matched between your labs and mine. The numbers are honest." She checks her watch and adds, "When Carter disappeared last time, you were close to him. What did you experience?"

Now we're coming to it, the real reason for her visit. But I can't tell her the entire story, how the air trembled and surged with energy, or how clear my mind had been. I dare not trust her with Jacob.

"He seemed to tense up." I'm sure she's re-watched the video hundreds of times and this is obvious already. "Then he slipped through the floor."

She looks at me, expecting new insight.

I shrug. "The floor was hot, really hot." I lean back in my chair, faking comfort, exhaustion from the sting closing in.

"You talk to him a lot when he's unconscious. Do you think he can hear you?"

An honest smile plays on my face. "When I was thirteen, my uncle was in an accident. The hospital staff allowed me to sit by him while he was unconscious. I told him stories for hours, holding his hand. When he woke up three days later, he knew the endings to all my stories.

"He said he knew someone was holding his hand, that he didn't catch everything I said, but it helped him to fight, to stay, to heal. That's when I decided I'd be a nurse. I've had excellent results working with patients that way. They need an honest connection and hope, especially when they're unconscious."

Sutton checks her watch again. They've certainly been careful to limit personnel's exposure to Jacob. Except for me. I guess we're both guinea pigs.

Sutton proves it. "I'd like to get a blood sample from you."

I nod. No matter the results, I'll fight to keep my place at Jacob's side. A thought hits me. *What if they suspect my allergy?* Clamminess spreads. *Is that why she came in to ask for this test?*

I swallow hard, grabbing my water bottle before answering. Caring for Jacob has become intensely important to me, even more than my own safety. What would my older brother Peter say if he knew all this?

"What are you testing for?"

"We'll run everything we've run on Jacob. You've had a lot of exposure." I find relief and greater concern in her words. If I'd covered the sting well enough, it's clear they expect that Jacob's condition is affecting me.

I blink hard. *How many times have they done this? How did they know they would need boats to pick up bodies?* A chill races across my skin.

These thoughts descend on me like a crushing revelation. Who would guess that men would fall through four metal decks and a steel hull? *They knew.* The knowledge sits like a brick in my stomach. I take the kit as she sets it on the table, tie off the tourniquet with one hand and my teeth.

"I'll take the sample," she says in a silky voice.

"No. I got it. Thank you." The thought of her touching me is repulsive.

I ready the needle. *What did she do to Jacob while I was gone?* The flash of anger covers the bite of the needle. I hold out the vials of blood but don't drop them into her hand.

"I'd like to see the results." The only reason I'd consented to this blood draw was to keep peace.

She shrugs. "Of course; you're doing a great job, Sage."

I nod, biting back what's in my heart. Yes, a great job keeping your super-soldier alive so you can poke and prod him. Figure out how to torture more of them. I breathe a sigh of relief when the door clicks shut behind her. Pressing a Band-Aid onto my arm, I go straight to Jacob, take his warm hand in mine.

"Bet you're going to be starving when you wake up this time, aren't you? What's your favorite food? Well, we'll know soon enough, won't we?" I rub his hand, so thick and square, dwarfing mine.

I wrap his limp fingers around mine with my other hand. There's a strong sense of energy flowing up my arm. *Is it my imagination? Watch yourself, Sage, maybe you're attributing more to this than there is.* I look into his handsome face, square jaw with a scruff of a beard growing. I guess I'll have to shave that soon.

The fierce protectiveness grips me again. He's not a number, not a project, not an experiment. Not to me. He's an incredible man who deserves to live, to smile, to be filled with success.

"Let's get that beard shaved." I check the IV in his arm, then ease his hand down, turning to gather what I need.

Brooks enters, hands me my labs, locks me in again. I scan the numbers; they are as crazy as Jacob's. Swallowing hard, I search for internal balance. Now that Sutton's gone, I feel fine. Actually, considering the sting, I feel great. The last sting laid me flat for two days, even with the EpiPen.

Sensing motion behind, I spin to find Jacob's head turned toward me. I gasp as his mouth moves, forming intelligible words. I leap for his chest as he jerks, his head rolling back and forth; then every muscle goes rock hard. He surges up as if I'm not lying on him, the IV pings out of his arm, and he leaps off the table. I find my arm twisted high behind my back, facing away from him.

"Jacob! Stop!" I cry as my shoulder rends. He releases me abruptly. I whirl, face inches from his chest. His eyes are wild, and then his hands come up.

"Sorry. That reconnection was rough," he says.

I nod, breathing hard. "*Reconnection?* Is that what it seems like to you?"

"It's not what it seems like; it's what it *is*." He glances around, then down at himself. "Sage, I'm naked again."

His earnest blue eyes lock on mine with a glint of mischief. My face goes red as the door slams open. Brooks and a fleet of nurses crowd the door, stopping short on seeing Jacob standing there in his birthday suit.

One corner of his mouth pulls back and he cocks his head. "Food, Brooks. All I need is food."

I shove the neat stack of clothes I'd prepared two days ago into his hands. Jacob juts his chin at Brooks, whom I'm amazed to see back out, and shut the door. I turn my back as he dresses, cheeks hot. Patients don't go from incapacitated to alert, and it's difficult to deal with. When he's still, I turn to him, his height imposing, the room seeming small.

"Did I die again?" he questions.

"Only once. Which, I thought, was pretty good compared to last time."

He nods. "Sage?"

"Yes?"

"Next time I come back, it would be nice to have some clothes on."

I nod my head in a circle, apologizing. "Yes, of course. So… you… think there will be a next time? I mean, you think you're going to disappear again?"

He holds my eye a long while before saying, "I hope so."

His words make me scowl. The door swings open and a Marine puts two heavy trays packed with food on the desk. Then he hands me a stack of papers. Orders for another full physical and tests.

Jacob sits down and inhales the food. All my easy words to him while he was unconscious dry up. He snatches the radiation tester off the desk, sweeps it over himself. The needle leaps crazily, as it always does; he stuffs another forkful of meatballs into his mouth.

"Broke," he says around the food, flicking the readout. I shake my head.

"Nope, it's you. That's the third one I've tried; it reads everything else perfectly." I take it and scan myself, finding the needle bouncing with only slightly less exuberance. Jacob narrows his eyes.

"Are you absorbing something from me?"

The answer sticks in my throat, so I push our blood tests side by side in front of him. He scans them. Grunts, taking in the similar levels.

"You haven't jumped yet?"

The strange word catches me, but I'm extremely aware of the surveillance, so I let it pass. "No."

"You need more magnesium."

His easy observation makes me laugh, pushing back the gravity of all the unknowns. How had he picked apart my blood test so fast?

"You always this smart, or is it a side effect of these numbers?" I tap the blood tests.

He stacks the full tray on top of the empty one before answering. "You don't become a SEAL by being slow."

"How are your lungs?" I ask, wondering if the jump had hurt them.

"Perfect," he says, flexing as he rubs one hand over his right hip where Sutton had cut him.

*I'm so sorry I left you.*

"I'm going to need to take some blood," I apologize.

He stretches out his arm, and I take the sample. The whole time he watches me with eyes deeper than the ocean.

"It's good to be back in my body," he says, nodding, rolling his shoulders.

I press gauze over the spot I'd pulled the needle from. Trying to hold his gaze. "That's an interesting way to put it."

"Yeah," he agrees, drawing a big breath, enjoying each sensation.

"I was going to shave you just before you woke up."

He nods, running his fingers across his scruff. "That would feel good."

I follow him to the sink, pestering him with the required medical questions and a blood pressure cuff. By the time he's done shaving, he's a little jumpy.

"Brooks!" he says into the air. "How about some more exercise?"

He drops to the floor in a set of push-ups, where he claps at the apex of each. Soon we're repeating the procedure of reaching the exercise yard under heavy escort. I don't like the fact that Marines have been tasked with menial jobs, like guarding our door and delivering food. I push the thought aside as Jacob pings up and down, bouncing on his toes, stretching. He can't contain the energy anymore.

His numbers on the course are a hint faster than last time. There's a smoldering pleasure in his eyes as I take his vitals; it's like he's got a deep satisfaction in the movement alone. For him, it's simple, normal; he's trained like this for years.

He runs the course twice more and enjoys every minute. I catalogued how long he'd stayed, well, *in his body* last time, and I watch him like a hawk as we pass the moment of his previous jump. Was it the exercise that had caused his last jump or the stress of seeing Rivera?

"Take a water break, Carter." Brooks turns on his heel, disappearing through a doorway.

I glance at our escort squad, satisfied that they're out of earshot of quiet words.

"Jacob, why do you think you and Rivera had such different experiences?"

It's a loaded question, and he takes a moment before answering. "Something he said makes me wonder…"

"Something Rivera said?"

"No." He holds my eyes, deciding. "A man I met on my first jump. 'You've got the light about you, Boy.'" A fond gleam shows in his eyes as he says the phrase. He studies me with that see-into-your-soul gaze, as he lets the implications of his words sink in.

"You're telling me you traveled somewhere and met a man?"

He nods.

"Did you go to the same place both times?" I ask, Rivera's screams echoing in my mind.

"Yes. Well, the same place in general. I landed in a different spot, but it's the same…reality." He's waiting for me to scoff, but at this point I'm not judging anything. Or ruling anything out.

"And he said you had light?" I squint, questioning, recalling the green haze and the intensity of the energy swirling on the deck as he jumped.

"Did you ever go to church?" he asks.

"Of course." I nod, taking the sharp turn in stride, willing him to keep talking. "Sometimes."

"So, you know God is three parts? Father, Son and Spirit? And man is made in his image?"

"Okay," I agree.

"Humanity is spirit, soul, and body, three parts—a sacred echo of Him." He ducks his head toward me. "What happens when a person dies?"

I wrinkle my nose, not sure I'm keeping up. "The heart stops, brain waves drop to zero."

"Nope." He lets the word hang there a moment. "The spirit leaves the body."

My eyes lock with his.

"So, you think your spirit traveled to a different reality?"

"Trust me; I'd have been the last person to believe what I'm saying till it happened. That's why my body keeps trying to die when I jump. Last time was easier. I'm getting better at handling it; plus, without the experiment's intrusion, it's not as…chaotic."

I blink rapidly, desperate to remember every word. "And Rivera?"

"He didn't have the light about him." Sorrow wells up in Jacob's gaze.

Is the light Jacob's talking about a mutated potassium? The mystery element I've begun thinking of as K-60? I look down, processing.

"What happened to your neck?" Jacob asks; he doesn't miss a thing.

My fingers find the sting, still an angry knot. I'm relieved to have someone else know, even if I might be the one saving his life any second.

"They ordered me on deck for a break." I can't cover the disgust in my voice.

Jacob scowls. "Ordered?"

"I hadn't left your side for five days." I can't hold his gaze; the comment seems too personal now that he's awake.

His brows go up, and I rush ahead to cover it. "I was only on deck fifteen minutes when the wasp stung me."

To distract him, I tell the story of my desperate rush for the EpiPen. But Jacob, of course, catches what I didn't say: my determination to stay with him.

"Thank you," he whispers. Reaching up, he eases one finger onto the sting. As the pain fades, my eyes widen. *What just happened?* A cool, clean sensation spreading from his touch covers the sting.

Jacob is scowling at the dark glass wall a few feet away. His hand falls to his side, fists clenching.

"What are you glaring at?" I ask.

"Admiral Ash," he says, voice like steel. "The man who killed Rivera." Anger smolders in his eye. "With friends like these, who needs enemies?"

I turn, looking at the highly reflective glass, hair standing on end. "We should check your eyes; all I can see is us."

"That would be a much nicer picture." His voice sends chills down my spine.

I'd hate to be Ash with Jacob Carter staring me down like that. His eyes move, following motion I can't see in the far room.

"Is he gone?" I whisper.

But Brooks reappears from the room behind the glass. "Time for some shooting, deck one."

We fall in line, descending into the belly of the ship. I can still feel the heat of Jacob's anger. We enter a vast space that's super quiet. Heavy metal plates set at angles protect the vessel from the rifle range they've set up.

Jacob steps up to a table and we don earmuffs. He breaks down a rifle, snaps it back together, motions smooth and practiced. I eye him, watching for tension to grip him.

"Targets in ten," Brooks says, voice eaten up by the strange room.

I check my watch; we're well past the time between Jacob's last jumps; it's possible there is no rhythm. Maybe he's back for good.

He tucks the rifle to his shoulder, then motion on the target range draws my eye. I jump at the blast of the rifle, muffled in the large room. Figures pop up, showing only for milliseconds. Each one explodes as Jacob moves, laser focused. Ten. Twelve. Fifteen shots. He holds off on one target, then pops three more in quick succession. The yard goes still and he sets the rifle down.

I stare at the target field as the black silhouettes of men roll back out on their automated arms. They dangle, shredded at varying lengths as the system forces them back into view.

"You missed one," Brooks says, his voice full of disdain.

"No, I didn't. That one"—he points at a smaller target, still whole—"that one's a child."

He's right; the figure has the distinct look of a child. I totally missed it the first time it flashed up. I eye Jacob, respect growing deeper. He'd been the one making the split-second life-and-death decisions and he made the right choice.

Brooks grunts, satisfied. "Let's move."

We climb another set of stairs, rising deck after deck until we step into the brilliant light of day. We round the rifle tower, and there's the *Engage*, waves breaking against her bow. I flinch, hearing wasps that don't exist.

Jacob stops, eyes locked on the ship. Brooks turns, decides not to say whatever is on his tongue. I tense; something is happening. Jacob's fists are clenched, the veins popping on his forearms. My heart slams in my chest. I don't have my med pack; I'm not ready!

But Jacob continues to stare at the *Engage* as an eerie green glow rises off the ship. His jaw clenches as the ship wavers like a road on a hot day.

"Jacob," I whisper, frozen in place, hoping he won't sink through the floor. His face is bathed in the green glow that mushrooms out from the *Engage* a heartbeat before it disappears. A huge dent remains in the liquid surface, with waves frothing against the nothingness of its invisible hull.

I reach out and take his hand, desperate to distract him. Jacob shakes out of the connection to the ship. His eyes swerve to mine. I hold his gaze, giving him all the contact with this world that I can. Out of the corner of my eye, I catch the *Engage* re-materialize, but I hold Jacob's eyes, palms sweating. I pull my hand away before Brooks can turn from watching the *Engage*.

"Carter, how'd you do that?" His voice is low, demanding an answer.

"Sir, I didn't, sir," Jacob responds with typical military volume, but his gaze is still on mine. In them I see the memories of all his experiences, mixed with a vibrant pulsing life, flaming up from his blue eyes. Rescue boats buzz as they swarm the *Engage*. Jacob's shoulders drop, the tension falling away; he breaks my gaze a half breath before Brooks looks at him.

"Carter, the Admiral will see you."

My gut turns at his words. Jacob says nothing as we drop to the third deck.

Our escort falls away at a tight doorway, and I breathe a sigh of relief when I'm allowed in. Admiral Ash stands, his short gray hair covered by a white hat with gold leaves on its black brim, his perfect uniform stretching around his middle. Pale-blue eyes brood under heavy brows and send chills down my spine. Jacob's words come to me: "The man who killed Rivera."

I glance at Jacob, find him stiffly at attention. But it's his eyes, guarded as if he's pulled down a wall, that make me nervous. I'd seen the rage boiling under the surface; I fidget; sure hope Ash doesn't push him any harder. Another figure shifts in the corner: Dr. Sutton. My skin crawls, all my senses hyper-alert.

"Carter, at ease."

Jacob's upper lip tenses; he lifts his chin, squares his shoulders a hint further. He's sticking it to Ash on purpose. *Come on, Jacob, we've got to play this right.*

Ash clears his throat, eyes colder than before. "Your numbers from today are impressive."

The admiral's effort to slake Jacob's pride fall flat.

"Sir," Jacob responds.

Ash watches him a moment. "I'd like you to meet Dr. Sutton; she's been responsible for your recovery."

I grit my teeth as Sutton stands, her knee-length white skirt and mid-height heels a direct contrast to my scrubs. *She's been keeping him alive?* A huge part of my mind loses it. She's done nothing other than order invasive procedures.

She reaches out to shake his hand and I struggle to keep my mouth from hanging open as he makes no move to acknowledge the formality. His hands remain locked at his sides.

"Ma'am," he says.

She nods, covering a flash of contempt at his slight. Sutton and Ash exchange a tense glance. The awareness that these two people are in total control of our futures settles until I have to force slow, steady breaths.

"You've served for six years, and as an elite operative, and your specs are very impressive."

Ash is used to dealing with these alpha males by gaining their trust with recognition of their accomplishments. Jacob Carter, however, is in a class of his own, and Ash is missing the mark.

"You have an opportunity to become an even more valuable asset."

Jacob's face remains stoic, but I can feel the heat pumping off him. He doesn't offer any response, forcing the admiral to continue. He shifts his tone from the admiring father figure to command.

"You'll be engaging in hand-to-hand combat exercises with an operative named Tex. He's been a part of my program for over a year now."

Everything the admiral didn't say flashes through my mind. Tex, an operative, a *super-soldier* under Admiral Ash's control. I shudder.

"Sir, I'm overdue for duty with team three." Jacob's words are tense.

Ash nods. "You will not be returning to the teams anytime soon."

Jacob's jaw clenches, and my eyes go wide. *Is he saying Jacob's no longer a SEAL?*

"We've got to get you stable first. Your labs are still quite concerning," Sutton interjects, trying to soften Ash's blow.

Jacob turns his head, gaze hard as he stares her down. She fidgets, smoothing her skirt.

"What can you tell us about your episodes?" Ash's gravelly voice pulls his attention back.

"It hasn't been easy, sir." Jacob's calculated response doesn't say much.

"Certainly. You did, however, manage to make the LCS *Engage* return to its cloaking state by merely looking at it."

I'd been hoping that the ship had been experiencing that disappearing act without Jacob's presence. Ash is finished talking when Jacob doesn't respond.

"Brooks," he says, pushing a button on a handheld radio. The door swings open.

"Carter," Brooks booms out his name, and I turn with him, eager to exit.

"Emerson."

I stop, cringing inside. *Shoot.* Brooks shuts the door, and I fight the queasy feeling in my stomach.

"Has Carter told you anything about his experiences?" Ash's question makes me scramble.

"He's not a very talkative person, sir," I say, avoiding an answer.

"It's of utmost importance to his health that we discover what he's experiencing while in his episodes. His EEG levels are completely inconsistent with someone in a coma." Sutton returns to her tone of motherly concern.

Taking a breath, I realize I'll have to leverage everything to stay by Jacob's side. I glance at them, gravitating to Sutton, just the way they planned.

"I feel the same way, especially his cerebrum activity. It seems as if he's learning. His return was much smoother this time. He called it a 'reconnection.' Strange. I didn't expect his sense of humor though, or his quick perception." I lay these words down like a row of aces.

He won't talk to them and I'll do whatever it takes to remind them I'm valuable to their goal. "He said it was easier this time. Plus, we're way past the time frame of his last episode, so, it could be we're in the clear. Have you run case studies on anyone coming out of a coma the way he does? Straight into action?"

"Yes. We don't have any documentation on what we are dealing with. And your labs, what do you make of them?" Sutton asks, her brown eyes earnest.

"We're missing something. I feel great. Actually, I have more energy than usual. Honestly, I think it's a potassium causing most of the anomalies, but it's a type we've not yet studied. Potassium-60." I let the name hang in the air a moment. "That's why the labs are grabbing it so inconsistently."

I nod, glad for the keen interest in their eyes. It was worth parting with my personal theory to gain their trust. Now I'm their best link to Jacob Carter. *Keep yourself relevant, Sage.*

I hurry down the hall toward the training deck, wishing my Marine escort would walk faster. As we swing left off the stairs, my shoulders drop; Jacob is at the far end, arms crossed as he listens to Brooks read off a set of orders. By the time I reach him, Jacob is alone; his eyes read mine.

"I do not like that woman." His voice is low at his reference to Sutton.

"Feeling's mutual. They're prying about what's happening while you're out."

He nods. "Brooks is bringing out their prizefighter from Ash's other projects."

My stomach rebels. *No.* Ideas surge: how can I get Jacob out of here? Could we fake an episode? The thought shocks me and my face must show it.

"Don't worry; hand-to-hand is old hat for me."

"It's not right. What's the point?" I cross my arms, trying to contain a hurricane of emotions. "Did you sign up for this? Is this what you wanted?" I have to know.

Jacob's chest pumps with a sardonic laugh. "No. They pulled Rivera and me from active duty." His mouth flat-lines at the name. "I'll play their game a little longer, but I'm not giving myself over to them. I've heard what Ash is into—mind control, physical fortification."

"What?" Fear grips me hard.

"Got guys jacked up with bone strengtheners, pain inhibition, brain enhancement. I won't take a chip. Sage, if I jump again, don't let them insert anything. I'd rather die than take that." His eyes hold mine steady, burning with passion, but the full import of his words makes sweat slick my palms.

I shift, mouth dry, thinking of what Sutton had already done. "I...I'll do everything I can."

Half of Jacob's mouth tips up, his eyes bright. "What would I do without you?"

"You might be in rough shape." Somehow, his words fill me to the brim.

"You know they had a particle decelerator on the *Engage?*" he questions.

"Yeah, I saw it, but I didn't know what it was then. Been researching, trying to find out what they did. I think we're dealing with a new type of potassium, one that interacts with positrons." The cavernous training room swallows our quiet words.

"Like a banana? They create a positron about once an hour."

I nod at his knowledge. "When you make a jump, you emit enough positrons to power a city for a year. You give off your own green glow."

"So, bananas and I have a lot in common?" There's a playful glint in his eye.

"Bananas don't disappear," I say flatly.

"True, I'm cuter too." He drops his eyes, which only serves to make him irresistible.

A smile plays on my mouth. He's dead right about that. I long for a fraction of his confidence. Across the room a door opens, and we turn as Brooks precedes a tall soldier in camo pants and a black shirt. My stomach twists; this can't be happening.

"Don't worry, Sage. I have a few aces up my sleeve."

I look at him, tears pricking my eyes.

"Lately I've got so much extra energy, it'll be good to burn some up. I could power a city, remember? Time to see what Tex is made of." He juts his chin at me, eyes happy, then sets off for the center of the room.

He faces off with Tex. Everything in me revolts at the sight of that man; a deep unease settles over my mind as I study the hardness in his face. Something's off with him. He's a few inches taller than Jacob, a little lighter; his pale skin is pinched tight over muscle and tendon. His strawberry blond hair's short, and his skin has a reddish tint.

He stares down at Jacob with a sneer. I can't make out what Brooks is saying; his eyes shift between the two of them. He gives a nod and heads my way.

They circle each other. Tex has a few inches of arm's length on Jacob. I twist my hands together, unable to cover my nerves as Brooks stations himself a few feet away.

Tex sweeps out with his arm, and they surge in and out, evading each other. They move like cats, supple, faster than I can keep up with. Jacob barrels in, taking Tex by the waist, shouldering into his stomach.

He drives hard until Tex takes the edge of a wall with his back, but it doesn't seem to faze him. Jacob's comment on pain suppression echoes in my mind. Tex grabs Jacob by the leg, heaves up, and they flip over, still grappling; everything goes wild. I can't tell what's what.

They spin, the wall blocking my view. I can't keep the grimace off my face; *I hate this.* They reappear on the far side of the wall, and Tex sweeps out with his fist, a solid connection with Jacob's jaw. I gasp in horror as Jacob shakes it off, tilts his head, expression deadly.

Something's changed; the rules ramped up a notch. Jacob dodges left, snatches a thick rope that dangles in the obstacle course. He tucks his legs up, momentum carrying him over a five-foot wall. Twisting in the air, his boots land a punishing blow to Tex's stomach. He flies back, skidding, but he comes up like a freight train. Their fists fly so fast, I can't count the connections.

"Brooks! This is crazy. Stop them." I resist grabbing his arm as I shout.

Brooks looks at his watch, shakes his head. "They're just warming up."

Tex's face is a mask of rage as he rains blows down on Jacob, who deflects most of them. Tex lands two solid blows one after the other, and the combined impact sends Jacob sliding across the floor. Possible kidney damage or torn intestines. My nails bite into my palms as they keep the distance for a moment, chests heaving.

Jacob dives back in, blood trickling down his chin. "Brooks!" I shout. "They are destroying each other."

Jacob's renewed attack drives Tex back.

"Time." Brooks booms out the command to no avail. He advances onto the course. "Time!"

I follow, running through the contents of my med pack the Marine had brought down. They flash between obstacles. Brooks has veins standing on his neck as he repeats his order. They spill over onto the far track out in the open; we round the last wall as Jacob spins, his high kick twisting Tex's head back.

"Time!" The word reverberates in the metal hull of the ship.

Jacob spreads his hands, but his eyes remain locked on Tex as he rights himself. A sneer curls one of the man's bloody lips as he crouches. Tex won't listen to Brooks. Jacob absorbs his punishing impact, deflecting blows, spreading his hands at every opportunity; Tex keeps laying into him.

Brooks advances till he's just out of range of Tex's swings.

"Tex, time!" Brooks unclips a small remote when he doesn't respond. "Five seconds," he threatens, but Tex doubles his pace, Jacob dodging and sweeping blows aside.

Brooks presses the button. Tex's neck twitches hard, his face contorting.

Jacob pulls back one swollen lip. "They turn your brain on, Tex?"

His words ignite his opponent, and he leaps forward. Brooks enters a combination of numbers on the pad. Tex's whole body twitches as he rolls off Jacob to stand at attention, eyes blank. Jacob leaps to his feet, chest heaving, staring at Tex.

"Tex, report to area four."

Tex sneers at Brooks, one eye swelling shut. Brooks shifts his feet.

*What on earth happens if he won't listen?* I chew the inside of my lip as the tension grows. But Tex turns away toward an escort of sailors similar to Jacob's.

"Carter, head to the bench. Emerson, full check."

I follow close on Jacob's heels. Spleen damage is the greatest concern. I need an ultrasound, STAT. If it's torn, I need to assess the bleeding to prevent a hematoma. Possible broken nose, check his kidneys; my hands are sweaty. *How soon will they let us up to the room?* Jacob sits on the bench at the far end of the track, elbows on his knees. I dig out gauze and wipe his swollen lip, cringing. His nose still looks straight.

"Sage."

But I still need to check it. If his spleen is bleeding…I need my equipment *right now*. I look back for Brooks; he's nowhere in sight.

"Sage."

His eye is swelling, his knuckles bleeding.

"Sage." He takes my shoulders till I make eye contact. "I'm fine. Take a deep breath." Half his mouth turns up. "I've survived a lot worse."

I snort at his comment.

He laughs, unhindered by the split in his lip. "A lot worse. It's nothing like melting into the floor."

I let out a slow breath, his easy manner breaking through my nerves.

"How can you laugh with your lip bleeding like that?"

He shrugs. "We train to control discomfort." He sits up straight, stretching, muscles standing out. "I'm not used to being pampered."

"Well," I say, wiping his hand with an alcohol swab, "you're going to have to adjust."

Jacob's eyes are bright. "You know, fighting with Tex…" He weaves from side to side as if he's dodging punches. "Was almost like I knew what was coming. That's never happened before." He narrows his eyes. "The only times he connected was when I ignored it, when I thought I could change it or dodge him. Normally, when you fight, you've got a split second to feel where your opponent is going, move by move, and stay ahead of it. This was like I was watching it on video a second ahead of reality. Not up here"—he taps his head—"but in here." His thick fingers land on his sternum. His eyes lock on mine; it's as if the experience has elated him.

"I found life. I know that sounds strange, but everything I've learned translates to this world. I didn't think it really would."

His EEG results with their incredibly high gamma waves make my hands go still: what if he possesses knowledge no one else knows?

"What do you do there?" The words come out as a whisper.

Blue eyes intense, he says, "Survive." He clasps his hands, the longing for that world clear. "There, everything is so raw, so real, the…" He looks at me, deciding. "Colors have sounds. And when you've eaten enough, just being there…well…it's what I was made for." He shrugs. "The lions are no joke though."

"Lions?"

He nods to himself. "You know what's weird?"

I smirk. "Uh, your green haze and the way you fall through the floor?"

"Right," he says. "You know *another* weird thing? There was an oil spill on the *Engage* before the experiment. It had lion tracks through it. Rivera and I both saw them. Were the worlds mixing even then?"

Brooks reappears at the far end of the room, heading our way. I take Jacob's blood pressure, in a hurry to speak.

"Listen, in our room, the audio quality is incredible. Don't say anything important in there. If you need to ask me something, jumble it up with something else. If the answer is yes, I'll sniff; if it's no, I'll cough. *They want to know.* More than anything they want to re-create you. We can't give them any knowledge that could make that happen."

He nods. "What about you?"

"Me?"

"Your tests are reading similar to mine."

Brooks is halfway here.

"The only side effects for me are increased energy. So far."

"They're watching you close." He glances at Brooks, lowering his voice. "Listen, if you make a jump, don't trust anyone who doesn't have the light. Eat as much scroll as you can stomach; and if you smell something dead, run as fast as you can."

My face reflects my horror at his words. They make no sense, and yet they are seared into my mind. Jacob's face becomes a blank mask as Brooks approaches.

"Emerson. Stats?"

"Looking good, sir. I'd like to run an ultrasound to be sure his organs are okay."

"Report back to A27 and get that done."

Back in our room, I smear cold jelly on his back, needing something normal, anything normal. "So, what's your favorite food?"

He drains another cup of water from his second pitcher. He grunts, thumbing through the Bible he'd requested.

"Right now, it's Hebrews 11:1. 'Now faith is the substance of things hoped for, the substance of things unseen.'" He grunts as if those words are a deep revelation, delicious even.

I hold the ultrasound wand against his back. His odd response is amusing. "I said, *food*."

"Oh." He gives a laugh. "Right." He thinks a moment as if it were a foreign subject. "Barbecue bacon burgers. You?"

"Watermelon." A slow sigh escapes me; his internal organs are fine.

"Happy now?" he says, sensing the tension falling away from me.

"Yes. Now I am."

"Told you I was fine." He twists around to look at me.

"Well, now I know."

He nods, eyes deep.

"A wise man once said, 'Knowledge is power.'"

His true meaning seems just out of reach; here's a man who might hold the secrets of the universe. I turn, wiping the ultrasound wand and coiling up its cord. Sighing, I slide its drawer shut with a metallic clang.

"You think…" My words dry up as I turn to find Jacob again clenching the exam table, chest heaving.

I blink hard in the green haze, scowling, as an intense twinge clutches my chest. The feeling shrieks down my arms as Jacob grimaces.

He starts to jackhammer, the table rattling under his abuse. Eyes locked, we struggle, caught in the intense energy. The pitcher of water skitters toward him, ice clinking as it dives off the edge. Time slows down as the waves of water and ice crash against his straining chest.

"Ah," he sighs. Relief covers his face before his eyes roll back in his head, and he crashes to the floor. Shaking, I rush around the table, skidding on my knees, forcing down vomit.

Pulse is steady, breathing regular. My muscles don't respond smoothly, as if I'm driving a car with sloppy steering. The surging energy fades as I draw in deep breaths.

"Brooks!" I twist, looking at the door. *Why haven't they already barged in?* "Brooks, I need to get him on the table." I wait, fingers on Jacob's steady pulse.

Not falling through the floor was a vastly better way to go. I replay the water's slow-motion surge and his expression as it touched him.

*Wait.*

I freeze as his jumps race through my mind; we've always found him in the water. Does he enter that state where a jump is possible, and the condition worsens until he loses solidity? Eventually he sinks down and hits the water; then he stabilizes. Sometimes it's better than others, depending on how long he was in that disintegrated state. *Is water the key?*

He's solid now with no need of the defib paddles. *Does the water allow him to disconnect?* Every time he's made a jump, I've gotten him back wet. It's possible that the water allows him to take the last step out of his body. If he melts through substances till he touches water, then getting him wet when he's in that state with the green haze around him might just save his life. The door swings open, and three nurses in full radiation gear enter. We struggle with Jacob's limp form. Orders for another blood test.

*For me.*

# 5
# JACOB



In the soft light of morning with dew soaking into my clothes, I grapple with two worlds, and everything I wish I was, surging between physical strength and the distance to gaining faith like Demyen's. At least I'd avoided colliding with the trees this time. The divot from my landing is before me. I must not have been solid when I connected with the ground.

Without the strength of my body, it's hard to find courage. I sink my fingers into the dirt, the deep throbbing bass of it vibrating up my arms. Demyen's words about faith run through my mind, so fresh, like I'd never made the jump, never missed a second. Life here is seamless. The fight with Tex seems so distant, I almost think it happened to someone else.

I sigh, replaying Demyen's knowledge, letting it break through doubts I didn't know I had. *What if I can't grasp the truth, and I fail?* I grapple with the implications: what if I lived the Word? Knowing only the Almighty's will? Is life like Demyen's even attainable?

I clench my jaw; there is no other option. I will not lose. Catching movement through the trees, I see Myah threading a path in my direction. Graceful as a doe, she continues through the mist till she reaches a small clearing to my left. I'm certain she is unaware of my presence, even the birds hop in the brush, inches from my face.

I slip a piece of scroll into my mouth, hunger gnawing at me. Myah gathers herself, squaring her shoulders, balancing. With even, practiced movements, she bends, warming up. Slowly at first, she stretches, seamless motion. She spins, reaching high, now low; she pauses with arms spread wide. Her thumbs flick up, and there's a sharp sound as long daggers appear from nowhere. Then things get interesting; I continue to peer through the vegetation.

For half of a breath, she's still, then in the next instant, she's a whirlwind of flashing blades and motion. In my mind, I parry every blow, even though I know I'd never keep up in my current state. It's hard to say what will be in the air next—feet, blades, or her dark locks of hair. She flips and kicks with infinite precision. Watching her ramps up my hunger, stirring a deep desire for the strength I'll gain from eating. Form, balance, and strength meld into one of the most incredible shows of prowess I have ever seen as Myah increases her tempo yet again.

Then, she's still as stone, only her lungs pumping for air. She lets out a breath, relaxing and shaking out her muscles. *Worship.* The word comes like a whisper. At first, it seems totally disconnected from the scene I've just witnessed; but, then again, maybe not.

*Is it a purer form of worship than anything I've ever imagined?* I nod, truth settling; it *was* worship to the Almighty. Hers was a form previously unknown to me, but potent, and it makes me long to have something to give.

She slips back toward the hut. Moments pass, tears pricking my eyes at the keen thirst for life, to truly experience it the way she does. I follow, not wanting her to know I had intruded. Back inside, she's once again timid Myah. *Tiny, but mighty.*

She works in the kitchen, filling bowls with steaming scroll. I join her, needing understanding. We work for a few moments until I grab the opportunity of her adjusting a slim strap that runs around her thumb and back under her long-sleeved tunic.

"How do they work?" I query, pointing at her hands.

Myah's eyes take on a gleam as she says, "My daggers?"

I nod, and when she continues, her voice is hushed in remembrance. "They were a gift. Long ago, I came upon a girl being torn apart by lions. I couldn't tell at first what they were killing, they were so thick; I just jumped in. Over my head too, I fought like a wild thing, but my arms tired." She bites her lip, "I didn't know what I do now. The tide turned and they almost had two victims that day; but I shouted for help at the top of my lungs."

She looks at me, but I know she sees that day.

"Watchers came. The light was piercing, and then we were free. The lions scattered, and I looked down at the bloody form in the dirt. A Watcher reached down to touch the girl's mangled neck, and the words he spoke…" Myah shudders as goose bumps rise on her skin from remembering. "They were so infinitely full of life—in another tongue, but so distinct, imparted into my soul, yet I cannot utter them." She covers her heart with her hand in reverence.

"The girl rose and walked away without a word." Sadness wells up in Myah's eyes. "She died recently—one year from that day."

"How?"

"A scorpion stung her and she passed within hours." Myah looks at me now. "But that was her choice, to walk away. I received a gift that day, too." She smiles as she holds up her hands, then spreads her thumbs in a swift motion.

The daggers appear so fast I can't tell where they come from. They seem to expand like a telescope, length upon length. Once they're extended, I can make out no layers or separation. My mouth must be hanging open because her grin grows.

"They still amaze me, too." She snaps her thumbs again, chink… chink… chink, and the knives disappear into a slim case hidden in the strap around her thumbs. "But weapons without knowledge are useless."

I nod; that's for sure.

"Myah, the fighter. I wouldn't have believed it until you went after Solomon." I shake my head in disbelief at the memory.

"Saw that, did you? Well, I'm not much of a warrior. It's just that I can't stand to see someone under attack. It isn't the will of the Almighty, and I can't abide it. I become a different person for a few minutes." She shrugs, brushing it off.

"Well, you're welcome to follow me around—just in case," I say, only half-joking.

Her gaze is sharp. "You need no protection, Jacob. You've grown in the time you've been here. The testing of your faith is as pure gold. You won't get stronger any other way. Don't fear, don't run, or you're already defeated. Stand your ground. You're the only one who can. I can't believe the Almighty's Words in your place. Each of us must stand firm on our own. All things are under the Almighty; He has all victory in His hands. He's in you, and the only way you can fail is if you think you will. Then you've joined the enemy, and he will have his way with you."

Myah thrusts a steaming bowl into my hands. "Come on; I'm hungry."

My golden thread is lonely. I wish it had converged with Demyen's. Myah's words run through my mind as I sneak through the thick forest. My thoughts are against me at every turn; fear creeps in, imagining evils that haven't yet happened.

I pull a wad of scroll from my pouch and chew. I halt, cocking my head. When I stop chewing, the faint sound ceases as well. After a moment, I resume chewing and walking and I hear the sound again. It's like a radio, badly tuned and far away.

I stop chewing to listen, but it's gone. *Maybe it's the other way around.* I work the scroll harder, forcing juice from it. Now it's coming in louder. "For…weapons…warfare…mighty."

Closing my eyes, desperate to hear, the sound continues. "To… to… the pulling down of strongholds…imaginations that exalt themselves…" It starts over, and now I catch almost every word: "For the weapons of our warfare are…but mighty through God to the pulling down of strongholds; casting…imaginations… that exalt themselves against the knowledge…God."

Implications swirl, mixing with what Demyen had said about faith and Myah's words this morning. It all works together. *Could simply believing it change reality?* I had seen it with my very eyes when Demyen had taken the scorpion stings. Yet my mind resists, unsure; *it's not logical.*

I chew, listening and pondering. "For though we walk in the flesh, we do not war after the flesh: For the weapons of our warfare are not carnal, but mighty through God to the pulling down of strongholds; casting down imaginations, and every high thing that exalts itself against the knowledge of God; and bringing into captivity every thought to the obedience of Christ."

A piercing sadness grips me; I know these words in my mind, but they have never become a part of me, never changed me. And yet now, I need them to live. Time passes as I slip through the forest, keeping ever on the golden line. The word *imagination* won't leave me. That's the only battle I've faced yet today, the dark imaginings of my soul.

*What if lions can only kill me if I believe they can?* I snort at the thought. They have more than enough power to. But the image of Demyen fearlessly facing Aseph makes me wonder if children of the Light have a different reality. Can they affect the outcome? *That could change everything.*

A stream lies ahead with its clear, laughing water. Kneeling, I spread my hands under the cool liquid. I shiver at the sensation, life coursing. As I close my eyes, I strain to hear. The voice sounds like another language. Now I hear more clearly… "All…all…all authority in heaven and on earth has been given unto Me."

I pull out my hands; the hair on my arms stands on end. The water has spoken the ending—the missing link, per se—spoken it into me *in response to my meditation.* Authority is the key; it's what holds all these ideas of faith together. I struggle against the thoughts. The desire to go back presses strong: to return to the world where I have control.

I grimace, fighting to turn my mind. *What good does wishing do?* It will make me weaker when what I need is strength, divided when single-minded focus is necessary.

Frustrated, I plunge my hands and my face under the water together. The electrifying energy of it flowing over my skin makes me want to suck it in. I resist, holding my breath until I feel cleared, clean.

As I stand, water coursing down my neck under my tunic, a tendril of stench curls into my nostrils. A surge of fear stretches across my chest. Frantically, I seek my path; *maybe it will lead me to safety.* I plunge up the hill on the far side of the stream, fighting my thoughts.

Myah's words replay in my mind: *don't fear; don't run. The only way you can fail is to doubt.* I grab at the truth that's so slippery in my hands. If all authority in heaven and on earth belongs to the Almighty, and He is in me, then…nothing is impossible. My heart pounds as the stench grows.

I release a frustrated breath. *No cover in sight.* The trees are fewer here but larger. I run, seeking some sort of shelter, but the trees are so large they have no branches growing low. *There!* In the distance stands a mighty oak with an immense girth.

I reach it, chest pumping, and flatten my back against its rough bark. The hated scent fills my nose; there is no clean air. Eyes darting, every muscle is hyper alert.

There, to the left, a tawny head with evil black eyes peers around a birch tree. Its thick lips curl in a snarl. It slinks forward, eyes locked on mine. It only has one goal: to kill me. I lock down my fear; my weapons are mighty, and I must convince myself of this truth.

At least it's not Aseph. This one is slightly smaller, with a massive, unhealed wound across his chest. I wish for something between me and it…*my sword!* I fumble for the hilt, steadied by the long hiss of its sliding free from my scabbard. *It's grown!*

I heft its weight, testing its balance, wishing I had put in some practice like Myah. I want to run. Everything tells me to; only Myah's words hold me still. *Don't cower.* I grit my teeth, staring hard into dead black eyes.

Twenty yards is all that separates us. The lion's ribcage expands, and I brace myself for the coming blast. Dead leaves on the forest floor tremble at his roar. My stomach twists and sweat beads on my upper lip. There is no time. *He comes.* A blur of motion, a single breath till he meets the upraised edge of my sword.

His momentum crushes me against the massive tree; I hear his claws raking bark away on either side of my head. I shout, drawing strength as my left hand finds the flat of my sword. The lion's fangs snap a hair's breadth from my face; his scent is overpowering, lips dripping. I push the flat of my sword up against his jaw, forcing him away.

We struggle; the evil sound of his claws crushing bark creeps closer to my head. In desperation, I clench my stomach and jam both feet into the lion's belly, heaving with my sword as well. The beast staggers back off balance, then turns away.

He circles before me. *The sword will work better if you use its edge.* He rushes again. This time, I sweep out before he can pin me against the tree. The blade sings as it slices through the air.

The lion is wise enough; twisting his paw with a deft move, he knocks the blow aside. I slice air again. He crouches, ears flattened, teeth and claws extended, growling. His lean legs move like lightning, trying to rip away my weapon, uncaring of the wounds he receives.

I add my left hand to the hilt, doubling my power. He seeks an opening, but I force my eyes to stay locked on his. His hind legs tense to launch forward and I almost hesitate, almost turn to run, but a battle cry erupts from my throat with the stroke of my sword. I find the satisfying bite of my blade deep into his neck and chest. His growl changes, higher pitched as his momentum carries us back against the tree.

The air leaves my lungs in a rush, but I finish my sword stroke, forcing the lion down. My blade drips blood. I smile. The lion looks up, indecisive now, and I roar at him again in defiance. The red pool deepens beneath his chest as he snarls, deciding. I lean forward; he turns and streaks into the forest. I let out a breath, sinking against the tree.

"Ah." I slump against the bark. My sword tip hits the ground and I gaze at the sky, just visible through the leaves, lungs pumping for air.

"Thank You," I whisper, closing my eyes in relief. *I won.* The struggle was worth the surge of life. My back hurts from the slam, but otherwise, I'm fine. I let out a bark of laughter. *Maybe it's all true.* I heave a deep sigh, clearing tension, and then I turn to continue along my path.

*"Eeeeaaah!!"* I leap back, startled.

A huge Watcher stands there. His luminescent skin glistens.

"Greetings," he says in a deep baritone.

I stare at him, wondering. Strength and life radiate from him.

I lower one brow in question. "Were…were you standing there the whole time?"

He smiles a wide, Cheshire grin. "That's for me to know and you to find out."

I scowl at his cryptic comment.

"You did well, Jacob."

I don't question how he knows my name. "Thank you."

He nods, muscles popping. "I'm sent for a reason. You fought your first battle and won."

"Didn't have any choice; it was do or die. Would…would you have helped me if I needed it?"

His smile grows in response, white teeth gleaming. "Let's just be glad we didn't tread that path. These are yours, Jacob. Wield them well."

He holds out a pair of long daggers with a short strap attached to each. My mouth hangs open. Even though they aren't engraved like my sword, they are perfect weapons with a bright titanium sheen. The length of the blades is around ten inches and flawlessly balanced.

"Hold out your right arm."

I step forward and raise it. The Watcher settles the odd-shaped hilt into my palm, a perfect fit. He lays the flat of the blade along my forearm and works with the straps at my elbow, wrist, and then around my hand. I can't fathom how he fastens them because as he finishes each, I find no buckle or tie of any kind.

"The next," he says, then repeats the procedure on my left arm.

He grunts his approval, now slipping leather sheaths from his tunic and clipping them over the sharp, naked blades lying against my forearms. Peering at one, I see that toward the lower side of my forearm the sheath is open along its length; instead of sliding out from the top, the blades swing out. I flex my forearms, surprised to find no restriction despite the straps; I have a total range of motion.

"Within, say *Hadena* as you clench your fists," he commands, stepping back.

I do, then suck in my stomach as the lethal blades whip out. The odd handles rotate up into my palms; the curved hilts settle into the valley between my thumb and pointer finger. I grip them firmly in a downward hold. Instead of the hilt coming up in a normal sword grip, the blade's point to the ground, the tips of the hilts sitting uppermost.

"These are offensive weapons. They belong to one who chases, not merely stands his ground. And no, they will never come off. They are now part of you. For the gifts and callings of God are without repentance. The blades will only unsheathe when you clench your fist and bring up their name within your mind. Do not fear the use of them, Jacob, for the chasing down of foes. Wield them well."

I shrug my shoulders, so disconnected from his words. *Me chasing down lions?* "How do I get them to re-sheath?"

The Watcher flashes that grin. "You'll figure it out."

Then he disappears. My hair stands on end again as I stare at the empty forest. The import of his words does not bring me joy. More battles are certain.

I heave a sigh: give me my body, and I'd be first in line. I reach with my left hand to test the right blade. A rivulet of blood appears at the tip of my finger. *Sharper than I thought.*

As I suck on my bleeding finger, I wonder at the Watcher's words. *I've got to figure out how to sheath them.* I set out along my iridescent golden path, chewing scroll, and tiptoeing through the forest, trying to control my new "body parts."

Hours pass and I can tell by the scent that I've turned back toward the hut. It's a long way off, but I should be there before dark. My green tunic has three slices in it; but my side is still whole.

"I can't pass the night with these things unsheathed," I mutter. If I clench my fists and think *Hadena* to open them, then what would be an opposite command? I try saying the word backward, to no avail.

When I reach the hut, my weapons are still out in the open. My hand finds the leather door strap; it's the first time I'm not desperate to get inside. I smile, trying not to stab myself in the stomach.

Ian looks up from a map he's studying. He smiles, unfolding his slim figure, a look of relief on his face at more company. Solomon sits at the table, mid-sentence.

"Good to see you, Solomon. How have you fared since your healing?" I ask.

"Healing? Oh that! Very well, never better. I've been down to Hidden Valley and enjoyed myself, I did." Solomon runs a hand through his hair.

As Ian nods, my eyes narrow. What is it about Solomon that puts me on edge? I see Ian is experiencing the same odd check as I am.

Solomon continues talking until Myah slips through the hut door. His stories are nothing but doubt, fear, and failure, and now I understand Ian's relief at my entry; at least he stopped talking for a moment.

I take quick stock of Myah; she has a sheen of sweat on her brow, her hair is tangled with leaves, and there's the faint red smear across her shoulder. I breathe in. Yes, lion's stench. She also has a spark in her eye, and one edge of her mouth tips up the slightest bit. *Hmmm...* There's a story to be told; but apparently, it's not one we are going to hear.

"Well, hello, beautiful! So long since I've seen you!" Solomon's words flatten Myah's mouth into a hard line. Myah turns for the kitchen, Solomon at her heels. Ian follows. I'm sure Solomon resents the threesome. The door of the hut swings open and I look up, expecting Demyen. Instead, a man with a long dark tunic and a thick cloak wrapped about him enters. His blond hair and short goatee fit his aura of seclusion perfectly.

Ian backs through the doorway with a steaming bowl in one hand. The man's light-brown eyes sweep the room and he gives Ian a curt nod. Ian returns the gesture and pulls out a stool for the man.

"Samson." Ian dips his head as he says the man's name.

Samson wraps himself tighter in his cloak as he takes the seat Ian offered. His skin glows bright, at least what little of it shows under his hooded cloak. Solomon's voice echoes from the kitchen, still talking. The door opens again, and Demyen enters, covered in sweat, full of life.

He slaps Samson on the back without a word and sits next to him. I sit opposite them as Myah and Solomon exit the kitchen. Solomon's endless stories continue, but I block them out as I sit, wanting to absorb the knowledge that the two men before me hold.

They are so different in looks, but so similar in their bearing and the light they exude. They have some undefinable quality that I'm determined to gain. Samson steps out of the hut after the meal and I slip after him. He stands, staring up at the stars, cloak still wrapped around him. I hesitate; his light is even brighter in the dark night.

"Jacob." His voice is quiet and welcoming. Relieved, I step forward, copying his position. Minutes pass as I soak up the strength flowing from him. He looks over at me, eyes full of knowledge. "It is possible."

"What is?"

"To be as you were in the other world, here."

My shoulders drop. "Got a long way to go, then."

He nods, looking up at the heavens again. "You already possess everything."

I frown at his words.

"When you awaken to the fact that He gave you everything you need, life will begin." He's silent for a long time as I try to imagine having all strength and confidence. Fail completely.

"This can only be revealed by knowledge—the *right* knowledge." I wait for him to answer my thoughts again, and he does not disappoint. "Knowledge unlocks the life you were called to—the authority, the dominion."

I shrug. "I've never been so powerless."

His keen eye catches the starlight. "I said nothing about *power*; I said *authority*. There's a vast difference between them. Consider: can you overpower a lion?"

I recall the bulk of the lion smashing me against the tree. He was definitely more powerful than any man, larger, stronger, faster. "No."

"Then all is hopeless without authority. If one cannot overpower the enemy, how do the children of the Light exist?"

"Because the Almighty protects us?"

Samson shakes his head. "No, not in the sense you mean. We must go back to dominion. The first man: Adam, what did he have?"

I squint one eye and stay silent.

"The Almighty immediately gave him dominion over the world. Rulership. But he soon sold out, giving his dominion to the enemy. The lions brought ruin to the world with it. Then, in the ultimate sacrifice, the Almighty bought it back. Now, children of the Light shrug off all responsibility by claiming the Almighty will have His way. Yet, He never intended to hold the dominion here. Waiting on the Almighty to move has caused more death than any other cause. They do not see that they must speak and act in order to see His will come to pass."

I swallow hard, longing to get it. "So, it's up to us?"

"We have a new agreement. A new covenant. The Almighty created a new path when Christ gave Himself. Legally, He took the authority from the enemy, but He is now seated at the right hand of Power. He told His people to carry out His will. A *body* is essential to complete the Almighty's work. NONE of it can happen without a human acting in faith. People claim the Almighty made them sick to teach them something, or that it was *His time* for a young person to die. But legally, His people must take action to allow His power to move, to make His will come to pass.

"Blasphemy is the attributing of evil to God. We must be very careful not to lay the blame at His feet, but our own. He created laws in the beginning, and He won't violate them. Under the new agreement, we must *carry out* His authority, doing the same works as Christ, and even greater. Otherwise, evil still rules. It's a stolen power, but that's what the lions do: steal, kill, and destroy. What you don't know is killing you."

He's pounded my previous assumptions about life into the dirt; the bruises are fresh. He looks over, sees it. "Let us go back to power. We must overcome the enemy, or we die. His single intent is to kill every one of us. Victory can only come through the authority the Almighty has given. I have no power in myself. Power does, however, flow through me because I understand how it works, and I walk in the light of that knowledge.

"I am a carrier. A conduit—the wire through which it flows. The power, by law, will not reach its destination without something to flow through. It is authority, the *proper* flow of His power, that allows me to conquer. I know the will of the Almighty and I act in faith until it becomes reality."

He nods. "Victory is the Almighty's will for His people. Remember that."

He strides off into the dark night, leaving me to grasp at his words. I return to the hut, relieved to curl up on the floor in the quiet darkness. I close my eyes, but I do not seek the odd, alert stillness of sleep in this place.

I almost ran Demyen through at the table; I have to control these blades. *What would be the opposite of Hadena?* What does *Hadena* even mean? Sudden thirst overcomes me, and I rise to scoop a cupful from the barrel. When it touches my lips, I know. *Hadena…Battle.*

Battle is the name of my weapons. So, if their name is *Battle,* what is the end of that? Thoughts swirl as time creeps past. I roll onto my other side, seeking comfort. Finally, it comes. The outcome of battle is *victory.* If I didn't have any doubt entering a battle, then to finish that battle would mean victory.

I shift, giving myself ample room. I tighten my fists and think *victory.* The satisfying hiss of the hilts snapping up into their sheaths brings a long sigh of relief.

Solomon takes his leave early. I feel lighter the moment we part company. Outside, the day is perfect—crisp and vibrant. A strange thing happens; our paths align. Demyen, Ian, Myah, and I trek together, passing through familiar territory. As we enter the forest, there's a tingling expectancy in the air. The day passes as we continue traveling, eating scroll, and laughing in amiable company.

A question burns till I can't contain it. "What was it about Solomon that rubbed me so wrong?"

Demyen snorts. "Well, he bootlegged his healing, for one. He's old enough to take hold of it for himself; but he waited for someone else to get his miracle for him. It's a temporary fix for him. We're each called to stand on our own faith, once mature. I won't even go into his current behavior." His eyes flick to Myah and his expression makes the rest of us smile. Solomon had been…greasy.

I study the ground around my golden thread; it's like a mirage or heatwave is rippling. I move my head like an owl to see more. It works too: the more I focus, the more paths I can see stretching out ahead.

Squinting, I can make out the vibrant colors of each one. Myah's is a metallic purple. Ian's is a pale green, perhaps emerald.

Demyen's is pure silver. The forest loam, threaded with long lines of gems, is incredible.

"Look," I say. "Do you all see that?"

Three pairs of eyes scan the forest, weapons drawn.

"No, on the ground out ahead? Can you see our paths? Not just your own, but all of ours?"

Ian's grunt is the only sound as the others study the ground. Myah's eyes narrow as she turns, searching deep into the forest on all sides.

"Tighten up; something's going on," Demyen commands.

No one hesitates. Peace is still in the air, but now it is mixed with…expectation. We push forward for another hour, watching and sensing.

It's Myah who breaks the silence, pointing ahead. "Four more."

I squint. Yet another group of glistening paths swerves nearer ours.

"Have you ever seen anything like it?" Ian's question hangs in the air.

"Long ago." Demyen nods, deep in the past, expectation overflowing. His next words draw goose bumps across my skin. "Prepare your hearts; make ready."

We push hard as the afternoon wanes, joined by more children of the Light. Now, out ahead, I see twenty shimmering paths. No, thirty-five! Soon, there are too many to count.

We've passed from the cover of the woods into a plain of short, soft grass. The paths are veins of precious gems that make the sand glow beneath the growth. To my right, the crowd travels in a silence of intense anticipation. Though so many, we make no sound. Not even the tread of our many feet in the deep grass.

Night descends. The darker it gets, the brighter seem the paths. Still, we press on. The number of paths still grows, converging and tightening. The ground glows like a million fireflies as the cool of evening falls, and with it comes an energy snapping in the air.

Breathing becomes intoxicating. As one, we, now hundreds strong, lean forward. Containing the bristling energy, the *life*, is impossible. My legs pound as I run faster than ever before, slicing through the air. In wild abandon, we surge forward, up a slight incline.

The air crackles with an otherworldly life; the glow of the paths becomes so intense it reaches my knees. We reach the top as one, floods of people converging from every direction.

A trumpet blasts, a wall of sound with a warm honey taste; we skid to a halt at its command in a wide circle around the convergence, light filling the center. As soon as the trumpet's voice ceases, there is perfect silence.

Anticipation rises in the charged air. Night has come, giving way to a volcano of light in the center. The ground vibrates.

At the gathering point on top of the converging paths, mist gathers—a swirling cloak. The light intensifies until I throw my arm up before my eyes, still unable to look away, peering through my fingers.

*There!* I'm sure I see an outline in the mist. The ground trembles and I hit my knees, uncaring if I perish in the air's intensity—*just so I see.* There is a flash of light like inhaling fire, parts of me burned up and blown away, cleansed. Before me stands THE LION OF THE TRIBE OF JUDAH.

His image is seared into my soul: massive, exuding strength, eternal power, His coat brilliant white. His eyes bore into mine; I cannot bear it. His head turns, and I see a man, dressed in tattered clothes, standing before a judge. I scowl at the image, breath coming faster: *it's me.*

The judge, robed in black, hands me a thick package of papers. "This is a legally binding will which grants you the sole possessor of all written therein. From this day forth, they are the express property of Jacob Carter." My fingers rub the manila envelope reverently. I nod at the judge as he dismisses me and another steps forward.

The image morphs and I'm watching myself walking down a dimly lit street, tucking the envelope into my backpack. I turn into a three-sided hut with holes in the roof. Heavy rain falls; I huddle in the corner, trying to stay dry, backpack on my knees, pitiful.

The scene shifts again. I'm older, with deeper lines of worry in my face, gaunt, full of pain. Now I'm standing in a doctor's office, blinking hard as he tells me there is no treatment for my disease. I limp from the office, hopeless, looking up at the warm homes with longing. At my dilapidated shack, three thugs jump me from behind; they hit me till I'm lying slack on the concrete. They take my pack, all I have. One tosses the envelope to the street, taking off with the rest.

I crawl over to it, clutching it to my chest, trembling. A man walks past, well-dressed and confident. He turns back, squats down before me. He's scowling at the envelope, reaches out for it. I clutch it. He fingers the edge, confusion on his face. Then he points down the street, lays out a set of directions, his gentle hand clasping my shoulder before he heads off.

I stand, hobbling down the road. By the time I reach the address he's given me, I'm bent low with pain. My arm wavers as I ring the bell. A guard arrives at the gate surrounding the large house, frowning. He tells me to leave.

I crumple to the ground, empty; the envelope slips from my grasp. He reaches out in disbelief and reads my name on the front, then calls for help. People rush out, help me up, and usher me within the gate.

I'm on a soft bed, fed and warm. A woman holds out the envelope. Insists that I open it. The paper's perfectly white. As I read, weeping overtakes me. This is my house. But when I reach a clause at the bottom, I break inside. There is a cure for my condition.

All these years, scraping by, suffering, when in my own hands was the provision, unable to succor me till I opened it. I clutch it to my chest, determined to memorize every word, so I will never live like that again.

The Lion's roar rattles the ground. The revelation is crushing; truly, I've wandered like a beggar when everything is mine. I must only dare to believe it.

Deep within, desire is born: to serve Him, draw near to Him, to obtain glory for His name. The Lion's eyes fall on me, burning

away weakness. My bones melt as His ribcage expands. His second roar knocks me back; the ground shakes until I know no more.

I lie on my back, staring into the morning fog. Burned into my retinas is the image of Him. I want nothing else. All I want is the memory. He is all. He IS. And though I had known this before, now it's mine.

I reach into my pocket and withdraw a handful of scrolls, still lying flat on my back where His roar had flattened me the previous night. I run the pieces under my nose, searching for the right one. Now I realize the scroll has *His* scent. Beyond the food smell, there is a lingering vestige of Him—the snapping life, the power.

I run another piece under my nose, inhaling. Another. *Yes, that's the one.* I put it in my mouth and chew, relaxing every other muscle. Listening. The longer I chew, the clearer come the words. "And his head and hair were white like wool, as white as snow; his eyes were as a flame of fire; his feet were like fine brass as if refined in a furnace."

I sit up easily. *Strength.* Yes, there is strength in my frame. Scanning the peaceful meadow, I see nothing but intensely green grass. Vibrations tickle the edges of my hearing. Green sound. *Time to get going.*

Standing, I feel almost too light. My path draws me forward, so I lean in and run, so fast the wind dashes tears from my eyes, exhilarating. Reaching the edge of the meadow, I slow, stepping into the forest without a sound.

As I push up the incline, my head rises out of the deep depression and I catch a whiff of something dead. To my right, forty yards out, there is tawny fur. Another chill races across my skin as I ease forward to lie against the incline, just the top of my head and my eyes visible at ground level. *He doesn't see me.*

My eyes run over his gaunt body—*so thin*, yet so strong. His is a desperate strength, a starving animal's determination to survive. Like the rest, he's crisscrossed with scars, full of open wounds and rot, pain and suffering. On the hip closest to me is a gaping hole, black against his mangled fur.

He pads through the forest, nose to the ground, searching. He jerks around, biting at his hip. A cloud of flies rises, and I catch the white glint of bone in the wound. He snarls, shaking his scraggly head as half the flies settle on his nose. The ground vibrates at his grumbling as he continues in his original direction. The flies torment him as he crosses my field of vision.

What a wretched, ruined creature! Death would certainly be better; yet I know he is without end. My stomach turns as a small breeze fills my senses with his infected mess. I can't look away, lacking the intense fear that always overcame me before as I study my enemy. In my mind, I see the Lion of the night before—huge, perfect, exuding strength and light. The majesty of His mane, His power, the intensity of his golden, fiery eyes.

I blink and there before me again is this wretched copy—a rotting imitation of His strength and His prowess. My lip curls with hatred; now that I've seen the original, I detest this counterfeit. The being before me is a sham, a lie against His truth.

Now, there's a whisper of desire to hunt down this lion, to disprove his power. I treasure the knowledge deep inside that this stinking apparition before me has no right to hunt me. He has no ownership of me. I am of the light, he of the darkness, and light always overcomes darkness.

I shelter this revelation like the first delicate spark of a fire. The lion's crooked tail disappears behind a distant tree and I twist to lean against the bank. Is this the knowledge Demyen possessed as he faced Aseph? Is this the flame that ignites Myah into such ferocity? Time passes as I lean in silence, fingering through memories.

A faint sound intrudes upon my pondering. Leaves are moving. I cock my head; it sounds like the scuffling of a rodent among the leaves, but no. The leaves are moving. *What is this?* Now I catch a glimmer among the leaves at my feet. *Water?* A swirl of liquid rises and breaks in my direction. It meanders past, growing every second. I lean forward in the cool pocket of air; my eyes slide shut as I drink in...*words.*

Its soft voice ebbs and flows at first, entrancing, but indecipherable. I wait, listening. Then "B...b...behold, I give you power to tread on serpents and scorpions, and over all the power of the enemy: and nothing shall by any means hurt you."

How long I kneel there, I do not know; but eventually I notice my hands are only resting on wet leaves. I open my eyes; *no more water*—only a damp forest floor to prove that it had sprung up at all. But now I own this truth: nothing shall by any means hurt me. And I have been given power over the enemy. *Dare I believe it? Can I?* I ponder these revelations as I continue through the forest.

I pull out wad after wad of scroll, chewing as I walk. I remember Demyen's stripping off his pants when that scorpion bit him. No harm had come to him, although just one sting had proven deadly to Peace. A faint crunch in the leaves grabs my attention.

"Eh!" A scorpion drops out of the tree next to me. His needle feet scramble to right himself, giving me enough time to jump back and avoid the first lash of the tail.

I dance to the side, putting distance between us. Like lightning, he launches toward me again and again. I draw my sword. It rings long and full length as I whip it from its scabbard. *Oh, beauty!* It takes only one swipe to cut the creature in half.

I stand panting, willing my heart to slow down. *Did my thoughts bring him here?* I reach for a handful of dried leaves and wipe my blade clean. I slip it back in its scabbard. *Coincidence? Has to be.* But then again, after another three hours of travel, I see no more scorpions. Peter's warning echoes: every thought is a seed, and what you've been sowing, you will soon be reaping. Can my thoughts have so much control?

Soon, my path cuts hard to the right and within an hour, I've passed into canyon country. The trees give way to cliffs and sharp-edged rocks. Moss clings to the crevices as I drop into a tight valley, stuffing a scroll into my mouth. I freeze, wide eyed at the rock face before me. *Up.* The word is etched in white. A shiver runs across my arms as I take it in. It must be an old message from long ago.

Visibility has dropped to a few yards. The sharp inclines on either side and the twisting nature of the canyon take all my concentration to traverse. The canyon floor is just a foot wide here and drops off steeply. Still, my path glimmers ahead, so I press on.

The lower I drop, the more the moss is giving way to scraggly bushes and shrubs full of thorns. The canyon widens but the overhanging thorns force me to slow, picking my way along, sweating in the chill air.

I slip down a drop-off, my palms burn as rocks cascade, and I struggle for balance. I suck in my breath as I slide to a stop, hands bloody. *How much farther on in this way?* Another hour passes; this valley might go on forever. I travel down another steep section, until an open plain stretches in the distance, beyond the tight mouth of the valley. I pick up my pace, skin pricking with an odd sensation.

Little pebbles ping down from above. There's the slightest stench of something dead. I freeze. *Up.* I'd been warned. Why wasn't I watching? *Up.* In dread, I retrace the pebbles' path to massive paws and a gaping mouth high above.

I break for the plain, sensing movement as a shadow races along the far wall. Uncaring now of sharp rocks or steep drop-offs, I lean forward—running, falling, all jumbled into one. I must not meet him here in these confines. The shadow above disappears and I brace against the roar of the lion, leaping from the edge above.

*My sword! Should have had it at the ready.* I reach for the hilt; then the weight of the lion crushes me to the ground. I struggle, ignited by the feel of stinking fur on my skin. His jaws snap at the back of my head, and a warm river runs down behind my ear.

With a savage shout, I rebound up from the sharp, rocky floor. With desperate strength, I force the beast off. He struggles, restrained by the tight embrace of the sheer rock walls. I race forward again; somehow my sword is in my hand.

*No!* Another lion drops to the canyon floor ahead, sending up a cloud of dust. There is nothing for it now. My momentum won't slow as I crash down the sharp incline. I shout again; he'll meet my sword edge first. I slash down with all my might, using my sword for a pole-vault.

It connects with his head as I leap high and soar over his back. *Made it.* I glimpse open land ahead. But I'm spinning crazily through the air as the first lion's claws embed deep in my calf.

I scream in pain, slamming face first into the rocks. Time slows as the claws shred my leg muscle. My sword spins away. Curling, I let my tumbling motion gain me scant inches from the enemy. Somehow, I'm on my feet again, face to face with two sets of bloody, salivating jaws.

My chest pumps as I watch the lion on the right coil back. I pull back my fist as he launches forward. Twisting my stomach, all in, my fist rockets past his teeth, slamming hard into the back of his throat. I force it farther into the heat. My left arm absorbs his momentum and swings whip-like around his neck in a deadly embrace.

I grip, my chest squeezing tight, seeking one thing; to cut off his air: The stench of his infected wet wounds rubbing my skin and the awful heat of his mouth crunching my arm fuel me as we roll and tangle. His idea changes now as he backpedals.

I tighten my bear hug yet again; he needs air, reversing direction. His massive head swings from side to side, trying to dislodge my fist, mouth open.

A wild rebel yell escapes me as he flips backward. I twist hard so he takes the fall as I force my body tight to his side, out of reach of his wicked claws. He scrambles, desperate. I open my mouth and bellow in his ear. His black eye, inches away, glazes over; he bucks a final time, heavy tail whipping around to lash me.

The second lion comes. I have too long to hear his claws propelling him in my direction, too long to feel the awful swelter of his rotten breath. My brain records each long tooth as they puncture my right shoulder at the base of my neck. I clench my eyes as pain explodes. My collarbone snaps as he finishes his bite. It becomes infinitely more difficult to keep my fist in the first lion's throat.

I'm screaming with only this one thought: *Don't let the lion breathe. Don't let the lion breathe.* No, I'm not shouting; I'm holding my breath hard against the intense pain. Yet a shout fills my ears. As the second lion grips my shoulder, his mane against my cheek, I hear his grunt that turns into a hiss of pain. He lets go.

Free of his crushing bite, my eyes roll back in my head as I fight the blackness rolling over me. Bone grates against bone; still, I hold the first lion with every drop of determination I have.

Dim battle sounds creep into my focus: lions roaring, a man shouting back, and the beautiful sound of a sword slicing air and flesh. *Someone has come for me.* The lion beneath gives a final twitch, then lies still. In a stupor of pain, I whimper as I draw my ruined right arm out of his throat. I glimpse the sky; the wound on the back of my head against the rocky ground is leaving a river of blood. My shattered shoulder is like a fire under me; everything throbs as hot rivulets of blood wrap around my neck, and my right calf screams in agony.

*Must have passed out.* A cloud of dust floats past, obscuring even the lion I'm lying next to. *Samson.* Crouched above, sword poised, guarding me. Everything is dizzy, drifting. He's chasing two more lions and lands a punishing blow against one's back. *It's okay now.* I let go, floating on a sea of calm as all the sensations of pain fade toward darkness.

*Stupid ground. Why are you shaking?* I scowl, half-drunken with pain, angered by the vibration causing it to flare higher. Tiny pebbles jump, and my shoulder screams anew at the minute motion. *Why?* I lengthen the focus from the pebbles, reddened with my blood, to a cloud of dust growing on the horizon. My thoughts feel like a thick soup as lions roar all around.

*Horses.* Horses are coming. Samson's shadow shifts over me. I roll my eyes to see his upraised sword, dripping red. The rumble of lions greets his defiant stance. I watch the shadow of his sword sweep out and hear the scramble of heavy paws dancing away.

As the dirt pounds harder, I clench my teeth, certain I feel every hoof strike the ground. *Right here. So beautiful…* the symmetry of their round hooves. My thoughts bounce everywhere. Then I feel huge hands roll me and the blackness closes in.

I open one eye, pain pulsing. Shut it again. *How do I return to the black nothingness?* My right calf throbs with urgent messages. I take a breath. *Oh, no.* At the slight motion, I hear my collarbone crunching against itself. I struggle, trying to keep my stomach down, trying not to move. I feel green, my lips pinched tight, sweat pouring. Time passes in an evil crawl.

I open both eyes wide, desperate. An old woman is seated next to me; her dark-brown eyes stare into mine. Her face is a wreath of wrinkles and fine, long white hair frames her face.

She cocks her head. *Listening?* Her bony arm reaches toward me, offering a piece of scroll. I want to turn my head, but I know better than to risk the motion, so I pinch my lips shut instead. A grin appears on her aged face, revealing a perfect set of teeth.

"I have been doing this for a long time, young man, and I have many tricks up my sleeve. Trust me; you do not want to be acquainted with a one of them." Her sweet smile tells me she would love for me to put up more of a fight.

I scowl, living on the edge. Then her conviction makes me open my mouth and chew. I have no spit; the scroll sticks to every part of my mouth it touches.

"Dry?" she queries. "Of course you are. Here now, this will help." Her voice doesn't sound as old as she looks.

Water from a wooden cup is a welcome relief, and I stave off a shiver as it courses down my throat. After two more cups, I take stock of my surroundings. I'm propped up on a couch, and the air—even through my filter of intense pain—is intoxicating, peaceful. I can't dislodge the thought that if I weren't breathing this air, I would have already died.

We're in a large room with an arched roof; the walls seem to be carved out of one solid piece of wood. Glowing green leaves are curled up, tucked into small recesses in the walls, casting gentle light.

A wave of pain overtakes me, and I groan. *Don't turn your head.* I shift my eyes back to the old woman. Her dark-brown eyes drill into mine.

"You are a strong young man. Many changes have come to you." She pauses. "This is your moment. We will see what is inside your heart. What is your name?"

Her words make me squirm inside; I have to get away from the pain. I blink. *Man up.*

"Jacob." My voice is unfamiliar, dry, and rasping.

"A suitable name for such a one. I am Mara. Do you know where you are?" Her eyes never leave mine and I find myself unable to break gaze with her.

Thinking back, I try to gather information about myself other than my own name. Nothing comes. *Not. A. Thing.*

"No," I respond.

Mara nods. Despite her advanced age, I sense no weakness in her.

"Do you remember what happened to you?" She leans forward slightly, intent.

"Happened to me?" I ask. Then I feel foolish. Obviously, something caused these wounds.

The old woman nods again. "It is the time."

She murmurs to herself as she brings the cup again to my lips. Next, she holds out a tiny scrap of scroll. I open my mouth, desperate for her help. The second it touches my tongue, I work not to recoil. I've never tasted something so bitter, not even the first bite of scroll I ever took. *There! A memory.*

Mara's eyes narrow, and her voice carries intensity. "Is it bitter to you, Jacob?"

I cannot answer. My tongue seems frozen by the scroll lying on it. Can't chew it up and I can't spit it out.

"We haven't much time then." Swiftly, she rises, moving about, gathering an armful of things, depositing them on the small table beside the couch.

She selects a tiny bottle, opens the lid with a pop, and the room fills with an incredible fragrance. She lifts it to my nose. "Inhale."

I draw in a slow breath, trying not to move my chest. The scent stills my racing thoughts and brings focus and courage. Now I can chew; she places another bit of scroll in my mouth.

"This will bring strength." Mara stands now, hovering over me. "The wounds…they are in just the right place." Her voice is so quiet I almost don't hear her.

She pulls back the thin blanket covering my shoulder. I lift my eyes, hating the sight of its mangled mess at the edge of my vision.

Her fingertips are cool and gentle against the hot edges of my wound. Mara leans in closer, her head weaving back and forth as she searches. "Umm hum…"

She's found whatever it is she was looking for. Now her face is still close, directly in front of mine; her ancient hands cradle my face. Her question is urgent.

"Quickly, Jacob! Tell me, what is it you want?" The smell of the oil rises from her fingers, bringing back the clarity.

"What do I want?" I echo her. In the strange emptiness of no memories, and the intense pain pushing me, I search deep inside.

*What do I want?* I sift through the dry places in my depths. Then I see it. At the very center, it's clear.

"I want to be sure." It's too simple when I say it. But it's so huge on the inside. Mara's eyes flash bright at my words.

"This great surety does not come easily, Jacob. Are you willing to gain it?" Her fingers grip my face now with her intensity.

My mouth opens. *Can I?* I'm already near the edge, unstable. Yet somehow, deep within, I reach out and take it. "Yes, for that I'll do anything."

I swallow hard as sweat pops out on my forehead. Mara is all quick motion again. Settling in her chair, she lays the strips of soft muslin across her legs. She nestles a wooden cup between her knees, next to a short knife and a small, thick stick.

Goose bumps race over my skin. "What are you going to do?"

Mara's dark eyes lock on mine. "Remove your doubt."

One white brow rises. *A dare?*

"Get it all," I grit out the words.

"Now," says Mara, "it shouldn't take long. I need you to be still; and when I have hold of it, you must let it go. I cannot tell you how, but you will know when the time comes. Open your mouth."

At her command, I do so and bite the stick like a dog.

"This is going to hurt," she states without apology as she picks up the knife, and I try not to pull away as her cool fingers probe into my open wound again.

She speaks, but I can't quite make out her words. I know I've heard the language before, but *now comes the knife*. The second it touches my skin, I gasp, clenching my eyes—not as much because of the pain, but the awareness of my tendency to doubt instead of believe. I've always acted on what my senses tell me. Yet, to survive here, I must live on the Word alone.

Pain takes me, and I writhe. There is no air, no breath—only the pain and an intense hatred of my carnal instinct. I gasp, gaining nothing. *Now!* It's as if hands have taken hold of the inside of my shoulder. My stomach lurches, and I fight the feeling of something being drawn out. *Taking out my bones! No! I can't take anymore.*

"Let go!" an urgent voice knocks at my consciousness.

I grit my teeth, fighting for control, biting the stick so hard it breaks, drawing blood from my lips. I feel like a supernova about to explode, condensing into a tiny mass. *Surety.* The word echoes in my chaos so loud—yet so quiet. *Yes, I must let go.* With a guttural sound, I expel it all.

Roots are breaking loose somewhere deep inside; I hear the ping, ping, of each tiny one snapping off. *Oh, the pain.* Then the long, awful moving of a bone being pulled out. I cry at the top of my voice…Then blackness descends.

Brown eyes gaze into mine. A smile layers wrinkle upon wrinkle. Everything is in my mind again—my history, the lions, Samson's standing over me, the knife, the pain. Yet as I now take stock, I find the pain so much less than it had been. Sadness overtakes me. *What good am I without my collarbone?*

"You did well, Jacob. You have much strength in you." Mara's voice is soft and kind.

"What good is strength without bones to hold it up?" I ask, fighting emptiness.

Her white brows furrow. "Bones?" she questions. "What do you mean?"

"I felt you pull it out. My collarbone."

Now her white brows shoot up in delicate arches. "You felt me pull something out?"

"How could I not?" I fire back, writhing inside.

"No one has ever felt it before. Not a one has perceived it." She peers at me closely, her eyes bright. "Mmm... Well, let me put your mind at ease. I left your bones alone. In all my long years here, I've known no one to remember." She squints one eye, leaning in closer.

A few days ago, I would have been uncomfortable under her scrutiny, but now I hold her gaze, seeing for the first time. *Really seeing.* The deepest wrinkles are at the corners of her mouth from a lifetime of smiling. Her white brows are finely arched, still beautiful even at her age, and all that's hidden in her eyes... *What secrets does she possess?*

Mara takes my left hand and draws it up to my right shoulder. She guides my fingers along the straight line of my collarbone. I let out a long slow breath, relief flooding. *It's still there.* She stops before too long though, and I know my ravaged shoulder is still hanging open and lacerated.

"I didn't steal your bones, but I straightened this one out while I was in there. A dip in the first pool will set you right as rain, young man." Her words lodge in my brain.

"The pain isn't near like it was. Thank you," I say, wanting to keep her talking.

"If you continue to eat, you will soon leave all the pain behind." Mara rises to gather a bowl of water and a plate of scroll. She settles on the creaky chair before me.

"Where are we?"

Mara's eyes light up as she answers. "Where I have ever loved best. As a little girl, I yearned to have a place at the Tree. We have no name for it, really; it's too magnificent, I suppose. Have you come here before?"

"No," I say, recalling the first time I opened my eyes in this world.

"Well, I suppose you arrived out cold from your battle. I shall tell you a bit of what I know, if you like." She dips a bit of scroll into the water and offers it to me.

I open my mouth and take it. *Ah!* I've never tasted its like. It's perfect and hunger has returned.

"It would honor me to hear it." I dip my head as I speak and I pay for the motion with a wave of pain. I wince, but increase my chewing to compensate.

"My first time here, I was young. I tilted my head up, trying to see the top, but oh! You can't see that far! It took me an age to run around the Tree's trunk. You'll notice something though… if you should be conscious the next time you arrive. As soon as you pass under this Tree's canopy, the air is distinct. All your worries fall away as you enter its life." Mara's eyes are distant, but now they lock on mine again.

"There is much for you here. You may receive as much as you will give. Remember, one cannot fill a full cup. The pools will change you. The stairs will enlighten you. Empty yourself, Jacob, for then you will be full." She pauses.

"But first, this must be fixed." She leans forward, peering at my mangled shoulder. "Yes, it is time." Mara's wrinkled hands clap once with a whisper of sound. Seconds later, a tiny bird swoops through the small window and lands on her shoulder. Its impossibly thin legs are jet-black, but its feathers are the brightest blue I've ever seen. The bird's minute head rubs Mara's cheek.

She whispers. The bird responds with "Tuk-tuk-cat!" The sound of its tiny wings somehow matches the color of its body, so strong I can taste it.

Mara stands, collecting her items and placing them back on the desk. She turns to face me. "The first pool is not far, but the trip will be painful. Gather yourself for it. Your wounds won't bother you after you take a good soak."

I peer down at the mess on my right shoulder. My stomach clenches at the bright white of bone. *Visible.* Yet even seeing and feeling what I do, I believe Mara's words. She's helped me more than perhaps any other.

"Thank you," I say, missing adequate words. "Mara. What you did, I needed. That's for sure."

Her dark eyes sparkle. "My part is simple, but yours...a soul must be in just the right place. Still, I've never known of anyone to feel it happening in all my long years." She peers at me again. "I should like to talk with you more, but your wounds…"

Hating to admit it, I respond, "I don't think I have the strength to get up. Where is the pool you speak of?"

Mara's hand flutters to the doorway. "They come."

The space is now blocked by the sheer mass of two giant Watchers.

"Raeuel, Adriel, would you help Jacob into the lower pool?"

The one with the darker hair responds. "Yes, he needs it, doesn't he?" He approaches. "I am Raeuel; we will help you."

I clench my stomach to get up and meet with a wave of pain. I grunt, focusing all my energy into moving when pain screams at me to be still. Raeuel's huge hand clasps my left arm and pulls me steadily up. Determined not to shout, I bite my tongue.

Blackness closes on my vision; I fight it, focusing ahead. Adriel is on my right. His massive arm snakes around my ribcage as I leave the couch.

*My leg.* I'd forgotten it in the intensity of my shoulder and forearm. My stomach heaves at the pain and the deep furrows of the lion's claws open afresh. My stomach continues to roll, and sweat drips off my nose; but now, two fingers are pinching my left earlobe. I focus on the feeling. It is as if Raeuel is pouring painkiller into my body through my ear. My lungs pump in relief as the waves of pain and nausea subside. I open my eyes. Mara stands with her hand over her heart, wincing in compassion. *Bless her!*

"How far?" I pant, leaning on my escort. Then I realize Raeuel had been whispering under his breath as he held my ear. *I interrupted.* Unperturbed, he finishes, then his fingers leave my ear.

"Only know that your pain will leave you when you step into the water," Raeuel's deep voice radiates through me.

*Only…only know that my pain will be gone when I step into the water.* No believing in the pain. No looking at it. No knowing it. Certainly, no planning on it.

Walking proves harder than I'd imagined. One thought… one thought only takes me past the arched doorway out into the dappled light. I lurch with my good leg onto a wide, flat expanse of living wood. Adriel takes my weight when my mangled right leg should have.

*The pain will be gone when I step into the water.* We follow the massive wall of living wood through a tunnel carved in it. At the exit, the pain overwhelms me again. Raeuel sees my sudden sweat and heaving breaths. His thumb and finger find my earlobe, and unintelligible words force down the pain.

I swallow hard and grit my teeth. "This pain will be gone when I step into the water," I growl. "Which way?"

Raeuel looks quizzically down at me. "Through this courtyard, then that tunnel."

I hop forward on my good leg, the jolt of pain… *No. It is not for me to know.* Only that this pain will be gone when I step into the water. We cross another court of massive size. This one is ringed about with arched doorways and tunnels. The flow of people passing through makes way as we hobble across the space.

Passing into the cool dimness of the last curving tunnel, I smell the pool before I see it. *Water.* Its scent fills me. *Water.* Then something sweet… *flowers?* Hop, groan, hop, groan. *Reach the water.* As we exit the tunnel, the floor is dished, creating a wide pool. The water has a tint of purple to it; the air above it wavers like heat rising on a blistering day.

The atmosphere is so heavy; I open my mouth to breathe. No, it is *alive.* It seems difficult to draw it through my nose. A shiver runs down my spine and the pool draws me in like a moth to the flame. *Step into the water and all my pain will be gone.* I hobble the last two steps on my own, desperate to reach my destination. As my body enters the vapor above the pool, I'm free.

"Uh-ah." The guttural sound encompasses it all. As my left foot touches the water, *no pain anywhere.* My right leg, till this point, had been hanging useless from the knee down. But now I command it with no hesitation. I step smooth and strong into the water on it. My body twitches hard. I've felt water's power before, but not like this.

Instead of its normal tingle, this is like touching a… *What is the word? A power line! Like grabbing a power line with both hands.* I take another step, unable to keep from it. When the first of the wounds in my lower leg goes under, I hear a sizzling sound. The surrounding water froths.

It's like burning without the heat. A sensation in my leg grips me, not pain—but so much feeling that it's an overload. I pull another breath through my mouth. My hips go under and now my upper body. The water is a neutral temperature; yet at its edge, the water rising up my body is so intense—like a frigid arctic dip.

My shoulder submerges, sizzling. The water froths, splashing my face. I close my eyes in the absence of pain. I take this new knowledge deep into my soul: that the impossible *is*.

The water quiets; and in the stillness, I float, eyes closed, searching. *It's not just the absence of pain. No, again, it's the presence of something too. Strength. Rock-solid strength.* The lions had attacked me, true, but they did not claim victory. Their works are now overcome as well.

I think about walking in the valley again, facing lions. Before, I'd been a tangle of doubts and what-ifs. *If.* It's a small word, yet so deadly. A new path emerges in my mind. *Even*…even if they wound me, I will be healed. *Even* if we fight, I will overcome.

In the valley, I was determined to hold on to the Words of truth, as if by repeating them I could force them to work. But it takes more than that. It takes a deep *knowing* that the Words are true: a determination to exalt them above what's seen and felt. The water's silvery voice echoes straight into my ears.

*But the Word preached did not profit them, not being mixed with faith in them that heard it.*

The Words must live in me, fill my deepest parts with their life. I've shifted, no longer pulling back, but leaning forward, ready to defend. I open my eyes, sit up, and look down at my shoulder. The fingers of my left hand run over new skin crisscrossed with scars. But there is no openness, no weakness. I flex my chest, testing; my collarbone is strong.

*Whole.* I think back to the scroll I'd chewed walking in the deep forest. *Behold, I give you power to trample on serpents and scorpions and over all the power of the devil…and nothing shall, by any means, harm you.*

I wince; if I had believed it, could the enemy have touched me? Deep down, I know the answer. No. Yet still the water speaks to me, releasing me from past failures to believe in the future.

*You shall know the truth, and the truth shall set you free.* Belief in the scroll makes all things possible. It's too simple in my mind; but in my spirit, that truth has exploded, shattering past expectations and creating a whole new scope of reality.

Before, I had been grasping at it like a dying man. Now I *belong* to it. I know that this suffering, this experience, wasn't necessary for me to find faith, but my thick-skinned heart wouldn't absorb the truth. But this cutting to the quick had allowed me to bypass the facts and step onto the truth.

Quiet footsteps draw my attention. I turn to see Adriel disappear through the tunnel-like entrance. Raeuel's brilliant white teeth gleam as he stands grinning at me with his massive arms crossed over his chest.

"You, I like," he states in his deep baritone.

"You seem surprised about that," I shoot back; his grin is contagious.

Raeuel shrugs. "I am. I have ever ministered to the Almighty's children; it is my command. But you…are different." His grin widens. He tilts his head toward the tunnel. "Come. You've much to see."

I nod, though this pool is difficult to leave as its precious water flows down my skin. I emerge from the pool, my head reaching his shoulder.

"You listened."

I glance up at him quizzically. "To what?"

"Since the beginning of time, I have helped countless people into this pool. I have spoken the same words to everyone. I can count on one hand those who actually listened to my words." He holds up three fingers.

I shrug, enjoying the movement. "I've learned a thing or two about words. There's more to them than I thought."

Raeuel nods as he walks toward the exit. I follow, noting the fact that we're *inside* the Tree. I run my hand along the cool, living heart of the Tree as we enter the tunnel.

"Here, you will learn many words. As you hear them, you must choose what to do with them. They will all enter your ears and into your mind, but only a few will sink into your spirit. These are seeds that will grow, much like this Tree." Raeuel seems brighter in the tunnel's dimness.

"Choose? That's different." Memorization alone won't complete the task. *How do I get them past my mind?*

Raeuel flashes a smile. "'In the beginning was the Word, and the Word was with God, and the Word was God. The same was in the beginning with God. All things were made by him; and without him was not anything made that has been made. In him was life; and the life was the light of men.' First, understand that you are made of words, and that everything you see, touch, feel consists solely of words. Have you ever thought of that?" He glances down at me.

"No, never."

Raeuel nods. "This understanding will change everything. It is a subtle shift deep within, but it has immeasurable ramifications. For…" He holds up one thick finger, eager. "…if this solid Tree is actually words, and you also are made of Words, what could have more effect than that Word? What can defeat the living Word, the source code of all things?"

My mind goes to my wounds. They had exercised domination over me; they had power over me. My fingers find the scars on my right shoulder and Raeuel takes note.

"The lions' marks were powerful, no?" He waits for my answer.

I shrug one shoulder, not wanting to miss this lesson. "Yes. They almost destroyed me."

Unexpectedly, he smiles. "Yes, that is a fact. Many have died in the facts, Jacob. The facts are obvious; seen, felt. Touched. These *facts*—they grip humanity." Raeuel's voice grows passionate; his fingers press together, punctuating his words.

"Yet the facts and the truth do not often align."

My face must reflect my struggle.

"Begin at the beginning. In the beginning was the Word. You were made by, to, and *for* the Word. Without it, you are not. Whatever the Words spoke, it is the *truth*. This truth is eternal— never changing, all powerful. Yet contrary to the truth, your body *was* ravaged by the facts of the lions' teeth and claws. But look at you now." Raeuel pokes my right shoulder for emphasis. "What changed? What forced the facts to line up with the Word?" He waits for an answer that I don't have.

"Uh… the water?"

"No." He's silent, and I sure hope he's not finished.

"It was your *faith*. Your belief. You walked the last two steps to the pool on your own. Had you any pain?"

"No, I didn't hurt at all."

"It is because you believed my words! I spoke the truth to you, and you believed; and even before the facts had aligned with the truth, you were healed. Those last two steps, your flesh was still ripped open—I saw it, but your pain was gone. Once it hit the water, the facts finished aligning with the truth. But you possessed the truth *with results* before that happened. How?" Raeuel looks down at me, willing me to have the right answer.

"Because of words," I say. "Because I believed them… because…" I pause, sifting through the deep waters. "Well, would I have been healed if there wasn't any water?"

Raeuel's thick, black brows shoot up. "Excellent question. What do you think?"

Our footsteps scuff in the quiet as I ponder. Deep in my soul, I hear the soft water voice as if I were in the stream with my hands plunged under. I cannot keep the Words within me; they fill me till I must open my mouth. "'By His stripes, we are healed.' So, water wasn't necessary because it was by *blood* that I was healed—not by water."

Raeuel's brows raise even higher. "Now you see. This was revealed to you, Jacob. True sight. It is a treasure few attain. Do not let time steal it from you. Think on it often, hone it as you would your knife's edge, and always, it will defeat the enemy." He's quiet for a breath. "Yet often you will see there is water along with healing. Why?"

I'm sensing a pattern here. I have no answer; but I enjoy shrugging my shoulders.

"Often the water aids in belief. Water speaks the truth, enlivens, and brings strength to the weak. Often you find healing where water is, especially when a man is first learning." He nods, satisfied with his point, as we pass into the atrium.

I look up, mouth agape, truly taking in the room. The living wood grain of the floor swirls toward the center in an intricate pattern. Light and shadows dance. I count five different exits and observe the mix of people and Watchers.

One aspect stands out above the rest—the lack of worry. There is no rushing here, no hurry, no fear. The pace is locked on easy.

Raeuel's square-tipped finger points toward another tunnel to our right. We weave through Watchers, conversing in low tones. The tunnel is quiet against the pleasant murmur of the atrium. Soon we pass onto one of many staircases worn into the living bark of the Tree. The second floor offers a view of the forest. The "stairs" are uneven heights and widths, knots and bark growing out from the trunk; we climb slowly.

I catch Raeuel shaking his head as we ascend. "I have to know."

He reaches over and grabs my wrist. We stop as he examines my forearm, his face incredulous.

"I can't figure it. When the legion of Watchers and I rode up and found Samson poised over your inert form, lions surrounded the two of you. But the most interesting aspect was the lion you were using as a pillow. I never have seen the like. Lions don't die; they don't get knocked out. Yet there you were lounging on a mostly dead, unconscious beast. We assumed Samson had done it somehow, so we asked him about it after the rest of that wicked bunch cleared off." Raeuel shakes his head, reveling in the memory.

"Samson said he ran up on you piled over with lions so thick he didn't know you at first. After he ripped the top few off, he found you under there with your forearm jammed down the lion's throat! The chokehold was so tight it couldn't free itself from you. *What?*" Raeuel's voice echoes, too loud in this quiet place. His gaze leaves the scars on my right arm and locks on my face.

"*What?*" he whispers this time. "Never in the history of ever have I heard of such a feat! A man suffocating a lion?" He shakes his head in amazement. A glint of humor leaps to his eyes. He wiggles my arm like a wet dishrag. "*Hadena.*"

Even his whisper is enough to make my daggers snap to attention. "Here's another thing I can't wrap my head around. How can a man with a weapon like this given *unto his arm* have scars like *these* on the same limb? When I gave them to you, I expected you to use them!"

My mouth opens, then shuts. Too many streams of thoughts flowing. My face reddens. *He's right.* I hadn't used them at all. In fact, I didn't once think about them. Also, Raeuel was indeed the Watcher who gave me *Hadena*.

"So, it was you…" is all that comes out of my mouth.

Raeuel grunts in affirmation. Waiting to hear my side of the story, he drops my arm, and we resume our slow climb. I think back to the hot, stinking breath of the lion against my face. The searing, slimy heat of his throat ignites the nerves in my arm. I was so focused on bringing that one lion down, there wasn't anything else.

"I… forgot they were there altogether. The battle started so fast; it was all I could do to fight. I was warned, but I didn't get the message."

Raeuel's dark eyes are serious now, fathomless. "You had not the hearing of faith. Many people have the Words in their minds, they can quote them, but these precious Words never make the jump from their mind"—he points to his dark hair—"down into their hearts." He taps his chest.

"Interesting, Jacob, that you should have such a thought in you at this level. Hearing the voice of the Spirit is the skill that keeps children of the Light from the mouth of the enemy. For 'faith comes by hearing, and hearing by the Word.'"

He snorts. "Nearly all the people have that wrong. They think faith comes by the Word. And that *is* the result, but the step in the middle makes it work. You learn to *hear* through the Word. This hearing of the Spirit is what brings faith."

We rise another few steps and he looks at me from the corner of his eye. "Yes, you are ready. Come, let's go in."

He points toward the trunk at my left. I scowl at its solid mass. *Wait…* A cooler stream of sweet-smelling air is flowing from it. I move my head to the side, *there.* It cleverly disguises the opening to another tunnel. I step in, wondering what lies at the end.

I climb the stairs for the third time. The last two levels changed me inside. Understanding is now within. I nod my head as I step up alongside Raeuel.

Have I ever lived before this moment? *I don't know.* I could add a million things on the end of that phrase. But I have *begun* to know. It's like seeing the inner workings of a watch: I don't know what each part does, how it keeps time, but I've *begun* to know. I've seen.

My scars are glowing. Curious, I twist my forearm. Every scar is as bright as Raeuel's skin. I think back to the first time I'd met Demyen. The light was why he had "adopted" me, been willing to take me in. It was so faint then.

I wonder at the beauty emanating from my scars. Looking back, I should have done things differently in the battle. But all I've learned from it, the change in my soul, this strength, is priceless.

Raeuel extends his hand toward the next opening, smiling. "After you, my friend."

I duck my head and start down the twisting passage. Soon, I step into the light of an open room. A bark of laughter bursts out. A pool filled with light-green water sparkles in the pure sunlight near the top of the Tree. At the far end of it, Demyen lounges, his huge meaty arms draped across the edge. His head, which had been reclining, comes up at my laugh. A grin slices through his beard.

"Eh, Boy!" he booms. "All patched back together? Come have a soak in the most delightful place you'll see this side of glory." His head lolls back as he half floats in the pool.

I laugh again, the odd lightness of his mood is contagious, and I can't wait to get in the water. The second my toes touch it, I hear its voice.

*The…the…the…the joy of the Lord is your strength.* Up to my knees, I hear: *Come unto Me, all ye that labor and are heavy laden, and I will give you rest.*

I dive under, and the shiver of energy is almost more than I can handle. The words slip straight into my spirit. *Take my yoke upon you and learn of me; for I am meek and lowly in heart.*

The desire to suck water into my lungs is *so strong*. I surface, filling them instead with the water's scent.

"*Smell it, Boy!* Did you ever smell such a thing!? Daha!" Demyen's voice is louder than ever, but somehow perfectly fitting for the energy of this place.

I drift to the far end near Demyen and, finding nothing better, I adopt his posture. Soon I find a humming happiness flowing through my thoughts.

"Humm…." Demyen's deep sigh of perfect contentment rumbles in my soul. "I don't think I'm getting out." His eyes stay closed as he says this.

"Ha. Well, it's proven almost impossible to move you these last three days," a big blond Watcher replies.

Raeuel speaks up. "Three days? Never heard of such a thing!"

The first Watcher snorts. "You should've seen him race me up here. Never struggled so much to keep up with a mere man!

"Eh!!" Demyen's satisfied sound accompanies his half-closed eyes and lazy grin. But I catch the odd look that passes between Raeuel and the other Watcher.

"Jaden, I have often made you run, have I not?" Demyen questions.

One side of the huge blond Watcher's nose wrinkles. "Yes, you have been one of my more challenging charges."

Demyen grunts in satisfaction. The Watchers exchange another solemn glance that I cannot decipher.

Jaden nods. "There is news."

Demyen's head pops up at full attention.

"Things are stirring." Jaden's voice has an undercurrent of excitement. "Ancient words. Soon is the time of their fulfilling. The two of you have been called. The work…it is one. It requires a perfect sight. It will be the saving of many and the beginning of the end. They will not be able to deny the power of the Almighty."

I know Jaden is seeing the future. Though he speaks in the present, he's not gripped by time. My skin tingles, bracing for what comes.

"Your ways…run not together yet; still, your work, it is *one*." Jaden's pointer and middle fingers entwine as he holds them up. I wait, hoping he will continue.

"What will we do?" I ask.

"This is not for you to know, only that you must prepare." Jaden folds his meaty arms across his chest, done speaking.

Demyen sits up, rippling the emerald water. "I've never known an oracle to come early or late. I suppose it's time we head out?"

Jaden and Raeuel nod in unison. Demyen sighs. He slides down under the water and stays submerged till I wonder if he has miscalculated his breath. Giving in, I join him. The water is intoxicating. Needing air, I surface. Demyen is still under.

"Should I get him?" I ask Jaden.

"Only if you wish to end your friendship."

I grunt. His dark head finally appears, water streaming from his beard.

"Boy! You've got the short end of the stick. Only got to soak in the pool for a bit. Eh! My first few times I didn't get long either. Tell you what..." Demyen's square thumb jerks toward Jaden. "He won't keep up with me at all the next time I come up here." A devious smile tugs at his mouth.

A deep grunt escapes Jaden. "Bring it."

# 6
# SAGE



I lay my head on the desk, let out a long sigh. It's conclusive. Jacob and I have a previously unknown type of radiation. Symptoms include increased energy, hyper wound healing, and possible increased physical performance. *When will the nasties show up?*

I stare at his PET scan results. The good news is he's not sick. But under the scan, he is lit up like a Christmas tree inside. It's easy to match the brightest areas to every bruise he'd gotten sparring with Tex. The K-60 seems to congregate around wounds. Standing, I study Jacob's face; his lip has a pink spot where the deep split had been just twenty-four hours ago.

"Emerson, break in ten minutes, topside."

I force my face to stay blank, but sweat breaks out on my palms. They've started using the intercom instead of opening the door so often.

Biting my lip, I turn, shielding the drawer that holds all my pharmaceuticals. I pull two of the smallest syringes I have out of the plastic case, draw five mL of bupropion to drop his GABA and tramadol to spike glutamate, then add diphenhydramine into each and slide them into my pocket. The drug cocktail *will* cause a reaction. I rub my thumb over the cold plastic, remembering Jacob's plea to keep them from inserting anything.

*What will they do while I'm out?* Crossing the room, I turn the laptop toward Jacob when a sudden rank scent hits me. I turn, searching. *Is there a dead rat in the vent?*

Jacob grimaces under the white EEG cap. I lean over him, but his face goes still again. The heavy rotten scent lingers, bringing back his warning: *If you smell something dead, run.* I scan his EEG, thetas gone wild, spiking off the top of the charts.

*What the…?* I lean in closer: is his neck twitching? No, what's… the skin on his neck bursts open, blood flowing. With a shout, I reach for gauze as more wounds appear; there's a loud crack as his collarbone snaps. Someone's shouting; my hands are covered in hot blood as four deep puncture wounds spew it.

Heavily suited hands join mine in the effort to control the bleeding. Sutton is behind the mask.

"Start a transfusion!" she shouts.

I turn; his lower leg erupts, blood flowing off the table. I tourniquet it above the knee, applying pressure to the muscle.

"What is happening?" Sutton yells, white suit splattered red.

"Get pressure on the shoulder!" I shout, horrified at his blood loss. More suits join the fight till we've got the bleeding slowed. I grimace at the brilliant white of his collarbone's sharp broken edge. *Not like this, Jacob, not like this!*

Sutton hasn't stopped swearing and it takes all I have not to slap her across her masked face as we argue.

"He needs to see an orthopedist; he needs surgery."

She shakes her head. "We don't have an orthopedist assigned to Project 157."

"I don't care who you have. He needs immediate transport to land and proper care."

"He's not leaving the ship." Her voice is icy.

I clench my fists, face red. "Navy sailors have the right to quality care and treatment consistent with available resources and accepted standards, including access to appropriate specialty care and pain management." I quote the naval patient Bill of Rights, each word louder than the last.

"He's been reclassified as a naval *experiment*." Sutton plays her trump card, voice hard.

"What?" The world's just turned upside down with my hands pressed against his fresh wounds.

"He's now under act 58309, stating any scientific anomalies resulting from medical or technological testing that are deemed unsafe for the public are thereby property of the Collective."

Blackness crowds my vision. *It can't be true!* But she stares me down, in complete control.

I rub my forehead as she continues. "Set the bone, Sage. His calf needs layered stitches; the puncture wounds must heal from the inside out."

My breathing is short and fast. I turn to the sink, the water running red as I wash, wrestling for control. *With my K-60 levels near his, have they reclassified me the same?* I grip the sink.

"Are you refusing duty?" Her crisp voice makes me tilt my chin in the air, defiant.

"No." I don't trust myself to say anything else.

"You'll have to wait for the swelling to go down, then set it. Put him on vancomycin immediately." She walks to the door and the lock clicks as she exits.

I crumple into the chair, head in my hands. All my worst fears are reality. Jacob belongs to Ash, listed as private property, rights denied.

I search for a way out, blinking back tears. Hours pass as anxiety settles over me, and I hover over his wounds. Will he live? What happened? What could prevent it in the future? We've got to stop this process; how can I reverse the K-60?

The old crushing weight settles inside. *It's all you, Sage, measure up, figure it out, or he dies. Just like so many others did.* I pull the gauze off his collarbone to assess the swelling. He's not ready for surgery yet.

*Lions. If you smell something dead, run. Why didn't you run, Jacob?* I pull up images on the laptop of victims of a lion's mauling.

The gruesome bite marks match with sickening accuracy. His stories must be true.

A sizzling sound snaps my head up. "What?"

The deep puncture wounds are frothing, as if I'd put peroxide on them. With a crisp sound, his collarbone solidifies, pink skin spreading over the opening.

I back away, hands in the air. *This is out of control.* A slight mist and a fresh clean scent rise from his wounds as they seal themselves; new scars cover his shoulder and leg. I press back against the desk, breathing hard. My nerves and the motion of the ship combine against my stomach.

"Emerson, did that just happen?" Sutton's voice over the com system lacks her previous cocky tone.

I nod, which is the only response I can give. Forcing myself forward, I scan his vitals. Steady as can be. His hands twitch. My fingernails cut into my palms as his chest jerks, mouth forming words. His eyes flick open, fists clenched. He sits up. It's his smoothest transition yet.

"Hello, Jacob." My voice trembles at the far edge of okay. I hold his eyes for a long while and it seems as if we say a thousand words. I drop my gaze to the fresh bright scars on his shoulder.

He looks down, frowning. His mouth opens as his fingers trace the raised edges. He looks back at me, but he's worlds away, remembering. Tears pool in his eyes as his lips move, but no sound comes out.

His gaze is present again, eyes flashing wildfire. He grips his shoulder, fingers spread wide but still not able to cover the long scars; his bare chest tightens. The hair on my arms stands on end, with no way to know what's coming next.

A groan escapes him, rising in pitch. He leans forward, condensing, coiling, till the sound explodes into a shout. I back up, terrified, skin prickling as the air crackles between us. He throws his head back, body straining, the veins on his thick neck standing out, fists clenched, muscles rippling. Still, the thunder of his roar grows till the room reverberates with it. Empty now, he hauls in air. I scowl at the wild grin I find on his face.

"It's true, Sage!" he shouts, point blank, beyond control, throwing back his head again. "It's all true."

He's still gripping his shoulder; his relief and elation make me question his sanity. He's off the table, snatching the clothes I'd set out. Now he's pacing the room, eyes scanning, seeing some other world.

The door unlocks and two full trays appear, but he doesn't touch them. I remain pressed against the desk, unnerved. He leans on the exam table, focused on me.

"Did I bleed here?"

I open my mouth, but nothing comes out. I try again. "Profusely."

He shakes his head, brows knit. "So, there is a connection."

My mind races. Sutton will expect me to be grilling him for information, not waiting for a private moment.

"What happened?" I ask, desperate for him not to answer.

He juts his chin at me, knowing. "I was hoping you'd tell me."

I fold my arms across my chest. "Never seen someone get wounded on the table. How did it happen, Jacob?"

*You'd better tell me later.* Internal balance returns with the clarity in his eyes.

"I was unconscious, remember?"

I nod, frowning. *I've played my part.*

Brooks steps in. "Carter, report to deck three for some pool time."

We swing out the door to find our escort tripled. Jacob hadn't eaten; this last episode has really bothered me, and I'm empty and worn out.

Brooks pulls open another small metal door, and the sharp scent of chlorine wafts over me. Jacob stands at the edge of the pool in a pair of shorts, hands on his hips, fresh scars standing out.

"Let's go, Carter," Brooks commands.

The water seems like a dragon waiting to eat him up. His hesitation tells me he's thinking the same thing. He takes a deep breath, dives in. I hold my breath with him until he surfaces in the center of the pool. He turns, making quick eye contact, then settles into a round of laps. Brooks paces the far side of the pool, keeping a sharp eye on Jacob. I nod, understanding this is a trial, a soft opening to see if he's back to full strength.

So, the water doesn't make him jump; it only facilitates a jump when he's in that state. Jacob flips at the far end, shooting back in this direction. No wonder they call them SEALs. He seems more at home in the water than on deck. Tears prick my eyes; he's not a SEAL anymore; he's classified property of the New World

Order. I force my hand away from my mouth; I dare not show emotion. It feels as if a school bus has been methodically driving back and forth over me.

As much as they thrilled Jacob, the scars are deeply disturbing. I've got to find some way to keep him from jumping. I pace the length of the pool, reading charts in my head. Each return has lasted longer than the previous. As time passes, will he eventually become permanent again? The further we get from the experiment, the less power it will have over him. I nod, grasping at this theory; it's the only one I can handle.

But what's stopping Ash from putting him through it again, or forcing him through the same procedures Tex has undergone? I miss a step, almost stumbling into the pool, stomach turning. *Get it together.* I take a seat on the bench at the far end of the room, pretending to be okay. Brooks calls time and we head back to A27.

I leaf through Sutton's fresh list of tests. There are two syringes taped to the paperwork, cyclosporine and azathioprine; cold sweat breaks out between my shoulder blades. They give these drugs before an organ transplant, immunosuppressants to keep the body from rejecting whatever they put in. I stare at them, seeing Jacob on the deck of the *Engage* before the experiment, whole. How far will this nightmare take us?

"You all right?" he asks.

I cough, *No*, and then say, "Yes," my voice tight.

He nods slow, finishing his food, hair still wet, eyes on me.

"Would you sit on the table, please? I've got two shots I need to give you." My back to the cameras, I blink tears away. His fork hangs in midair.

"Are they something I need?"

I cough hard and loud, as if something is stuck in my throat. "Yes." His mouth twists as I continue, "Maybe you'd like to use the restroom first?"

He nods even slower, mouth turning down as he studies my face. As soon as he closes the door, I bend over the desk gathering papers, slipping a Post-it note over my charts and shielding it with my body. I scribble as fast as I can, stick the note up flat on my palm, then flip the cover of my chest pocket open, and stick the note to the inside. I finish the motion by scratching my ear as if it had been my intent.

Jacob comes out and hops onto the table, deep-blue eyes studying me. I gather alcohol wipes and the syringes, set them on the table beside him. I reach up to scratch my ear again, flip my pocket flap up with my forearm as I do, and the bright paper catches his eye.

"Can't give it to you. I'm going to put it all the way through the skin, shoot it out behind you. It will hurt."

One brow goes up as he hints at a nod, then rolls up the short sleeve of his black shirt. I let out a shaky breath, force the flap of my pocket closed with my elbow, then scratch my eye. The second I touch his arm, the grip of dread loosens, and my hands stop trembling.

He smiles at me with half his mouth the way he does, and I return it, flicking air out of the tiny syringe. I try to pinch his arm to make it easier to poke the needle through the skin, then back out again as if I'm sewing. Of course, there's no give, even with his muscle loose. I aim the needle toward the back of his arm, hoping cameras can't pick up the angle. He doesn't flinch as the needle dives in, and I torque it until it reappears. I squirt the contents onto the table behind him.

"Ready for one more?"

"Sure thing, thanks."

I flick my eyes up to his; he's enjoying this. I give an empty laugh, shaking my head. We're playing a dangerous game, but it's the kind he's always won.

"All done?" he questions.

"Yes, sir."

He scoots back farther on the table, sopping up the evidence with his pants. I nod at him, smiling. *That's right, Jacob; now I just have to prevent the procedure you're not prepped for.* I gather up the garbage, swipe the note out of my pocket, crumple it into my pants pocket, and dump the rest in the can.

Brooks enters and stares us down. "Training floor, STAT."

His eyes are cold. I swallow hard, grabbing my med pack. Jacob exits, but Brooks steps in front of me. I lift my chin, pretending I have nothing to hide. He reaches out, flips open my chest pocket.

My eyes snap fire as I step back. "You want me to take you down for sexual assault, sir, I will."

They're empty words. I have no rights here; but he backs off, nods toward the hall. I breeze past him to find Jacob watching for me over his shoulder, dragging his feet. His shoulders loosen as I fall into step behind him; we're up to a fourteen-sailor escort.

Jacob hits the track, blowing off his previous times, still not giving it everything.

"Course!" Brooks booms, and Jacob cuts into the obstacles.

I enjoy watching him, wondering at the return of my internal balance when I had touched him. Motion at the far end of the room catches my attention; my skin crawls. Tex ducks through the doorway, crossing the track low and fast.

The light blinks out.

"What?" I whisper, muscles clenched. *They'll get the issue fixed.*

But understanding dawns in the dark. This is a fight. I suck in a breath. "JAC—"

Brooks clamps his hand over my mouth. I struggle, but he locks me hard against his chest. He pulls me back behind a screen where I can see Jacob and Tex in the bright red, orange, and white of an infrared screen.

They're still separated by a few obstacles, but Tex is honing in on Jacob, who is crouched at the base of the wall.

"You gonna stay quiet? Field trials are the only way to see what our boy is made of. This is a training scenario; nobody's gonna die," Brooks whispers in my ear.

I twitch, trying to yank away… His grip loosens, and I pull back, panting. Tex leaps the wall Jacob is behind. Jacob rolls to the side, enough to let him land, then pounces, sending Tex headfirst into a thick post. He's on Tex before he can recover, but the infrared blurs too bright as they grapple to tell what's happening.

They separate. Jacob's figure is shorter and thicker; he's warmer too, showing more white than Tex. He crouches, moving fast behind obstacles. Tex is searching, moving forward low and slow.

Jacob stops, still as stone. Tex doesn't know he's there, moving parallel to the left. Jacob explodes into motion, scaling a wall in the pitch dark, twisting at the top to descend, his cooler green boots plummeting down. Tex hesitates, leaps to the side. Too late. Jacob collides, riding him down, forcing Tex's arm behind his back. They struggle and Jacob forces Tex's arm higher.

A sharp pop echoes in the perfect silence of the dark. Tex rolls, one arm hanging limp, swinging with the other. My mouth goes dry: *Sage, you've got to get him out of here.* The image blurs again as they tangle. The lights snap back on, piercingly bright, but the men don't flinch, swinging and grappling. I break forward, desperate, but Brooks catches my wrist.

"Don't go out there. Tex will kill you; you would be an anomaly in this program."

My heart sinks. *Program.* Tex is just a piece of equipment to them. Brooks pulls out a tablet with a video of only Tex on the screen.

"Brooks, this is madness! Stop him."

But he won't; the savage fight continues.

I can't rip my eyes away from the small screen. A green bar at the top advances with every blow Tex lands. As they move throughout the tight space, the program outlines Tex in green; to one side, there's a selection of moves and strike positions. Brooks taps the icon of a backhanded thrust. Tex twists to the side and executes it with his good arm, catching Jacob in the ribs.

I've got Brooks' arm in a death grip. "Stop him! This isn't right, and you know it!"

I catch his eye; tears glint in mine, desperate. A frown flashes across his face; he knows. The outline around Tex turns red as he leaps onto Jacob, driving him hard into a wall.

The tablet shows a pop-up that reads, *Backdoor?*

He swipes it away, glancing at me.

"Time!" Brooks calls.

Tex's outline remains red. He's enraged, veins bulging, far outside the training parameters, as Jacob flips him to the floor. Tex sweeps out with his boot and they roll across the track.

"BROOKS!" I can't contain the scream.

He hits a red button at the top. No response. He switches to the small remote he's used before, punching in a code. Tex jerks and swings again, but Jacob dodges it. Brooks resends the command. Tex stands, chest heaving, staring at Jacob. I lunge for the track.

Brooks takes my upper arm. "Wait."

Tex shifts, standing at attention, the outline turning green again.

"Carter! To the bench."

Jacob stares at Tex a second longer. At the bench I fuss over him, mind revolting at the knowledge of what they've done to Tex.

"Are you okay?" My voice wavers.

"Yes."

"Did you break his arm?"

"No, I only dislocated it. I wasn't going to be a punching bag again; that guy is not a friendly." His face is free of swelling, eyes bright.

I try to convince myself he's all right.

"I smelled him coming, like the lions." He works his mouth, remembering, life brimming over.

I wish I had the same. I pin him with a look, unwilling to back off until I know. "Jacob, you've got to level with me. What happened to your shoulder?"

"I..." He shakes his head. "Failed to take some good advice."

"You weren't kidding about the lions, were you? Those bite marks are an exact match."

"Oh, the lions are real. You remember what I told you if you make a jump?"

I nod. "Jacob, so help me, tell me what's going on while you're unconscious."

"Listen, in the spirit, you can see everything, who you really are, your enemies, the truth. It's all plain instead of being hidden, shrouded the way it is here. The lions want to kill you. Flat out. It's the same here; only we're so blind we can't see it.

"In the spirit, I have to fight. I have to believe the Almighty's Words above what I see and feel. If I can do that..." He clenches his fists, eyes intense. "Then anything could happen. Everything hinges on how much scroll you eat and how deep you let it settle. I know, I know."

He shakes his head at the absurdity of his explanation. "The truth is, I thought the lions would get me, and they did. If I'd been able to turn that thought, shut that door in my mind, the outcome would've been different." He stares at the floor, as if listening.

"'As a man thinks in his heart, so he is.' That's why eating scroll is so important; it changes what you see inside, which allows for a different outcome than you've ever experienced before.

"But listen, I'm serious. If you make a jump, steer clear of the lions at first, until you get your feet under you."

"What will I do then? Shoot them?" I joke, his words like machine gun rounds.

But his gaze is serious. "There are no rifles there, Sage; you've got to do it with a blade."

My mouth hangs open. He's one of the smartest men in the military and he's not joking. I blink hard; there's no way around what he said.

"With the right knowledge, you can. But without it..." He shakes his head. "If we're not together, find a man named Demyen. He'll help you."

"I cannot believe we are having this conversation."

"You'll be glad enough if you jump. Wasn't easy figuring it out on my own. You'll have some scroll in your pouch; I know it's tough at first, but you've got to eat it—as much as you can stomach."

"You keep saying 'scroll.' What do you mean by that?"

"The Almighty's Words. The children of the Light always have access to them; how strong you are is a direct correlation to how much you eat. But, at first, it's tough to stomach."

"You mean the Bible?" I'm trying to get it. Really. Trying. "Here," I say, digging the small KJV Bible out of my med pack.

I'd read it some while he was out because it's been so interesting to him. It's been years, but the familiar words were comforting. *Is the K-60 a result of the scroll? Is it possible that what he's doing in that other experience is giving him the edge here, an ability beyond what he had before?*

He laughs, taking the book in his wide hand. "Thank you. I was hungry."

He flashes a full smile, the first I've ever seen. It imprints on my soul.

"You're welcome." My stomach drops.

I'm anxious to get a sonogram done on him. I take the blood pressure cuff off his arm. He flips the book open, eyes scanning. One square finger jams down on the page; he gives a quiet laugh, then a shocked sound, his mouth open.

"What?" I feel as if I'm ten steps behind, still in the dark, while he's in the brilliant light of day.

He gazes out over the course. "It's true."

"I've heard that before." My comment makes the corner of his mouth tip up.

"'But you have an unction from the Holy One, and you know all things.'" He blinks rapidly. "First John 2:20. When the lights went out, I knew Tex was coming. I could smell him. I think he's had bone enhancements, and they've bumped up his vision, but I couldn't see a thing."

"Looked like you could." He frowns at me; I shrug. "They had infrared on you."

He grunts. "I couldn't see my hand in front of my face. But in the quiet dark, I paid attention to my spirit." He taps the page. "That's what it says right here. My spirit knew everything; where he was and when to move. As I kept my mind under, I was able to face him *without* physical knowledge." An expression of awe takes him. "It's everything, the Words the Almighty gives. They're infinite. Infinite against our finite."

I let him absorb the moment; it's flat to me, but it means the world to him. "So, a lion tried to kill you. How did the wounds heal so fast?"

I can't get myself to believe it on a logical level. But still, I'm staring at the imprint of massive fangs on his forearm.

He flips the pages. "'Surely he has borne our sickness and carried our pain…and by his stripes we are healed.' I know that's not an answer that going to satisfy you, but it's the truth."

I purse my lips. *He's right.* I shake my head, Sutton's news taking the forefront of my mind. *What will he do with it?*

"We have enough to deal with in this world. You've…" Bile rises in my throat at the thought. I force it back down. "You've been reclassified as 'government property.' A medical experiment they've deemed unsafe to the public." I put my hand over my mouth.

He grunts, lacking the anger I thought he would have.

"Figured it was only a matter of time. Sage, you've got to keep them from implanting anything while I'm out." He takes my hand for a moment, making my breath catch. "Please. You're my best defense." He gives me a grin. "I know that's asking a lot."

He lets go of me, fingers tracing the scars on his forearm. *How can he take this in stride, as if it didn't affect him? A good portion of his life has been somewhere far from here; his scars say that much. It's like his real identity is in some other realm.*

He's waiting for an answer. I nod. "I'm ready."

"Thanks for what you did today. What did Brooks say to you?"

"He was looking for the note; they saw you reading it. They're watching that closely. But they missed my little sewing trick. We've got to do something soon."

"The right thing will come at the right time." He's so sure, no fear.

I'm consumed with it.

"I hope so," I whisper as Brooks reappears; we've only got a second, locking eyes with him, heart in my throat. "Jacob, I'll do whatever it takes to keep you safe."

His half smile reappears. "I know that, Sage. Stay close, all right? I'm gonna rock the boat."

It's no empty threat.

"If you sink it, make sure I'm not on it, will you?"

He laughs. "That's the plan, though I have to admit the gel coating they have on the shooting deck is impressive. I've heard it makes ships unsinkable. It's thicker than I thought it would be."

"How do you know how thick it is?" I'm still weirded out by his "knowing all things" comment. *Maybe he does.*

"Kept falling through it, remember?"

"Oh, right." Someday, we might have a normal conversation.

Brooks steps close. "Ash will see you now. I'd suggest answering his questions this time, Carter."

Jacob stands and Brooks takes a half step back. My eyes widen; he's afraid of Jacob. He can control Tex with his little box, but Jacob had more than held his own with Tex and currently is not controllable. They're going to implant a chip soon; I know it. I force a slow breath as we file up the stairs.

Ash sits in a large room, Sutton and the male nurse to one side. The Marines stop at the door as we enter. Jacob stands at attention in the center of the room, muscles tight. *Oh, Lord, help us.*

Ash twists in his swivel chair and snaps on a screen attached to the wall. The infrared replays.

"Right there," he says, as Jacob rolls out of Tex's way and clobbers him before he can gain his feet.

"How did you know he was in the room?" Ash spins back to Jacob, thick brows low, eyes hard. "The light in that room was less than 1/1,000 lux. Pitch dark."

*Come on, Jacob, we've got to play this right.*

"Sir. I smelled him, sir."

My shoulders drop in relief at his answer; at least it was something. Ash grunts, turning back to the screen. Jacob's bright-red-and-white fist drives Tex hard into a protruding corner.

"And that, Carter? You couldn't see him, but he could see you. He has extensive vision enhancement," Ash says.

We watch as they wrestle; Jacob strains back, dislocating Tex's shoulder.

"No worries. He'll heal up in two days, good as new. Dr. Sutton's made certain of that. He didn't feel it either; he's impervious to pain. That sounds nice, doesn't it?"

Ash's being so open makes me nervous. All the cards are on the table, and they are holding all the aces. Sutton opens her mouth, but Ash levels a glare at her, and she shuts it again. *Good move, lady, he despises you.*

"Imagine what would be possible for you if you had those enhancements. You're the first soldier to hold your own with Tex, much less injure him. A very impressive performance—all with no biomedical enhancement." Each word he speaks is calculated with heavy intent.

"Figure, sir, that I'm set with what the good Lord gave me." Jacob's voice is tight.

"It can't compare with what I can give you." Ash leans forward, his eyes cold. A bright pin on his chest lapel catches my attention. It's got a strange symbol on it, with a pointed top and a tool on the bottom. "Take a seat, Carter."

Jacob turns toward me, jaw clenched, ignoring the one near Ash and taking a chair at the far wall and putting as much space between them as possible. His eyes are hard but controlled.

*Have a little faith, Sage.*

Sutton approaches him. "Jacob, we are very concerned about these episodes you continue to have. As your doctor, I have a list of recommendations for you."

Jacob's eyes narrow, gazing up at her. "I won't sign your consent form."

Sutton drops her eyes and shifts her weight to the other foot. She clears her throat, casting a quick glance at Ash. There's a sheen of fear in her eyes. I lean in; sure enough, on her clipboard sits a medical consent form. A shiver runs down my arms.

"Brooks, give me the stats." Ash's voice is hard as Brooks steps forward, and Sutton takes her seat, unnerved by Jacob's words.

I glance at him; his hands clench the armrests, every muscle straining. *No.* A thin green haze hangs on the floor about his feet. Scanning the room, I slip forward toward a table with water bottles lined up along the far edge.

I twist off the cap. Sutton glances up from following Brooks's report, then goes back to her papers. The veins on Jacob's neck stand out; he trembles, determined to conceal his jackhammering muscles.

I hold out the bottle; there's no way I can dump it on him without their catching on. He grimaces, chest heaving as his quivering fingers grip it. His eyes find mine.

*Thank you.*

I nod, wishing I could save him.

Bottle vibrating in his hand, he gets that half-crazed, half-hungry expression as if he can't wait to go. I scoop my charts off the top of my med pack, pretend to trip as I turn. The papers shoot skyward, all eyes on me. I kneel to gather them, apologizing. Brooks looks down in disgust, then continues his report.

I steal another glance at Jacob. He raises the bottle to his lips, dumps it down his chin; a smile plays across his face, then he goes limp, crashing to the floor.

Sutton shoots out of her chair. "Emerson! Take his vitals!"

I'm already there; his pulse is strong, breathing regular, just like last time. Water works like a charm.

# 7
# JACOB



Horse scent fills my nostrils.

"Climb up, Jacob. It is time." Raeuel's huge hand reaches down from his mounted height.

This jump was smooth, the travel enjoyable. I dust off my pants where I'd plowed a trough in the ground, landing. It seems no time at all has passed since we stood at the pool.

I send a suspicious look at the sharp expression in the horse's eye. *Gotta do what you have to do, Carter.* My hand finds Raeuel's and he heaves me up onto the white horse's bare back. Before I can settle, the beast leaps forward.

"Eh!" I grab Raeuel's shirt in a desperate grip.

"Easy, Haseleph. Easy now; you must bear him a little way." The wind rips Raeuel's words past my ears. The horse needs no bridle or urging as it gains speed until the gust whips tears from my eyes. There is so much energy in the creature below; I think we could fly.

Haseleph snorts, stretches out even more. Leaving propriety behind, I wrap my arms around Raeuel's thick waist, clinging like a fly to his back. I've never been so glad as when I slide off that smooth hide. When Raeuel dismounts, the horse buries its nose in the Watcher's elbow.

"Err, now, 'twas not that bad, was it?"

The horse answers Raeuel with a deep nicker, disagreeing.

"All right then, off you go. I'll call you when I'm ready."

One large, limpid eye peers around Raeuel's shoulder at me. Haseleph snorts, wheels, and takes off. Clods of dirt explode from his hooves, pummeling me from head to toe.

"Oh!" *Should've kept my mouth shut.* As I spit, I note Raeuel hadn't been hit with one clod of dirt, not a one. "Good aim," I state, between spits.

"Yes." I hear no remorse in Raeuel's voice. "Come, I will walk with you on the way yet."

I'm glad for the company. Stepping out on my glimmering path, I think about Jaden's words. "How do I gain perfect sight?"

Raeuel looks down, full of compassion. "An excellent question."

I wonder if that's all he will say on the matter.

"First, you must know what sight is. You have eyes. Yet do you see?"

I've learned a bit in my time here. I'm taking in plenty of information from my eyes. So, there's more. I've seen things beyond my wildest imaginations. Yet, out of all these, the memory of the paths converging is strongest. It's like holding the most precious treasure in my hands. The sight of HIM—the Master. *His eyes upon me.* I shiver; there's no expressing it. The memory is too great for me.

Raeuel's voice breaks in. "Yes! Yes, that was *sight.*"

His words snap my attention back to the present. "What you see oft deceives you. But a man with true sight looks beyond what is first revealed."

I nod, taking in the words. *Through His eyes.* Quieting the clamor of my own thoughts, I chew a bit of scroll and listen; louder come the words into my ears: *I…I…I know your works that you are neither hot nor cold: I would that you are hot or cold. So…so…so then because you are lukewarm and neither hot nor cold, I will spew you out of my mouth. Because you say I am rich and increased with goods and have need of nothing and know not that you are wretched and miserable and poor and blind and naked.*

My head jerks up. *You know not that you are blind?* I roll the mouthful to the other side.

*I…I…I counsel you to buy of Me gold tried in the fire that you may be rich and white raiment that you might be clothed that the shame of your nakedness does not appear and anoint your eyes with eye salve that you may see.*

I swallow hard, the words now burned into my soul. "How do I get eye salve?"

Raeuel's eyes flash bright, and a grin appears. "That is the right question, Jacob."

And *poof.* Just like that, he's gone—vanished.

"Hey!" I shout in shock. "What…?" I whisper under my breath. A disgusted sigh escapes me. I do a 360° turn… gone. *I'm alone.*

Without the Watcher's massive bulk next to me, I pay a significant amount of attention to my surroundings. Haseleph carried us far, and the terrain differs from what I've encountered before.

I stuff another wad of scroll into my mouth. The scattered trees are short, maybe fifteen feet tall, crooked, and wind-wizened. They are some sort of pine, odd but beautiful with all their bizarre shapes. The ground is pebbly, almost sandy, and light-colored. It's dry, both the air and the ground. Scorpions come to my mind. I keep my step light, remembering with vivid detail how the concussion of our digging had drawn them.

Even without a sun for direction, I can tell night is drawing near. The air changes as the dark approaches; a hint of coolness precedes it. Squinting, I try to follow my path as far as I can see. *This should be an interesting night.*

Soon, I stop and crouch down, studying the huge pugmarks of lions. Sniffing, I find no rotten scent. I place my hand flat on the hot, rocky sand, trying to gather any nuance of what comes. *Keep moving.* I increase my pace; finding a place to spend the night is imperative. I stuff more scroll in my mouth, nodding as I chew and pondering the change within. I'm deep inside lion territory, seeing more prints all the time…at night with no company…yet I am not afraid. A deep sense of satisfaction fills me.

As I chew, I listen. *Lo, I am with you always, even to the end of the world.*

A smile tugs at my mouth. One thing I know: *I will stay on my path*, and the Almighty, He will keep me, and I will take authority over His enemies. As I drop down a slight hill, the air mingles with a hint of stench. I lean forward into a jog, steps leaving tiny puffs of dust even though I tread as soft as I can. Cruising up the next incline, I pull back.

My path runs right up to a scraggly tree, then dives below it. I circle the rough bark; my path reappears on the other side. *Hmmm.* There is peace at the thought of climbing it.

The tree's branches are thick, even though it's not a huge tree. Its twisting trunk reaches full height, then takes a sharp curve to the south, its scraggly top half almost horizontal.

The day is waning. *Up I go.* Stretching to reach the lowest branch, I grunt, grinning because my shoulder is *so strong.* So whole. I shut my eyes for a moment, remembering the broken collarbone, the exposed interior. I flex harder, rejoicing. *How?* It's not possible, yet it *is.*

Holding the limb with my legs sloth-style, I work up to the top of the branch. I test the pine's strength as I gain altitude. Reaching up for another branch, my fingers find something smooth. A soft, hollow sound accompanies my fumbling in the fading light.

Soon I'm peering at a small wooden bowl carved from a deep-purple heartwood. Balancing as I turn its domed lid, it fills my nose with a potent scent of pine. Inside is a thick paste. *It will cover my scent.* Dipping my fingertips, I scoop some up and rub it into my skin.

Replacing the lid, I climb farther, reaching the horizontal top of the tree. The day is almost gone. In a hurry now, I break off handfuls of long needles and pad a scant nest for the night. I settle in as silvery starlight replaces the fierce heat of day. The wind picks up, stirring at first, and then rising to a tempest. I readjust, putting as much tree between me and the gusts as possible.

As I sit, perched on the limb, my chest tightens and the fabric of space seems to warp. Through the green vapor, I see the *Olympia*. I blink hard; the ship rides heavy seas, straining against its anchor. Then it's gone, just a wisp of a memory.

That's when I hear the first roar. I hunker down, trying to separate the sound from the shriek of the wind in the pine boughs. I needn't have tried; soon the very tree reverberates with the wicked voices of lions. I stare with soft eyes over the landscape, searching for movement.

As soon as night firms her grip on the land, the lions come forth en masse. They wander from every direction, some in groups, the bigger ones alone. *So many.* They don't seem to have any path to follow; they pass my tree and continue on.

I use the time to study them. They're wretched, mean, and hungry—pinched almost. At random, with no provocation, they attack each other. They seem like ghosts in the dim light.

I work to quell the roiling of my stomach as the stench of them fills my lungs. Time marches by as an army of lions continues to flow past my tree. Later, their tide ebbs; and scanning my field of vision, I count only twenty. These have no desire to move to better hunting, and they loaf, harassing each other.

Five of them wander past my tree. The others wind out of sight. I will them to continue, but no. With deep sighs, two of them flop down at the trunk of my tree, while others snarl and swipe at each other, and one sniffs the ground.

*My scent.* He treads along my exact path, his shredded mane dragging the ground. He reaches my tree. I hold my breath, ready. As he rises on his hind legs, a chill runs along my skin. His long, blood-crusted claws scrape the bark as his huge snout weaves back and forth.

His eyes, glowing in the silver light, fasten on me as I remain perfectly still under his gaze. He huffs, sniffing with his open mouth, revealing one broken lower fang. His head turns, searching a lower branch. *No, he hasn't caught sight of me.*

Still as stone, I sit with a few precious feet separating me from the massive jaws below. But he drops back to all fours, his front feet sending up twin puffs of dust. Without warning, he swats the other lion, and the tree quakes at the snarling and snapping that ensues.

*Breathe.*

Then things get interesting; they begin to speak. My first seconds in this world surface, scared stiff and listening to lions whispering. I hear only a few words among their raspy, growling tones. *Blood, kill, hunt.* I close my eyes and listen, letting the whispers flow past, and they clear.

"Ran screaming, looked back at me, and right into…mouth. Never heard so many bones crunch! I took his legs…didn't stop screaming till the silver cord was severed." The other four lions half-cough, half-wheeze in what could be laughter.

Another voice joins in. "Caught two out after dark. Chased them for miles with just a nip every so often, worked them this way and that till they climbed a tree. Had such fun pulling them down bit by bit."

I swallow hard, hating their words and the night. The dark creeps by at a snail's pace. The hours wear on me; my skin against the scruffy tree bark burns, and my legs scream for movement.

I work to tune out their grating evil words, but I can't, no matter how hard I try. The lions' conversation takes a turn for the worse. My mouth opens in horror.

Five giant noses sniff the air. The lions' eyes glow bright and eerie in the midnight. Their heads weave back and forth, searching for something. They caught the scent of my breath! I stay stock-still and shut it without sound.

They circle the tree, hunting. *Me.* I grimace. *That was a stupid mistake.* The scant height of this tree seems no separation at all.

Certain that I must battle five in the night, I tense. But something changes, as if a switch has been flipped. Now the air is rank. The lions sense it too. Instead of searching for me, they sink lower to the ground. My hair stands on end. *What is going on?* I can't see anything different, but the atmosphere is full of dread.

All five lions look to the south—the direction my path continues past the tree. One lion is trembling. *Trembling?* The stars dim as if someone pulled a shade over the sky. Its eyes widen; it turns, slinking on its belly toward the west. A new stench permeates the air, entirely different from the rotten smell of lions. The other four belly crawl after the first.

I watch them go, snakelike, heads low to the ground, trying to be invisible. *What would make them run like that?* It gets darker again; yet there are no clouds between me and the stars. I shift in the tree, my muscles thankful for the movement.

The darkness spreads from the south, or at least it's deeper there. A fresh wave of stench fills my nostrils, and I grimace. *The lions can't compare to this.* This is more like Iraq, in Ramadi after the Jihadists had committed genocide, leaving bodies in the streets.

My stomach roils; I haven't eaten in a while, so I grab a huge handful of scroll; its pleasant bread-like scent stills the churning in my belly.

I chew, watching the darkness thicken when I expected the light of morning soon. A piece of scroll over my nose acts as an air filter. I chew and listen and watch.

*Nothing…nothing…nothing shall by any means harm you.*

My brows lower at the words as I chew the same bite again. *The lions have harmed me.*

*Nothing shall by any means harm you.*

What to do when my thoughts and the scroll are in direct opposition? I grit my teeth. The scroll's the truth; it *is* reality. If I can grasp it, I will live in it. My experience was not according to the truth, because I was not walking in the truth. I expected them to harm me, so they were able to.

*Nothing shall by any means harm you.* If that's the truth, then it changes everything. It would mean no more fear, no wondering, no hesitation, no doubt. *If I had believed those few simple words, would it have kept those lions from attacking?* As soon as I'd seen them above me on those cliffs, fear gripped me. I'd done well to fight, but maybe it was my very first thought where I'd gone wrong.

I ponder Demyen in the meadow watching Aseph stalk up to him. Why hadn't the massive lion exploded out of the woods at full speed? Why hadn't he swiped with his claws? The revelation comes that perhaps he *couldn't.* Demyen's rock-solid knowledge that "Nothing shall by any means harm him" had prevented the lion from trying. That's why he'd blustered like that: he was trying to get Demyen to run.

The stench thickens, as does the oppressive veil that is falling over the land. I hunker down, making sure I'm solid on my branch. It feels like knowing a hurricane is rolling in and all I can do is wait, perched in the open. My senses are piqued, but inside I'm quiet. I smile through my scroll-breathing mask. *Free.*

Watching the approaching blackness, I ponder my experiences in this place. I was filled with fear—at my enemies, my own atrophied body, thoughts running wild, killing me on the inside. What a different place my mind is in now. It's that simple. Thoughts of fear and doubt stink just like the lions; it's their own kind. I shudder, realizing the connection, the open door. When my thoughts match theirs, they have every right to hunt me.

I flip another piece of scroll into my mouth. *It's so good.* The taste clears my nose of the stench for a few moments.

*The…the…the mind controlled by the Spirit is life and peace.*

It's a test. If the Spirit does not control my thoughts, then fear and death reign. That gives the lions legal rights to me.

But when the Spirit controls my mind, I have life and peace. It's that simple, black and white. I flex my arms and strength is there. My bones no longer show. But now it's time; whatever comes is near. The air seems to press down, the blackness complete.

*Thud.* My tree shivers a bit. *Thud.* Footsteps. *Thud.* My eyes burn from the smell. *Thud.* Waves of intense heat roll past.

A slight hiss makes me strain to hear. *Is it breath?* No, it's more like…something dragging. *Thud.* The pine needles rattle against each other and, remembering the lions, I clamp my mouth shut, relying on the salve to keep my scent hidden.

There! A red glow about ten feet higher than my perch in the tree draws nearer. *Thud. Drag. Thud.* The glowing orb blinks out for a second, then reappears. An eye? But it's so high.

My skin feels as if I sit in an oven and the tree takes a violent jolt as the creature scrapes past. The sound of twisting, groaning wood shrieks in the dead quiet between footsteps. I grip the branch as the tree bucks at the impact. *It holds.*

The tree sways again, and the gripping heat and squeezing pressure of the air release. I let out a breath, still careful to keep my mouth closed. The dark wanes, the stars reappear, and the long night marches on.

*Lion territory.* My path leads me deep into their lair. Crouching at the peak of the hill, I peer over a valley filled with lions. A haze of dust hangs in the squalid air, kicked up by their constant brawls. My path dives straight down the hill and disappears around a sharp outcropping of boulders. A scorpion scuttles past. I watch it, but I'd reapplied the pine salve before I'd climbed down from the tree, and it seems oblivious to my presence. The heat climbs to a scorching peak as the day brightens.

It's only getting hotter. Thirst grips me. The lions rest in what scant shade they can find, warring over the best spots. I ease backward down my side of the hill, soaked with sweat under the blistering heat of day.

I chew some scroll, and find courage…and an idea. I lie down and roll. Holding my breath, I take a handful of hot powdery dust and throw it on my face, elephant-style. My hair comes next. I work the dull-colored sand into it and shake the loose powder out.

My arms are indistinguishable from the drab ground. *Almighty, preserve me.* I slip over the brink of the hill and creep low and quiet along my path. Keeping a sharp eye out for movement, I pick my way down to the boulders. It takes an age to go ten feet because I'm surrounded by scorpions who scuttle over the hot rocks, seeking small slices of shade.

Maybe it's my lack of fear, but they don't seem to notice me. I move sloth-slow, *one step, pause, then another.* I wait for a clear place to set my foot. Skin burning, I inch forward; the air is almost boiling. My throat sticks together, eyes stinging.

I crouch down; my path curves to the left of the blistering valley. It crosses an open area for a hundred yards before disappearing behind a series of small hills. I scan the valley. The stench of hundreds of wounded hides fills my nostrils. *So many.*

"Nothing shall by any means hurt me," I whisper.

I step into the open. Moving one limb at a time, I will my dust-covered outline to blend into the dirt. Halfway across, I'm so thirsty I can't think straight, and my sweat is long gone. By the time I slide behind the first low hill, my tongue is stuck to the top of my mouth. As I lean against a rock, water consumes my thoughts.

Hunched behind the curve of the hill, I move with desperate speed. *I must find water.* A jolt of adrenaline shoots down my arms; I almost trip over the massive nose of a sleeping lion. My senses come back in a flash. I teeter, clamping down the urge to run, then pass in silence.

The sharp awareness fades, and I struggle forward, muscles cramping, delirium setting in. I stumble, my legs refusing to continue. My hands hit the ground, sending up choking dust. As I groan, a motion draws my gaze to the left. A massive black snake lies coiled not two feet away. *No.*

His slitted tongue flashes; then he hits my arm, faster than I can follow. The force of the impact drives me to my stomach. The massive snake coils around me, clenching the air from my dry lungs. I wheeze, but it clamps down harder. My eyes roll back in my head, arms locked at my sides.

The coils press my gut into my throat; my eyes bulge. Everything tingles; I follow the sensation, exhausted, giving in. *I can't fight this enemy.* The green haze takes me, but it lacks the usual pleasant freedom of a jump.

I open my eyes to intense pain and cold. Sage hovers over me as my body burns. I turn, struggling against the deadly grip of a fever. I *must* fight this enemy, but not here, where I don't know how.

"Help me," the words rasp from my parched throat. She slides a dripping cloth over my forehead; I long for just one drop in my mouth. But now I'm caught in a nether land, hovering between worlds where there is no pain. I tilt forward, and the inevitable pull of the spirit draws me with ever-increasing speed.

The snake cinches tighter, no air, so dry. *Hadena.* But the blades are trapped, just like my arms. Face crushed against the powdered dirt, I can't even whimper. *Hadena.* I grit my teeth, straining against the bone-crushing force. *Nothing shall by any means harm me.*

It's laughable, those words beneath this grip, life ebbing.

No! I believe. *Hadena.* I hold the name in my mind, veins on the verge of exploding, refusing to let go of the truth.

"Hadena." With no air, it's a weak whisper; but I feel the blades move. A surge of energy rises.

"Hadena." I won't let go; it's what the Lawgiver said, so it *must* be. I imagine the sharp edges snapping open, cutting through the coils, bending all my will toward it. Hadena inches forward again. In my mind, I stab the snake as it struggles to slither out of sight.

"Nothing..." I mouth the words as Hadena snaps open, warmth flowing from the glistening black scales.

I drag in a desperate breath, twist the blades, driving them deeper. The snake hisses, and its slitted eye ignites with pain. My numb arms find room to move; Hadena's bite flays the coil of muscle, and the snake's grip falls away.

It slithers past with a halting motion and I make the last stab I'd envisioned. Lungs heaving, I get to my feet before the exhaustion renders me inert. *Water.* I must have it. I stumble forward, leaning on the blistering heat of a boulder.

The sight of a rank pool of water with a rim of white foam at its edges consumes me. I freeze, shrinking behind the rock; a lion crouches at the far end, lapping. My dry tongue longs to move in unison with his. Statue-still, I hide until he finishes and turns away with dirty water dripping from his mouth.

Waiting till I'm sure he's beyond sight is almost more than I can do. In a crazed rush, I drop to my knees, scooping up hot water to guzzle. Intense burning clutches and I choke, spewing and roiling at the searing salt of the vile water. I wheeze, my throat swelling at the punishment. I roll with my cheek to the dirt, retching.

Empty. Curling on my side, I fight the intense burning of the salt in my mouth, nose, and throat. In the emptiness of my soul, I cry out in desperation. *Savior, my Hope, ALMIGHTY. Help me now.*

The black fingers of death close in, so dry. Unable to move or speak, I wait, shifting my focus with herculean effort. The Lion, the Almighty, *I see Him*. My nose twitches, *water*.

My muscles screaming, I try to turn my head. Sniff… *Water. Where?* I flop onto my back, searching for the scent. *Water.* Not two feet in front of me, the ground is wet. The damp spot grows.

Arms like rubber, I inch forward on my belly toward the spreading wet. My fingers tingle as they dig into the soft, enlivening muck. Like a tree drinking in the rain, life spreads up my skin.

A smile cracks the thick crust of dust around my mouth. This is victory, this *knowing*.

*For you died, now your life is hidden in Christ.* The water's voice ripples up through my arm. Freedom from fear…from… *me.* Receiving Him.

I roll in the shallow puddle, muscles twitching as they revive. Lying on my stomach, I scoop a shallow impression. Soon it fills and spills over. It clears as it flows. I dip my chin and suck up the sweet, fresh life.

*Behold, I will do a new thing; shall you not know it? I will make a way in the wilderness, and rivers in the desert.*

Even in this desolate place, I'm not alone. Surrounded by lions, He's here. Even when I'm weak, He's enough. I gulp, jerking as the cool water flows down my throat. Still, it continues to gush up under my belly and flow beyond my chin. *Hold on!*

Within a few seconds, the rising water scoots me forward as the flow grows in volume. My path glitters under the flow. Now I slip downhill on a steady stream, reaching down at arm's length to walk on hands and knees in it. Slurping as I go, my mind getting sharper by the second.

*You have prepared a table before me in the presence of my enemies.*

I lift my gaze, scanning as I float downstream around the bend. And enemies there are. Scarred, war-torn heads pop up as I whisk into full view. Dead eyes lock on to me from every direction. The closest three jump up and rush forward. I observe them, without changing position. The biggest lion bobs his head, trying to figure out how to reach me. He steps forward, one paw dipping under the flow.

His reaction is astonishing, shooting straight into the air as if something electrocuted him. A smile curls one side of my mouth.

The other two sink to their bellies, watching as the first one writhes on the ground.

The lions drink the bitter saltwater that had sent me over the edge of dehydration, but they can't abide this living water. I duck my head under, eyes open; my path still glimmers under the flow of water. Protected by the vibrant life, I sweep along at a fast clip, the depth still swelling by the second. It's not a wide stream and just a few feet separate me from the lions, but the water is deep. As I glide by, every so often a lion tries snatching at me. Each one blasts into the air as soon as their paw touches the water.

I settle in, not watching the lions so close, trusting the water. It still speaks; I hear its voice, yet somehow, I'm still not catching it all, as if I understand only a fraction of the words.

Taking a deep breath, I dive under, swimming with the current. The thrill of being submerged is stronger than I expected. The water is intoxicating; its life seeps through my skin, my mind sure and focused. Too soon, my lungs are bursting for air. I fight surfacing for as long as I can. My head breaks the water, the feel of the air almost hateful. I inhale a giant breath and dive again. The words come.

*He…he…who would…save his life…life…life will lose it. But he…he…who would lose his life…life for My sake will save it.*

Understanding comes. The words combine with my lungs' overwhelming desire to suck in the water. Yet I resist, surfacing to haul in air. I twist hard to the side as a lion's claws part my wet hair. *That was close.* The width of the river has tightened up, allowing them to reach my head. I dodge another wicked swipe from the far side. When I dive again, the words are louder.

*He who would save his life will lose it, but he who would lose his life for My sake will find it.*

I stay under until my lungs are screaming. Another few seconds and I won't be able to keep from sucking in. I look up through the distortion of the surface to find lions lining the banks, rushing to keep up. I must breathe.

Tilting my head back, I try to let my nose and mouth escape the safety of the water. *BAM.* A lion braves the punishment to reach me, catching me in the face. I spin crazily at the concussion. The river doesn't run red; but I didn't get a full breath, and I struggle for air right off. Nearing the surface, more claws rake down at me. The lion shoots into the air, but another takes his place. *Can't surface.*

My brain goes wild, scrambling for survival. A chaotic moment passes as my muscles buck. My empty lungs pull hard. *Can't hold it.* I let go. Give up. *I don't want my life anymore; I want the water's life.* I open my mouth and water pushes at the gate of my throat. My eyes are wide open as my lungs fill with water *so heavy.* I struggle, blackness descends like a blanket; but seconds before I'm gone, everything changes.

Instead of blackness, I see light. *Light within the water.* The sound of a mighty wind pummels me, thundering in my chest. There's a brilliant explosion as I breathe out water and suck more in. The second lungful blasts more words straight into my depths— clear and fluent.

*But you will receive power when the Holy Spirit has come upon you, and you will be My witnesses…even to the remotest part of the earth.*

I open my eyes, *Sight*. I have never known such. I inhale another breath of water. Waves of life ripple and flow through my being—every cell, every thought. I had been, all my life, seeing, living through a fog, making out hazy outlines.

The truth is revealed as the veil tears away. Things I struggled so hard to believe before, now they simply *are*. The truth—I breathe it in. It is not of my world, it's foreign, but so real. Words flow from my mouth. I speak them into the water, uncontainable, another tongue. With water flowing through my lips, they are pure life.

Power surges, spreading from my chest out to my fingertips, and it keeps going. Unable to contain it, I swim, slicing through the water. There is no end to this strength. The infinite has overtaken me and all my own limits have fallen away.

Arms stroking hard, flashes of light emanate from my skin. The pale glow I'd had before has increased to an undeniable brilliance. The power builds; I can't move fast enough to use it all. I open my mouth, shouting in sheer joy.

Then, the water dives into the ground. My knees and palms scrape the ground, liquid flowing off me. Eyes wide, surrounded by air, I wonder what to do with my lungful of water. The lions circle up, their evil eyes waiting for the now ankle-deep water to recede. I exhale, water running down my chin. *Will I make the switch back to breathing air?* Empty now, and breathing in, there's another explosion of energy.

I roar, throwing back my head, loosing the power. The lions respond and the ground shakes at their combined roar.

I grin. *"Hadena."*

The smooth slicing sound of my daggers unglues me. Crouching, I catapult forward. *Hadena* flashes a silvery light as I drive hard into the wall of lions. My blades flare as I fell lion after lion. One rises, towering on his hind legs.

Bellowing, I surge inside his reach, raking his exposed stomach, twisting. I force Hadena into the jaw of another springing from behind, keep driving it until his teeth snap shut. Under the brute force of my onslaught, the lions fall and shy away. I pursue them as they scatter, hissing, ears flat against their heads. I can't contain the energy in my legs, so I run like never before. The wind of my passing draws tears from my eyes.

A war cry escapes as I fly down the valley. Running like a machine, I crash into a group of snarling lions that hadn't seen me coming. Bowling one over, I leap clear of his massive bulk as he sprawls in front of me.

*Hadena* slashes the other two; I duck under a nasty swipe, claws raking my shirt. Chest heaving, I stand, staring down at the lion. He sinks to the ground, dropping his gaze. Submission.

"Ha!" Both daggers catch him in the back and all three tuck their tails and run.

I soar through the valley, leaping over boulders. Exhilarated by the sheer speed, I lean forward; the lions are mere blurs now.

The landscape changes, the dry and dead giving way to green. My pounding feet hit lush grass. Splashing through a stream, I can't contain a shout. As the water touches my legs, the energy multiplies again.

A wall of trees rises in the distance. The pine needles scrape as I pass. Under their onslaught, I slow, grinning from ear to ear. I'd never known life before the water and I became one. I'd felt life on the outside; I'd eaten life. *Thought* I possessed it, but now it is *in* me. It's the water that gives life and keeps me alive; but now it's no longer working from the outside: it fills me. Every fiber given to it.

The soft pine mulch sends up an incredible scent, and the hush of the forest engulfs me. I stop to listen to the silence. Eyes closed, I wait. Knowledge comes without words. I hear nothing; but I know, ahead I will climb a mountain, and there something awaits. My eyes snap open, ready. I step out along my path.

Climbing invigorates me as the ledge thins, clinging to the rock that glitters with a myriad of gems. My golden thread clings to the slim ridge of stone ahead as a fierce wind buffets with nothing but air below. Turning sideways, I shuffle, belly and fingers scraping the rock.

Soon enough, I'm standing on a wide, flat ledge. I shake out my calves and hands, stepping forward to where my path disappears into the mouth of a cave. Hands outstretched, fingering the cold, wet walls, I follow the golden thread deeper into the cave.

A wavering light ahead draws me. With bated breath, I reach the bend, peering with one eye around the rough wet rocks. Centered in a small, domed room is a small table. A thick candle wavers in the cool air. Next to it sit a cup and a plate. I stare at the scene. Something's different. Scowling, I study the small space. The place contains a deep sense of gravity.

Studying the cup's smooth wood, there is nothing intricate or special, only a short, wide-mouthed vessel. The plate matches. On the plate sits a small loaf of bread. *Bread? Not scroll, but bread.* That's what seems so strange. Stepping into the room is like entering a cloud. A strong sense of awe and reverence overcomes me. I drop to my knees.

Raeuel steps forward from the shadows; I flinch at his sudden presence. We speak no words. In his hands, he holds a tiny platter—but not the one from the table below. He offers it to me.

I'm relieved to see two pieces of scroll upon it. My fingers tremble as I reach for them. They are cool on my tongue and even before I chew, I hear the words in my soul.

*Take, eat, this is my body… This is my blood of the New Covenant, which is shed for many.*

The image of the Lion of the Tribe of Judah comes to me, so far beyond the reach of pain or suffering. Yet He humbled Himself, became sin for me. I take the second piece.

*As often as you eat this bread and drink this cup, you proclaim the Lord's death until he comes. Whoever therefore eats the bread or drinks the cup of the Lord in an unworthy manner will be guilty concerning the body and blood of the Lord. But let a man examine himself and then so eat of the bread and drink of the cup. For anyone who eats and drinks without discerning the body eats and drinks judgment on himself. That is why many of you are weak and ill and some of you have died. If you judged yourselves, truly, you would not be judged.*

On my knees, I close my eyes; the severity of this act settles in. I lay it all before Him; anything that is of me, so finite, I don't want it. He meets me here, within. Goose bumps rise on my skin. I lean forward and my forehead rests on the cool stone.

"Now is the time; take and eat." Raeuel's hushed voice breaks the silence.

Lifting my eyes, I look at the bread. *Real bread.* My hand trembles as I take it. There is no explosion of energy or light as with the water; but as I chew, life is entering every place. Tilting the cup, I shiver.

*No weapon fashioned against you will prosper.*

I am one with Christ. It is a treasure beyond compare.

Now upon the table I see yet another cup. It hadn't been there before. I look around for Raeuel, but he's gone again. Getting up, I find a thick paste inside, much like the pine salve. Lifting it to my nose, I find an alluring soft scent. *Eye salve. Perfect sight.*

I dip my fingers in, smear the salve over my closed eyes, forehead, and temples. At first, I feel nothing; then the salve burns icy-hot. It tingles, creating more heat. I clench my eyes shut tighter.

The sensation becomes so intense that I drop to my knees again. Soon I'm curled on my side, light dancing inside my eyelids at the heat on my face.

Time passes. The sensation subsides. I dare to crack open one eye, searching for a difference. Though I see nothing new, there's a perception; maybe connection would be a better word. The memory of my life as a SEAL, where my body is on the *Olympia*, has been almost unreachable by willful memory here in the spirit. But now I have an awareness, as if the parts of me are now linked.

If I think on it hard enough, I can see Sage holding my hand, watching over me, though the image is wavering. I shiver; if this sight carries over to the physical, so that I can see into the spirit when I'm trapped in the flatness of the world....

The mountain lies far behind, shrouded in mist. Familiar land stretches out ahead. The knowledge of the physical still hovers in my consciousness. I stride through the deep woods, thinking hard. When I reconnect with my body, the physical is so strong, so overwhelming, it sweeps the spirit under. I imagine remaining in the spirit while walking in the flesh. *The original order of man.* Man was created this way. Spirit, mind, and body. In that order. I cradle the image in my mind.

The *Engage* is there, glowing green. The picture is so crisp, I can study the turrets empty of weapons. Now I'm on the deck of the *Olympia*, staring hard at the *Engage*, remembering Project 157. The ship disappears, and my skin glows with a soft white light. The vision fades, losing me.

I shake out my hands. The hut lies to the south; my path leads that way and the thought makes me smile. I step over a rock ledge to find a row of lion prints on a small shelf of sand.

My eyes narrow, scanning. *Ready.* I would have been sweating before. Not so now. Last night I'd caught sight of two lions stalking an old woman as she shuffled along. They had borne *Hadena's* punishing blows till they turned tail and ran.

Pushing forward, I stalk through the forest. Time stretches out in this place, *familiar.* I take a step, misjudge the strength of a log as I step over it. The fibers snap under my foot. A half a second later, another snap echoes. *I didn't make that one.* Every muscle is at the ready. *Hadena.*

Daggers snapping out, I turn with fluid motion to stare into black lion eyes. *How did you creep so close?* I study the beast not five yards behind. Massive, pure evil, left ear torn—*Aseph.*

I swipe with *Hadena* at the space between us. Nodding. *This is my time; I am ready.* He crouches, condensing; I match his movement, uncoiling a second before he does.

Using my momentum, I twist, right before impact, deftly maneuvering away from his paw swipe. We circle, each seeking an opening. His massive jaws drip scant inches away, but *Hadena* flashes and Aseph shrinks back, wincing. I know the truth.

He lunges; I give to his forward motion, letting him come, rolling under his weight. I sweep *Hadena* up, feel the sudden drag as the blade connects with lion hide. The ground shudders at his roar of rage.

I clench my stomach, rolling to my feet. In the blink of an eye, he's on me. The air leaves my lungs in a rush as my chest hits the ground. With desperate speed, I twist; *Hadena* flashes up, twin edges forced hard against the soft "v" of his lower jaw. One more centimeter, one more ounce of pressure from the beast's bulk, and *Hadena* will spear right into his brain.

"Do it," I hiss at him through clenched jaws. "It will be the last thing you remember."

Hot spit drips onto my cheek as two huge paws frame my face. The lion straddles me; his massive mouth closes for a second as he swallows. His minute motion draws a drop of red.

"I don't belong to you," I whisper.

"Yesss, you do," he growls. "I'm going to eat you slow, one piece at a time."

His head is so much bigger than mine. The fear presses in, turning my muscle to liquid. I don't feel any of the power or authority. But I won't fall into that trap. It doesn't matter what I feel.

"Liar. I have authority over you," I say, full of fire, because it is so.

The lion's eyes widen as *Hadena* goes up along with my knees, lifting Aseph; he twists away. He hisses in pain as his mouth slams shut on his tongue, twin blades biting through his jaw. In a flash, I'm on my feet; Aseph crouches, dripping blood. I lunge, he whirls away; with a battle cry, I chase him as he darts through the trees.

I stand, panting, watching him run.

Muscles supple, I turn. As I pass through the forest, I hear a dull pounding. The rhythm is familiar. It grows steadily louder as my path circles around massive trees. In a small clearing beyond, I catch sight of Demyen's massive arms flexing as his axe falls. A log explodes under his punishing blow.

I hold back a bark of laughter. I've missed him. My grin grows as I time my shout of "Hey!" with the pop of his next axe strike.

He pauses, head cocking as thick chunks of wood land a few feet away. Seconds later, he strikes again.

"Hey!" I shout, along with the blow.

This time his mouth pulls to the side, questioning, and he scans the clearing. I stay tucked against the massive tree trunk next to me. Seconds inch by as Demyen scours the wooded edge around him. Seeing nothing, he wipes sweat from his brow and turns back to his woodpile.

I shout louder this time as the log bursts apart.

He turns in my direction, leans on his axe handle.

Grinning wide, I step out into the clearing. Demyen's nonchalant slouch on his axe shifts to full attention. As I approach, a grin splits his dark beard on recognizing me. As I near, he leans forward, his eyes studying my face and my arms. His shout takes me off guard.

"Baptized, Boy?" His voice carries it all, the intense joy in the knowledge of it and the relief as of a father's receiving a son. He throws back his head and looses a wild whoop. The hair on my arms stands on end.

Still, he shouts until the veins in his neck stand forth and the air crackles. Twenty feet still separate us as he refills his lungs. The sheen of tears in this mighty man's eyes undoes me.

Unable to contain it, he throws back his head again, and I twitch as the sound hits me. I can do nothing else; opening my mouth, I tilt my chin to the brilliant blue sky.

The heavens thunder back. A wind stirs, swirling and tugging at the sound of our bellowing voices. Then something I have never known in this world hits my forehead. *Rain?* It pours down. Each drop is a shock—an intense concussion of life. I raise my arms, coveting each one as we shout, intensifying the sound.

The pounding, drumming voice of the rain is unlike any other water voice; I can't speak the words it utters. Demyen's war cry morphs into laughter as the rain fades into a patter.

I cross the distance to him, and we embrace. Demyen's square hand slaps my back and I'm shocked to find my bulk almost matches his. He holds me at arm's length, his green eyes searching deep.

"Ha!" He slaps my chest. "Eh, Boy, you've grown! Baptized! LORD ALMIGHTY!"

# 8
# SAGE



I sit, watching Jacob breathe. It's only been three hours since his last jump, but I dare not take my eyes off him. Sutton's been in twice. She's definitely prepping to implant something. I've been playing along; it's imperative that I'm in the room when she does.

*Is Jacob sweating?* I press my palm against his forehead, hiss through my teeth. I grab a thermometer; it reads 104°. I turn up his IV to full speed and administer Tylenol, then swab his throat.

"How high is it?" Sutton's voice fills the room. She gives me the creeps over that comm system.

"104°." I check it again. "And rising." My hands fly, rushing through the flu test: it's negative. It's not your average fever. *Shoot.*

"I'm bringing ice," Sutton says.

"Hurry." Panic sets in. *What's causing it?* The fever came so hard and fast. If it's a side effect of the project, it may prove uncontrollable.

Jacob twitches. *Coming back already?* "Jacob!" I take his hand. "Fight, you hear?"

His glassy eyes slide open, agony clear. He groans, shivering. Gritting his teeth, he curls to the left, straining to move; the green haze rises off him again.

I strain to catch his voice. "I'm going back."

"What?" I bite my lip. "Can you do that?"

If I believe anything he's told me, then this is a battle he has to fight in some other world. I freeze, remembering his combat with Tex in the dark; it *must* be true.

"Help me."

I snatch a cloth from the sink, hands shaking, dunk it in the pitcher of ice water. I scarcely squeeze it, just slop it onto his forehead. He shivers hard, eyes sliding shut, going limp.

"Battle hard, Jacob. You've got to win this round." I rock back and forth, watching him. *Lord God, have mercy.*

Sutton bursts through the door, followed by the male nurse pushing a cart of ice. She whips back the sheet and we scoop ice. His skin is so hot it melts on impact, water flowing to the floor.

"Come on, Jacob," I whisper. Sutton presses the thermometer against his skin. "106.4°." She pulls a syringe from her pocket, readies the IV tube.

"Wait!" I say. The flush has left his skin. "Take his temp again."

I nod, positive; his chest is cooler under my fingers.

Sutton runs the temp again "102.2°." She holds it there. "101°." She shakes her head, letting out a slow breath. "99°. We're in the clear." She purses her lips in frustration. "What was that? We've got to get a handle on this."

"Whatever door you unlocked with that experiment is wide open. His EEGs agree: things are happening to him while he's out."

Sutton eyes me. I have to get into her good graces, so I can attend whatever implant she's planned.

I have to give her something. "He said it's his spirit that leaves, which I can't disagree with. Gamma waves are always associated with spiritual perception."

"Yes, but a soldier who falls unconscious is useless." She clears her throat, adding, "He'd be a detriment to himself and all involved. It's imperative that we stop these episodes."

I nod with enthusiasm. "Absolutely." I run with the implant theory. "Have you noticed how his theta waves spike right before he wakes up? We've never had an EEG running when he makes a jump. But controlling those theta waves might accomplish that goal."

Sutton sighs, studying me. "I have something I want to show you."

Sweat breaks out on my back as she shuffles through her paperwork. "You were right." She hands me a sheet of paper with a chemical diagram at the top. K-60 typed next to it. "Didn't seem like there was a better name."

My mouth hangs open as I peruse the information.

"So, it's interacting with the mitochondria?"

She nods. "Nearly doubling the normal energy output."

"That explains his speed increase and wound healing." I stare hard at the page, thinking about positrons created by K-40. My eyes go wide as the pieces fall into place. *Is it possible that a positron is part of the spiritual world? That a normal molecule is its physical counterpart?*

*Is that why they annihilate when they meet? What if Jacob can jump onto the spiritual side of the world because the K-60 assists, allowing a previously unknown bond between the two primary sources of matter in the universe? Which enables him to move between two realities?*

Sutton continues, "You've only slept 8.4 hours in the last 6 days. Your levels of K-60 are almost as high as Carter's. You should be exhausted, but you don't seem to be."

I stare at the paper, trying to conceal the fear that leaps up at her words. She knows how many minutes I've slept. *Classified property.* My heart rate picks up: guinea pig. Thoughts racing from one dark imagination to another, I clear my throat. *Get it together.*

"With his current K-60 levels, his wound recovery rate is a little over doubled. We are very excited. Now that we know what it is, we've found K-60 present in every human blood sample we've tested. But in a normal individual, it only exists in minuscule amounts and its effect is negligible. K-60 seems to activate a link in the human genome, increasing cellular energy outputs, and allowing neurons to fire faster. No one has ever bested Tex before."

I cover my revulsion at her hand in all of this. "Jacob seems to have gained some sort of insight; he knows things he shouldn't."

She studies me for a moment. "I'm going to let him stabilize for twelve hours after this fever; then we're going to implant a chip in his brain that should allow us to prevent future episodes by controlling those theta wave spikes."

I nod. *No, you're not.* "How can I prep him?"

"He's already had the cyclosporine and azathioprine. Monitor him extra close. If the fever so much hints at returning, we'll have to reschedule."

"Yes, ma'am." In ten hours, I'll draw blood and hide the vial to submit later. That way, they won't know what I've done.

Sutton comes through the door with an entourage. My stomach squelches. *I've got you, Jacob; I do.* Two nurses wheel equipment into the room, setting up. I sterilize at the sink, shrugging into a surgical suit.

"We shouldn't have to shave him; the procedure should be complete in forty-five minutes. Rathmore, roll him."

The male nurse who always accompanies Sutton steps forward. I stare at the imaging system Sutton is positioning next to the exam table. *Wait for it, Sage, wait for the right time. It will come.*

I help ease Jacob onto his stomach. Rathmore adjusts a pillow so he can breathe while on his stomach, keeping his neck straight. Sutton lays out her scalpels, measures his vertebra, and marks his skin at the base of his skull. I wipe sweat off my nose with my sleeve, don't want it to show.

Sutton is gloved up and sterile, opening a small box. Within is a tiny cylinder with four minute wires protruding from one end.

"1.4 million." She glares us all down. "Once the procedure is underway, there can't be any mistakes. If he comes to in the middle, we'll most likely lose him and the chip. Emerson, monitor his theta waves. If they spike, administer phenobarbital ASAP."

I nod, turning to draw a vial of it and setting the loaded syringe on the table.

She takes a deep, steadying breath, readying her scalpel.

*I'm sorry, Jacob.* Stepping close, I take one syringe of the cocktail I'd made from my pocket and stab him in the front of his arm, motion concealed under the table. I stash the empty needle in the back of the drawer. Her knife descends. Jacob shudders.

"Emerson!"

"No! He's not coming back; his theta waves are steady." I hold him down as he seizes. "This is something else!"

Sutton swears. "Give him the phenobarbital now!" I reach for the syringe; Rathmore snatches it from my hand and administers it. The seizure subsides. Sutton slides the lid over the box, swearing again.

"Clean it up; we'll have to wait." Her motions are brisk as she packs up. She stares down at Jacob, and I long to step between them. "Next time he's alert, we are going to run some mental aptitude tests." She chews her lip, deep in thought. "It's possible there is another way."

She whisks out the door, and I plunk into my chair as soon as they're gone, hands shaking. What if he never wakes up? What if the drugs prevent him from jumping? There is just too much I don't know. If he stays in a coma, it will be my fault. *Please come back, Jacob.*

Sutton's voice is crisp over the intercom. "Full round of stats, Emerson. Check your email for the testing instructions." My mouth goes dry. *She suspects.* I force myself to nod, moving to obey. "I need a fresh blood test from you as well."

*It's not a request. I feel like a lab rat curled up in its cage.*

I draw Jacob's blood sample, slide it into my right pocket. Shielding the drawer with my hip, I pull the blood sample from a few hours ago and slip it into the same pocket. It's cool in comparison, easy to tell which one I need.

His vitals are good. But a major problem is, I can't get rid of the evidence. I've got the empty cocktail syringe and a fresh blood sample proving I administered it. It's not like tossing them in the garbage can will do any good. They are watching closer than they did with the note. Squatting over my personal bag, I tuck them deep into the bottom. I cross my arms, watching Jacob sleep.

With a twitch, he rolls off the table into a crouch, eyes full of fire. I jump at his sudden motion. Now, anything could happen. I deflate, shoulders sagging; the drugs hadn't disrupted his reconnection. Relief floods my chest, and I bite back tears. He's okay, brimming with life, in fact. I lean with my arms stiff against the exam table and blow out an enormous sigh.

"You come back stronger every time," I say.

"It's not for the reason you think, though. Not because of K-60."

"No?" I question, wondering how much he hears while he's unconscious.

"No, it's because my spirit is stronger. Potassium-60 may be a physical result of that; but it comes from my spirit." Looking into his blue eyes, I can almost believe it. "Sage, I owe you."

I sniff. *Yes.* "What for?"

He nods, that mischievous light jumping to his eye. "Many things, I suppose."

He lets the words hang in the air for a moment. They shore up my bruised emotions. *It's enough that he's standing here whole. It's all been worth it.*

"I was thinking about waking up with pants on."

But I know he doesn't mean just that.

One side of his mouth curls; mine can't help but match it. "It's against the rules, but this nice guy kept asking me to do it so…" I toss a shirt at him. "There, now you should be even happier."

He pulls it on. "I am."

And he is too. Brimming with joy, in fact. It makes me long for the same. *How can he, with Ash holding his future?*

"He doesn't," Jacob says.

"What?" My eyes widen; I hadn't spoken the thought aloud.

"What you're thinking…he doesn't. My future's in much better hands than that."

I stare at him, goose bumps racing across my skin, soaking up his confidence, feeling small and average. I don't read people's thoughts. He picks up an apple I'd left from my lunch off the table and takes a huge bite. "Um. That's good."

I turn to the laptop and ready the WAIS-IV IQ test, that's the first of a long list of intelligence and physical ability tests.

"I am way too hungry to tackle that thing right now."

I nod; only seconds pass till two full trays appear.

"So, previously, you scored a 130 on this test." I flip through his records while he eats. "That's only two points away from a membership in Mensa. Impressive."

"Losing is impressive?" He shakes his head, scraping his plate.

"In this case, yes. The test should take you under two hours. Do you think you'll be able to contain yourself that long?"

He arches one brow at me. "Maybe the mental expenditure will draw off some energy."

Talking to him makes it so tempting to forget Sutton's plans, to pretend for a minute that he will heal and return to duty.

"What?" His gaze is quizzical.

"After watching you shoot, I'm looking forward to watching you do the REST-SPER test."

"That's the one where you have to click only relevant selections, right?"

I nod, chewing my lip. *Why would Sutton want these done now? What's her angle?* "I'm required to draw an EEG while you're testing. Let's get you started on the WAIS."

I adjust the white cap over his dark hair, studying his face in the blue glow of the screen as he begins.

"You're making me nervous staring at me like that," he says, not looking up from the test.

"I highly doubt that."

"If I get a low score, it will be your fault." He flicks his gaze over to me.

I shake my head, turning back to the test orders. I let out a long breath; it's the last one that catches me. I'm in it. The orders are for another nurse to set a list of objects in front of Jacob, give him twenty seconds to study each individually, then record as many details as possible. The two objects listed I can't figure are me and a huge steel bolt. *What. On. Earth?*

"Done."

I read the clock. Sixty-two minutes to complete the WAIS.

"That was fast."

He flexes his arms, getting up from the chair.

"Can you contain yourself through some more?"

"Yeah. What's next?" He drops to the floor in a quick set of sit-ups, burning energy, white EEG wires slapping the floor with each movement.

I open the REST-SPER test. "Objective: click on the relevant stimuli on the screen as rapidly as possible, ignoring irrelevant objects."

"Sounds like a video game."

"Pretty much."

"Just warning you… I never play them; they're a waste of time."

"I'll note that in your file, sir," I say as he takes the chair. I mutter, "To whom it may concern, please note this test is viewed by the subject as a waste of time."

I click start and stand behind him. I keep up with him at first, mentally clicking the white circle appearing around the screen. As the seconds pass, the screen populates with more objects, and he easily outpaces me. I want to study each new item, but he remains focused on anything relevant to the white circle.

When the time is up, he pushes back, arms across his chest. "Let me do it again."

"You didn't know that video games are addictive?" I tease, as if we're not prisoners here, while I reset the test and bump it up to the hardest level.

He lets out a slow breath. "Okay, start it."

As he works, a distinct vibe flows off him, as if the air were fresher. He finishes and I move to the stats page, my mouth falling open.

"What changed?" I ask, studying the readout. His second score on the harder test is *15 percent* higher.

"You really want to know?"

"Desperately," I say, while thinking, *So does Sutton*.

He reaches over for the Bible and thumbs to the end.

"And I was in the Spirit on the Lord's day," he reads, nodding like it should explain everything.

I pull my mouth to one side. "That's not much of an explanation."

"I never got it before, either. But a human in covenant with God has access to the infinite. The knowledge only comes through the Spirit. I've lived just in physical and mental awareness, but that's not what I was made for. Now, new life is here."

He taps the screen on the higher score. "In the covenant, mankind already possesses everything. They have access to all wisdom and knowledge. Even physical ability." He crosses his arms again, nodding to himself. "But it takes practice to live in it." He flips the crinkly pages again. "'According as His divine power has given to us all things that pertain to life and Godliness through the knowledge of Him who called us to glory and virtue.'" He smiles at me. "But I'm preaching. What comes next?"

Right on cue, Rathmore backs through the door in his white lab coat, pulling a small cart through the doorway.

"Looks like just one more test," I say, eyeing the random items on the cart.

"I'm Philip Rathmore, and I'll be administering this test. Carter, please take a seat on the exam table." Rathmore explains the test and sets the first object on the small sink. Jacob stares at him till Rathmore has a sheen of sweat on his upper lip.

"You have twenty seconds to study the object."

Jacob turns to the dive mask Rathmore set out. We go through five more random items until Rathmore holds his hand out to me. Face red, I step near the sink.

"You're the next item?" Jacob asks.

"Twenty seconds," Rathmore says.

I bite the inside of my cheek as Jacob's blue eyes lock on mine. Nervous energy swirls through my chest. I clench my fists, breath coming harder; now the air is snapping, and I'm struggling to stay still. Trapped in the surge of energy, I can't look away. The green haze comes next. *Will he jump, or will I? Please, no.*

"Ti…" Rathmore clears his throat. "Time."

Jacob drops his gaze to the clipboard he's been filling out. I lean back on the sink as the grip of the contact clears. Rathmore, in his radiation suit, is staring at me wide-eyed. He felt it too.

I lift my chin and arch a brow at him. "Am I finished?"

He nods, using two hands to set the massive bolt on the counter. I narrow my eyes as Jacob studies it. Turning to the EEG machine, I examine the last hour's readouts. His gamma waves spiked at the exact time of his second REST-SPER test, and again, a few seconds ago, while he was watching me. I peer over Jacob's shoulder as he writes, read his list on me.

5' 6"

CAUCASIAN

BLONDE, BLUE-EYED

# SAGE



I stifle a gasp, covering the small scar where the bowstring had caught me as a beginner.











My face flames at the details. I move on to his commentary on the bolt.

Rathmore sets the bolt back on a small cart. As he steps forward again, Jacob jerks into action, snatching Rathmore's wrist and slamming him against the sink.

"Jacob!" I shout, shocked at his abuse as the EEG cap falls to the floor.

Jacob's growling in Rathmore's ear. "What was it?"

He reaches down and pulls an empty syringe from Rathmore's grasp.

"What was it?" His voice is even lower.

Beneath the suit, Rathmore's trembling.

"Zolpidem." His voice comes out too high.

Jacob looks over at me, questioning.

"That's a powerful sedative and hypnotic." Each word comes out quieter.

*Maybe there's another way.* Sutton's remark comes back full force.

*No!* Rathmore had sideswiped the injection into Jacob's arm as he passed. Tears jump to my eyes as Jacob releases Rathmore and takes an unsteady step back. Everything comes crashing down; he's just a science experiment to them. The door bursts open as Marines with thick black clubs fill the room.

"No! Listen to me! Stop!" But they don't.

Jacob takes three of them down; but they fall on him en masse, striking hard with the clubs as he struggles against the drug's effects. It takes six of them to hold him down.

I jump at Brook's voice behind me. "Put him in the wall restraints."

I turn. "What?" I spit the words, "He needs immediate medical attention."

"He'll have to get it in the shackles, Emerson."

I clench my jaw, rage right at the surface. He frowns at me as the guards force Jacob's limp form against the wall, cinching him in tight.

"Just get him cleaned up, Emerson. Sutton will be in soon." He turns on his heel and exits, leaving the door wide open.

*This is adding up to a disaster.* I reach high, holding Jacob's head up so he doesn't choke with his throat hanging against the neck restraint. My heart's racing, hands trembling, as I rip open an alcohol wipe with my teeth.

His eyes flutter as I clean his swollen lip, then inspect the swelling at the base of his skull, where the two hardest blows had landed. I need to check his spinal cord. A tear spills over as he groans.

"That wasn't cool," he slurs, but I'm relieved he's functioning, somehow forcing past the influence of the Zolpidem.

I shake my head; he should be out cold. "Jacob, how many fingers am I holding up?"

I put three in front of him.

"Twenty-five," he groans.

I sigh; at least he's still got his sense of humor along with his concussion. I snap my fingers at one guard. "I need an ice pack from next door and a dose of Ondansetron." Jacob blinks at me. "You have a concussion. I'll give you something for the nausea."

"No, I don't."

"Don't what?"

"Have a concussion." Each word gets stronger as he yanks against the restraints, getting nowhere. I let go of his head; he's holding his own now.

I frown at him. "Uh, you do actually."

"That's a fact; but the truth is, I don't. Soon enough, the facts will align with the truth."

I stand in front of him, open-mouthed as his pupils go from dilated to normal; he nods his head. My stomach heaves, but I swallow it back down.

Sutton steps in, pushing a cart loaded with an unfamiliar device. She doesn't acknowledge me as she steps up to Jacob and draws blood from his arm. She sticks him twice before she hits the vein. I hate her for it.

She hands the vial to Rathmore, who inserts it into a small handheld machine. They study the readout, heads together, matching charts. Jacob stares at them, eyes dark, at war with the drug. *He should be unconscious.*

"All right, average it against his EEG from the last hour," Sutton says, snatching up his answer list from the last test. Her eyes widen as she reads it, but she steps close to Jacob, brave now that he's locked down.

"All your smart-aleck comments will soon be a thing of the past. We are going to reverse the electromagnetic field that seems to be responsible for your episodes of unconsciousness." She sticks fresh electrodes from the machine near his hairline; he glares at her till she clears her throat.

"Rathmore, finish with the electrodes." She plugs in the thick cord, then powers up the device; I read *Transcranial Magnetic Stimulation (TMS)* on its side. Those are used to treat brain abnormalities by sending concentrated magnetic pulses into specific areas of the brain.

I shake my head at Jacob, tears close.

He gazes back, gives a hint of a nod. *It will be all right.*

I sniff, *yes.* Maybe I can read minds.

Sutton double-checks the blood draw, adjusts the knobs on the TMS. I'm breathing too hard, as if I've been running sprints. Rathmore clips a heartbeat monitor to one of Jacob's pointer fingers and a lead from the TMS to the other.

"We're ready," he states, leaning toward her, voice low. "The chip would be a far better option."

Sutton lets out a deep breath, hand on the dial. "This procedure may prove to end his episodes and provide a workable project. We cannot proceed with him as unstable as he is. The Zolpidem should allow us to access his hippocampus and correct the theta waves."

"Nothing you're going to do will have any effect on me." Jacob breaks into their argument. There's not one trace of doubt in his voice, though I know he's struggling for control.

"Well, I certainly hope to find a way to help you." Sutton's tone is sickening sweet.

"You can't take what I have. It's not tangible. It doesn't matter what you change in my body. I'm not like Tex, living by your hand."

"Isn't that quaint?" she says. Then she cranks the knob, expression smug.

Jacob strains, head tilting, jaw tight. Sutton nods at a guard, who steps near and takes hold of my upper arm. I wince, powerless. The machine spits out a reading similar to an EEG, and the section labeled *hippocampus* spikes with activity. Jacob pours sweat until it runs in rivulets down his arms. He arches his back, muscles standing out.

"Sutton, shut it off!" I shout as the intense energy of a jump overtakes me, but there's no green haze falling from him, no sense of expectancy in Jacob's gaze. Still the feeling grows, shrieking through me; my stomach clenches, biceps straining hard under the guard's grip.

I look down; there's a pool of green so thick I can't see my feet. *If you smell something dead, run. Oh, God, no! Please, I can't.* The guard looks at his hand on my arm, scowling; I know the tingling sensation he's experiencing.

Jacob shouts, eyes clenched, fighting his own battle.

"No!" His roar fills the room.

A spark sizzles from the TMS; everyone jumps.

"NO!" he bellows.

Smoke rises from the electrode leads that connect him to the machine, which sends off a bigger spark. The lights blink off. There is the unmistakable sound of pistols being pulled; all I smell is smoke from the fried machine. The intensity fades and I suck in heavy breaths, clearing the sensation.

One guard snaps on a flashlight, right into Jacob's face; he's sagging once again, shallow breath chattering against the neck strap. Every gun in the room is aimed at his chest. I shrug out of the guard's grasp, rushing forward to push up his head, his swollen lip hanging.

"Run an EEG immediately. We need to know how successful we were. I need a full readout on his beta waves as soon as he's alert." Sutton steps forward, drawing another vial of blood.

I seethe my skin crawling at her nearness. *How long will it take them to re-watch the video and see how close I was to jumping?*

"He already told you it wouldn't work," I repeat his statement, solidifying it. "I need him on the table right now. The injury to his skull needs immediate attention."

She snaps her fingers; the guards jump forward, eager to do so before he wakes up. I bite my tongue hard. The guards shift him to the table and file out. Sutton is still in the doorway, watching me.

I hold her gaze, refusing to back down. She frowns, the door clicks shut, and I fall apart inside.

Jacob peers at me, one eye swollen, lip protruding. "How long was I out?"

"Fifteen minutes. Is your vision blurry?"

He squints at me. "No."

"Are your ears ringing?"

"No." His arms jerk against the restraints. "That made me angry." He sighs, eyes sliding shut.

I put my hand on his forehead. "Just rest now, Jacob."

Twenty minutes later, he mutters in his sleep, mumbling at first. Then I catch the words "has borne my pain."

He shifts, and I wish I had a normal bed for him. I slide another folded blanket under his injured head. Gasping, I run my finger over the base of his skull, where I find only normal bone and no thick swelling like there had been minutes ago. It sends a shiver up my spine.

The grip of the energy and green haze isn't far enough away for me to ignore. I couldn't stop it, couldn't force it to go away, just like the sting. Terror makes my thoughts jumpy. I strain to remember everything he's told me.

The likelihood of my surviving a jump is extremely low. Fear clamps down hard. Jacob barely made it the first few times. A new thought hits me: what if my experience matches Rivera's? I lean hard on the table, knowing my face portrays my struggle. Sutton can think what she wants; I can't contain it.

I slide into the chair, lean my head on the desk, and do something I haven't done seriously since high school, words catching in my bent elbow. "Oh, Lord God." Memories surface from the youth group at First Baptist; I swallow hard. "Please save Jacob and me from these people. Make a way where there is none."

With a deep sigh, I feel the tension drain away. When I raise my head, the clock reads four hours later.

I turn, blinking, to find Rathmore watching Jacob's EEG readout.

"Sorry, I fell asleep," I say, horrified to find him in the room.

He looks at me, brown eyes soft behind his mask. "You were exhausted. It's been a long road. His readouts look good." He studies Jacob's face closely, leaning in, and says, "His lip and eye are almost healed."

*He's right.* I fold my arms, cradling the peaceful knowledge.

"His K-60 levels have jumped since the procedure. Do you think they rise in response to injury?" he asks, as if we're friends.

"Well, the last scan showed higher concentrations at the site of injury. There's so much we don't know. What's stimulating its production? Is it even what's responsible for all this?" I shake my head.

"I know. If he shows any sign of brain injury, we'll take him over for a CAT scan. But at this rate, I think any damage is already cleared up. His recovery is even faster than Tex's and he doesn't even have the S5 serum."

I shudder at the word. "Can I unstrap him?"

"Not without clearance." He frowns down at Jacob, then adds, "We're..."

I cut him off. "...going to need a blood sample from me."

He nods. "Yes, do you want me to draw it?"

"No." Minutes later, I hand him the warm vials, detached from whatever the results might be.

"I'm also going to need to give you this." My eyes fall to the syringe in his hand. "We've synthesized the K-60, but we can't get it to survive once it's injected into other subjects."

"And you want to try it in someone with already high levels." I cross my arms, but the peace is gone. "Do I have a choice?"

His eyes soften further as he shakes his head. "I'm sorry."

I heave a deep breath. "I'll take it without the beating, thank you."

I drill him with the memory of their savage behavior toward Jacob. He drops his eyes, knowing. I bite back tears as the needle pricks my arm. I shudder as the cold tingle spreads up my arm.

"Finished?" I ask in an icy voice.

He shuffles out, the motion awkward in his radiation suit. I stretch the tension out of my back, ignore the sensations in my arm, then take Jacob's hand.

"Well, it's been quite a day," I whisper.

Jacob's eyes slide open and he takes a deep breath. "It's not over yet."

"Oh." I'm not sure I can take any more.

"Brooks, I'm hungry. Are you going to let me out of these things?" He jerks his arms, voice solid, waiting for a response.

Long seconds tick by. The door swings and two trays of food slide onto the desk. It's a good sign.

After locking the door, Brooks says over the comm, "Emerson, unstrap him."

I heave a sigh, rushing to do so. When he sits up, I take his arm.

"I'm all right, was just worn out. Spent a lot of energy at once." He eases off the table, stretching his wide chest. "Whew. Come on, when was the last time you ate?"

I break out of scanning him for signs of brain trauma, shaking my head. "I don't even know."

"Well, you're dropping weight like crazy. Which one do you like better, beef stew or lasagna?" He settles into the chair with a wince, shaking his head in disgust. "There's no watermelon."

*How can he be so casual when our lives are on the line?*

"Beef stew." I smile at him with a corner of my mouth, so glad he's conscious, his mood wearing off on me, taking the bowl. "It's actually pretty good," I say, hungry for the first time in days.

He inhales the lasagna, and I shove the bread in his direction. "I'm not a big carb fan."

"Good for energy." It's gone in three bites. I enjoy watching him eat, debate telling him about the K-60 injection. The color comes back in his face, as if the foods flipped a switch.

"It's time," he whispers, with eyes deeper than the ocean.

"Ash!" he barks. "Permission to go topside, sir."

Goose bumps rise on my arms; I feel as if we're sliding in front of an avalanche. We wait in a long silence; a sense of doom descending on me.

"Jacob, what are you going to do?" I know he can't give an honest answer.

"Sage Emerson. I'll tell you something. It is the Spirit that gives life; the flesh counts for nothing. There's a lot of life yet to live, and we're going to live it."

The door opens; the hall is lined with the entire crew of armed Marines, their faces nervous, pistols drawn but pointing at the floor.

"Topside granted, Carter." Brooks waits in the hall, at attention.

As I pass him, sticking close behind Jacob, I notice the sheen of sweat on his brow. Jacob remains uncontrollable; Brooks has no button to push. *Thank You, God.* We clip up the metal stairs; I'm not winded when we reach the top, even after days of relative inactivity.

The seas are rough; a dark cloud hangs on the horizon, the waves white-capped. I hug myself against the cutting wind. The *Engage* takes the ocean's battering in the near distance, rocking but anchored solid. The aft deck of the *Olympia* is full of sailors, all eyes on Jacob.

He stands at attention, staring at Brooks with an unnerving intensity. There's purpose flowing off him, as if he's following a prearranged plan. Jacob turns to the *Engage*, takes a deep breath, and lets it out.

Tense seconds pass as the ship glows green and wavers, but I dare not take my gaze off Jacob. The surging energy reaches out to us across the distance; the sailors shift, drawn by the spectacle of the glowing ship. They throw their hands up to ward off the vibe flowing from the ship.

Jacob seems translucent, his skin glowing with a soft light. I blink, and the *Engage* disappears in my peripheral vision, the water crashing into the imprint of its hull. Jacob looks over his shoulder at me, so beautiful, transparent and full of light at the same time. He nods once, then disappears.

I snap my attention back toward the now-flat ocean where the *Engage* had once sat as if nothing happened.

Brooks turns, shouting, "Carter..." Finding him gone, chaos breaks out. "Hunt him down!"

The men spread out, pistols leading. Brooks pulls a device out of his pocket. His thumb trembles as he swipes it open.

"He's on the second deck in Ash's quarters."

Now I know what Sutton did when I got stung. I join the crazed rush down into the ship. Jostling for position, I elbow my way next to Brooks in front of Ash's door. It's locked from within. Brooks pounds on the door; his radio flashes.

Ash's voice echoes, lacking its usual confident tone. "Stand by, Brooks."

I look up to find his jaw clenched tight. He turns to one guard. "Prep some blasting caps."

My mouth goes dry. I swing my med pack off my shoulder and dig way down for the stethoscope at the bottom. Brooks reaches for the earpieces as I press the end against the metal wall; I relinquish one but keep a death grip on the other. Our foreheads press together as we strain to hear the low voices beyond the metal wall. I readjust the end until I can hear.

"You're government property now." Ash's voice is strained.

I imagine Jacob is not being gentle.

"No, sir, I never agreed to that. Remember Tony Marks?"

Brooks goes pale; it's clear he does, although the name means nothing to me.

"The question is, how you live with yourself with the blood of all these soldiers on your hands? Tony Marks, David Sutherland, Steve Rivera?" Jacob's voice grows with each name.

"You forced Marks past the edge of sanity before you killed him. Deemed him an obsolete experiment after all your torture."

I press my forehead hard against Brooks's as we strain to hear; his skin is cold and clammy.

"I won't be among them, *period*. You hear? I'm out. And Tex—with all the mind control you think you have over him, he's playing you."

Everything goes quiet, and I clutch the earpiece tighter. Sutton barrels in; we ignore her, pressing against the wall. The location device beeps as the door unlocks. Ash steps out, pale as a ghost, looking like an old man.

"He's on deck three. No! Four."

I scoop up my med pack. That's where the pool is; we've got to hurry. Sure enough, Jacob is floating face down. Four guards dive in, rolling him over the edge. He's pale, not breathing. I clamp his nose shut; two breaths later, he's breathing on his own.

Sutton monitors his pulse. "He's stable. Rathmore, take over for Emerson."

"I'm all set, Dr. Sutton, thank you."

She pulls the empty syringe of my seizure cocktail and Jacob's blood sample from her coat.

I stop breathing.

"Put Carter in the wall restraints, Rathmore. Lieutenant Smith, Emerson is now under arrest under the Uniform Code of Military Justice. Take her to C29. Delaney, get a full blood draw from her now. You'll perform a spinal tap and PET scan at 600 hours." Each word a link in the chain, she condemns me.

I am worse than a defector, on the level of a scientific experiment. Smith forces my hand behind my back.

"No, Sutton, don't do this."

Smith forces me around; all my fighting only makes my shoulder sore. Everything crumbles down; I have no control and no voice. I balk at the door of a small empty room; its one bare light is too bright. I finger the syringe of my last seizure cocktail deep in my lab coat pocket. Even if I take Smith out, how would I get off the ship with Jacob's inert body?

"I do not give you permission to take that. I have the right to speak to an attorney." I glower at Delaney as he preps to take my blood.

"Not here, you don't. You'll have to wait till you're landside. Orders are orders."

I sink to the cold floor when he leaves, trembling as the door slams shut. I put my forehead on my knees as I picture Jacob shackled to the wall. *Oh, Lord God Almighty, have mercy.*

# 9
# JACOB

THAT WHICH IS CONCEIVED IN
THE SPIRIT CAN BE REVEALED
TO THE MIND.

~BARRY BENNETT~

I land hard, right near the hut.

"Demyen!" I bellow. "Demyen, I need you now!"

The huts door slams open, bottom hinge snapping loose.

Demyen's green eyes are intense. "What is it, Boy?"

"I've got to get back. Things went sideways. I have to jump now."

He nods, searching. "There is a way, Boy, but it is far from here."

"I have to go now!" I'm still shouting, over the top, but this time the other world hasn't faded as it usually does.

It's hovering all around me with pulsing urgency, infringing on the beauty of this place. "Can you tell me how to get there?"

"Aye. To the north, there is a cave. I've heard the pool deep within is open, always able to carry the children of light," Demyen says.

"Raeual, I need you." I roar at the top of my lungs and Raeual appears, reins in his hand.

"Jacob…" He waits till he has my full attention. "They've taken Sage. Hurrying won't cut it. Take Haseleph. I must go request additional help."

"What?" I stare at the glistening white beast who shakes his mane.

"If you would save her, it must be so. There's not much time. We have only a slim chance of success."

Gritting my teeth, I take the reins. The horse pins his ears back. I feel the same way.

Raeual puts his palm on the beast's head and whispers into his ear. "He will carry you. Sing him a little song while he runs; he will like that."

I shake my head as Raeual disappears.

"Come, boy, I'll give you a leg up."

I step to Haseleph's side; he stomps one hoof down hard on my instep.

"Ugh." I groan in pain as I smack one hand on his neck, pushing him away.

He leans into me, but Demyen curls one finger, jams the knuckle into the horse's side. His long white tail flashes in anger, but he steps away.

"Ah." I suck in a breath.

"Up you go, Boy, before he takes off without you."

I bend my knee and Demyen hoists me up, then takes the creature's head and whispers, "The caves of the North. Fly."

With a snort Haseleph spins, wind whipping as he settles into a ground-eating gallop. I cling to his heaving back; trees and rivers flash by, but I can still see the ship. I lean forward, finding balance, letting his white mane whip my face.

I focus on the image of the ship and parts of it become clearer. *Sage.* She's curled on an empty floor of a room midship on deck three. I look up at A27; my body is strung up against the wall. It's so strange to see it.

I clench my fists in Haseleph's mane, the pulsing urgency to get Sage forcing me back to Raeual's comment. I'm not much of a singer. I make a bad start but Haseleph's ears flick up from where they been pressed flat in anger against his head.

I try again, forcing myself to focus on the time the paths converged, and He stood before me. The words come, of worship. The horse's stride lengthens. Louder I sing, not because I must, but because He is so worthy.

There's a high bank ahead; Haseleph splashes into the stream under it and I gather myself. He leaps, sucking in a great breath. Seconds of complete silence pass as we soar up. I shut my eyes as his hooves scramble to gain the high ridge, surging forward.

Finally, sides heaving, he stops at the base of a rocky outcropping. I slide off; he gives a buck in my direction. I dodge the dirt clods, and he's gone, vanished into thin air.

I turn to find my path shimmering away through the boulders. The heavy hush in the air makes me cautious. I press forward, scrambling up the altitude, frowning when my way dives into a fracture in the ground.

I lie on my stomach as I peer inside the crack in the mountain. It's dark, cold, and close. I chew on a scroll. "God has not given us a spirit of fear, but of love, and of power, and a sound mind." I take another; this one sweet as honey. "Behold, I am with you always."

It's time. I push past the intense desire to turn from this fissure in the ground and seek another way, sliding in. My chest won't fit. *Come on, Jacob.*

I study the image of Sage curled on the cold floor again. My path shimmers right before my face as I lie on the rocky ground. I expel the air from my lungs, compressing. Inching forward one shoulder at a time, rocks spearing everywhere, I clench my eyes.

*For Sage.* By the time I'm fully in the crack, it feels as if the whole mountain is pressing down on me. There's no way to turn around and forward doesn't seem to be an option either.

"Go," I growl at myself. I push forward one muscle at a time, rocks pinching my back and stomach. "I am power, love, and a sound mind," I mutter, hearing the water before I feel it. Its voice is clear and strong, drawing me forward. My outstretched fingers find its icy current.

Words come, instructions. *Deck three. Wait. Sage. Deck two. Wait. Deck one. Jump.*

I slide my chest into the flow. "*No…no…no weapon fashioned against you will prosper.*"

If I go any further, the ceiling will force me under. I inch forward into the flow, rocks forcing my face under, and take a deep breath of the cool, wet life. *The spirit.* The stream draws me forward over the slick bottom.

My lungs are so heavy, full of water; the energy surges, filling every cell. There must be a waterfall ahead; the thunder of it echoes and I surge faster in the current. My chest leaves the solid bottom at incredible speed and I plunge into the darkness.

I fall with the water, close my eyes, memorize the freedom. Tucking my arms tight around me, I twist till I'm falling feet first. The speed of a return takes me. I study the vision ahead, so clear; the *Olympia* rocks on the rough surface of the ocean far below, a bank of black clouds poised to overtake her. Straining for focus, I cut through the distance, centering in.

I search the ship, find everything exactly as I'd seen. My body hangs limp in the wall shackles. A ripple of longing surges and I leap into it, blink hard. At my core I resist the iron hand of the connection, at war with the overwhelming desire to solidify. But I see it, the way, as if my golden thread is shimmering straight ahead.

Exhaling my lungful of water, it splats onto the floor, running down my chin, making everyone jump. I clench my stomach, pulling away with everything I am, refusing to stay solid, seeking that secret middle place where realities mix. Using the massive energy from breathing the water, I'm able to move and take my body with me.

The room is full of people, except Sage. The green haze filters up. I grin wildly at the shock on Sutton's face as water drips from my chin, right before I pull back through the wall and brace for the incredible slipperiness of movement in this between place. Balancing between worlds, I know I only have so much time before the effort drains me and I slam back into a reality. Last time, the pool had literally sucked me in; I have to steer far from water.

I drop through the deck, slowing my fall with hands skidding through the walls as if they're made of putty. I push straight through two more walls, slip sliding; walking on ice would be infinitely easier. Pressing forward requires intense focus, as if it's my thoughts alone that create the movement.

I ease through the wall into Ash's quarters, find it empty. I pull the drawer that had been open last time I appeared in here. Trying to grasp the flash drive is a battle in itself. It slips through my fingers like a wet fish; I snatch it in midair over and over before I finally have it in my fist. Reaching one hand through the wall, the motion is slower, the grasp of the physical bearing down.

Sage should be just ahead. But that's it; body trembling, I have to return fully before I fall completely back into the Spirit. Leaning forward, I focus hard on the ship, the feeling of the deck under me, the scent, allowing the physical to grip me. That locked-in grip settles over my body and I stand, shoulder against the hard wall, panting and exhausted. I slip the drive into my pocket.

"Go."

Easing one eye out the door, I see an empty hallway; I turn left, midship. A voice reverberates ahead; guards are joking to pass the time.

I pause, it's coming from a recessed entryway. *Sage.* I explode into the space; two Marines crumple as I take them down. I pull keys off one, open the door. Sage huddles at the back of the cell, face a mask of fear, then rushes forward, and I brace for her impact as she wraps her arms around me.

"Jacob, we have to get off the ship." Her eyes are wild.

"Move."

We run down the hallway, back the way I came.

She takes my hand, grip desperate. "Jacob, wait. I need a knife."

She ducks into a room, searching through the desk, emptying drawers.

"We have to go now." My voice is low, still gravelly from the water.

"Here!" She comes up with a letter opener. "Turn around; this is going to hurt."

"What?"

"Listen, they've got a tracking chip in you; we don't stand a chance with it in there."

I turn, with a disgusted sound.

She pulls up my shirt. "They did it when I got stung. Wasn't sure what it was till Brooks tracked you straight to Ash."

She digs hard with the tool.

"A dull spoon might work better." I grunt the words as she saws at my right hip.

"Sorry." She comes up, fingers bloody. "Got it." A micro-sized silver tube sticks to the blood on her finger. She rushes to the head and flushes it down.

Her brown eyes are bright. "That ought to give them a run for their money."

A steady tread of footsteps echoes in the hall. Almost here. I draw a deep breath, honing in, pushing everything else aside until I'm clear and ready.

"Stop! He's dropping to deck four," Brooks shouts, so close.

Sage grips my arm as the footsteps reverse direction.

"Good thinking."

She smiles, "Handy that you usually fall through the floor though. They'll be diving in the septic tank for you. Now you're a J.E.E.P. again."

"What?"

"Just Enough Essential Parts."

Her expression makes me laugh. "Come on, we've got to make it to deck two, low and quiet."

She slips her hand into mine. It's so familiar. All the hours she spent caring for me at her own expense, I know she'd had my hand in hers. It condenses into desire: get her off the ship.

We make it halfway up the staircase before I engage three Marines. Two go down quickly; the third has some skill. Within three moves I level him with a crushing punch to his throat.

I pull the batteries out of their radios and toss them into the abyss under the metal staircase.

Easing onto deck two, I slip one eye around the corner. "Clear."

Vast experience with Navy ships leads me to the left. We duck into a room full of scuba equipment.

"You dive?"

"No," she answers, face white, going still.

"You do now." I breeze down the row of regulators selecting what we'll need. "Pull this on."

"You're serious, aren't you?"

"Swimming out is the best answer. Stealing a boat would be messy."

She blinks hard.

"I'll take care of you, Sage." I half-smile, holding the wet suit out.

"Jacob Carter, I do not like sharks." Still, she takes the suit and struggles into it.

"Sage Emerson, I prefer sharks to Ash or Sutton."

She blows out a hard breath, agreeing, and I zip into a suit, then help her finish, clipping her buoyancy vest on tightly. I shoulder the tanks, clip two sets of fins and masks to her vest.

"How did you know about Tony Marks?"

I look down at her, surprised, "How do you?"

"As soon as you disappeared, Brooks started tracking you. We got to Ash's quarters and I used my stethoscope to listen."

"Remind me not to underestimate you." I arch one brow at her. "Something happened when I was in the spirit; it was like the two worlds were reconnected and saw either at will." I shake my head, cinching down my BCD vest. "Sometimes, lately, knowledge comes, like I'm watching it on a screen. Those words came out of my mouth and I was hearing them for the first time too." Opening a cabinet, I find dive knives, lights, and a waterproof pouch. I slip the drive into the pouch.

"Listen, if we get separated, avoid capture at all costs; use any force necessary. Any option is better than being a science experiment. The seas are high and that's good for us. It will make us next to impossible to see. We'll swim at a depth of 20 feet, below the chaos at the top; it'll be nice and smooth."

She nods and swallows hard, left shoulder high, tension tightening her eyes. I study her face, wishing I could impart the assurance that we're on the right path. "It's time to move; ready?"

"Jacob?" Her brown eyes brim with tears, "Don't die, okay?"

"Yeah, Sage, we're going to make it just fine," I say, holding her gaze.

She shakes her head and steps forward. Crouching, I lead out the doorway; everything is quiet until the main ship's alarm blares, making us both jump. I pause, hand on the door to the aft deck. "If things get heavy, hit the deck and stay there until I clear the area."

"Oh God, help us."

"He already has, Sage." I push open the door into the dark night, straight into the arms of four Marines. Training takes over and I drop the first one, pulling his Glock from his belt; I use it to pistol whip the next man. I duck a punch, spin with my foot high, catch the third in the chin. The other levels his pistol at me, but I duck into a somersault, counting on his slight hesitation. I drive my knee hard into his stomach and he slides across the deck.

"Sage, now!" We break forward toward the high railing.

A bolt of lightning turns the deck into daylight for a split second. *Tex*. He stands like an apparition between us and the safety of the water. I shove Sage down behind me, dump the scuba tanks.

A sneer covers Tex's face as the floodlights fight a losing battle with the storm. The ship heaves under me; I use its pitch to close the distance and we meet in a flurry of blows.

The surging urgency to get Sage off the ship fills my mind. Tex lands a crushing blow to my stomach; I have to get past the mental sense to survive him. The deck tilts as I strike hard inside Tex's tight guard.

Arms flashing, I search for the quiet voice of my spirit. He spins, boot catching me hard in the jaw. I skid through the rain across the deck, fighting off the blackness closing in. Within it, I see him in the air, elbow and knee plummeting toward me. I roll, obeying it, and he materializes from the darkness, ship rattling from his impact.

I twist up, in the flow now, somersault backward a hair's breadth before he sweeps out with a bowie knife. I shift to the right, throw my boot high, mind screaming: he's not there. I force the thought down, continue the strike at nothing, then my boot connects with his knife hand as it surges up and the blade spins away. I grin at him, fists ready. He shouts, throwing himself forward.

I drive hard for his right shoulder; speed healing or not, it's his weakest link. I let him swing, rain pelting, driving my shoulder into his, and I hear a satisfying crunch. I land two swift punches to his gut then twist away.

He pursues, face a mask of rage. I dance around his punches; it seems he's in slow motion, but I'm still in real time. I lean back, watch his fist sweep by, have more than enough time to bend my right arm and secure it with my left. I clench my stomach as my elbow falls like a battering ram, biting deep into his shoulder past the muscle, tearing tendon. He crumples back, skidding through the puddles.

Scanning the deck for Sage, I can't find her. I duck; the sight within shows him come up swinging, I drop into a crouch. Tex's right fist whistles over my head, connects with the steel bracing. He bellows, enraged, doubles the pace of his blows.

But I sense them all coming; the wet deck affords me an opening and I slam him hard. We skid, water shimmering. Landing punches, mind clear, in the spirit, I see Sage, crouched above on the short roof of the control room. Surging in, I take a few serious hits to force him back in that direction.

Sure enough, lightning reveals Sage is on the roof, crouched low, a syringe poised in her fist, rain streaking down her face. She nods and I catch the gesture in the corner of my eye.

Shouting, I grab Tex around his waist like a linebacker, all in, till he slams hard against the metal wall. Sage's hand grips his hair, pulls his forehead back, and she plunges the syringe into his exposed neck.

His arm shoots up, tangles in her hair; she screams in midair, slamming to the deck on her back between us. I leap over her, pummel Tex, giving her time to crawl away.

Tex starts to shiver, muscles jumping. His eyes roll back in his head. The wall next to him punctures as a bullet slams into it. Backup has arrived. I spin as Tex hits the deck, convulsing. Snatching Sage by the back of her BCD vest, I run for the abandoned scuba tanks.

Brooks stands over them, pistol steady on my chest. An image flashes; the gun goes off, bullet spinning in slow motion off to my right. I lean left as Brooks pulls the trigger and I feel the blistering heat of the shot sweeping by.

I hit Brooks solid in the chest, right hand falling like a hammer, knocking the pistol to the deck. He scrambles on his back crablike, face a mask of fear, hands high.

I snatch the pistol and shoulder the tanks; Sage gains her feet, clinging to my arm. Brooks nods once, rain pelting his face, *letting us go*. I return the gesture, turn for the railing. I set the pistol on my left forearm laying down suppressive fire on the squad at the far end of the deck.

As we reach the railing, I find her hand. Sparks fly; the bullets rain as they return fire. I surge over the barrier, wrenching her higher. We start the long drop and I locate the flailing regulators with my left hand, pull Sage in with my right until she's tucked tight against my chest.

I wrap my legs around hers, rock back so I'll take the water's concussion. In the freefall, I squeeze her until I know she can't breathe. Still, on impact, the wild ocean tries to tear us apart as we plunge into its swelling power.

Miles to shore, water temp is 52°. *Better make it a fast swim.* I find her face in the dark water and slide the regulator into her mouth, make sure bubbles rise before I bite onto mine.

The waters erupts with gunfire. Got to get out of range, a few feet will do. I tow her toward the safety of the ship, gaining depth. Under its belly, I snap on a dive light and check her BCD; her eyes are terrified behind the mask; she's clutching the regulator hard to her mouth.

I give her a thumbs up then slide the fins over her feet and tighten them down. I take her hand in the heavy current; she's shivering already at the start of a long swim. About halfway to shore, her movements grow sloppy, her core body temperature dropping. I check her tanks with the dive light. She's used twice as much air as I have. I stroke harder, pulling her toward the distant shore, calculating how many minutes she has left. Time crawls in the dark water and I fight the currents until the breakers crash over the beach, and I lose my grip on her dive belt.

Frantic on the dark sand, I search, the concussion of the waves sounding like cannon fire. *There.* A lightning strike reveals her black suit, half-submerged in the pounding surf. I haul her onto the sand, ripping off her mask.

"Sage!"

She groans, movement slow, face pale, one side of her neck raw from the sand. I scan the rows of beach houses, choose a dark one with no cars parked in the drive. Scooping her up, I find her limp in my arms. Sand sprays everywhere as I run up the steep dunes, past a sign, *Topsail Island, public beach access #41.* Satisfied that the house is empty, I reach the door, out of the impact of the shrieking wind and rain.

"Sage, stand up. I need your help."

She struggles at my words, eyes rolling, "Help you," she slurs.

I set her down, and she leans heavily on the wall but stays upright. I redirect the security alarm, shaving the wires and twisting them together, looping the system. The dive knife is too thick to pick the lock.

Breaking the face of my pressure regulator I pull out its gauge needle. It's almost too short, but eventually I hear the lock click open. I gather Sage, pushing past a washer and dryer, pausing to bump the thermostat to high.

I set her in a tub in the massive bathroom upstairs, run the water as hot as I dare. "Come on, Sage!"

Her eyes flutter. "Inside?"

"Yes, we're off the ship. You're safe now, Sage."

She shivers again, warming up, blue tinge leaving her lips. I run a blanket down to the dryer than get her out of the tub. She curls up on the bed under the hot blanket, delicate face peaceful in sleep. I clench my fists, pulling a chair up next to the bed and gaze over the pounding surf glinting in the lightning.

The storm intensifies, raging up the shore; but inside, there's peace. Everything I was a month ago is gone. All the years of training and dedication to the SEALs, all my goals have been stripped away by forces beyond my control.

Thinking back to my first jump, the truth is, there are now greater things possible than anything I could have achieved on my own. Nothing can replace what I've learned and it's a wealth I intend to protect.

All my life I've been at war with fear, trying to prove it has no hold on me. But really, all I'd done was prove I was brave in the face of it, able to keep it under. The thing I'd always wanted is what Demyen has, a heart without fear. Now it's within.

A helicopter flies low through the lashing rain, spotlight trained on the beach, flight erratic in the heavy squall. We're hunted now, exiled, a red flag in the shadowed world of military secrets. It will take everything I've learned in both worlds to stay out of their grip.

I clasp my hands, elbows on my knees as I watch Sage sleep. How many hours has she done the same for me? I clench my jaw, "Ash will never touch you again."

Plans flow; we'll have to move soon. The US won't prove a safe haven for us; but I'm ready, I'll follow the path. Lightning strikes close, all the details suddenly visible, just like the Spirit's become to me. The path *never* terminates. Two worlds wait, where anything is possible.

*I see it.*

# What's your lion?

If you're ready to learn more, go to shilocreed.com and click Got Questions.

Don't forget to grab your copy of the Plunged Study Guide, for personal  study or small groups. It's time to dive deeper into the laws of faith.

I'm excited to hear your thoughts on Plunged. Please leave a review on Amazon or other retailer!

# Author Bio

Shilo Creed is a follower of Christ Jesus, with a passion to
share faith with others. After being healed from
a heart condition, seeking the kingdom first became a lifetime
goal. The gospel is the power of God
unto salvation, believe what it says, and you
will find all things are possible.